Beneath Contempt

Of Magic and Contempt Book 1

Jade Thorn

Readers may also find some scenes distressing.

Copyright © July 2020 Jade Thorn All rights reserved

The characters and events portrayed in this book are fictitious. Any similarity to real persons, living or dead, is coincidental and not intended by the author.

No part of this book may be reproduced, or stored in a retrieval system, or transmitted in any form or by any means, electronic, mechanical, photocopying, recording, or otherwise, without express written permission of the publisher.

ASIN: B086SSR5JH

Cover design by: Natasha Williams of DAZED Designs
https://www.dazed-designs.com/

Edited by: CB Editing Services
https://www.facebook.com/CBlackEdits/

Please note that due to its content this book is not meant for readers under the age of 18.

❦ Created with Vellum

ACKNOWLEDGMENTS

In the writing process there are always people who help you along. In the publishing process, there are even more! There are some people who I need to thank for helping me.

First and foremost, thank you to my husband for supporting me in my creative madness. For listening to me mutter into long cold cups of tea, for taking the kids to the park to allow me writing time, and for supporting me as I create. You are my rock, you have been for 30 years, and I hope we will last at least 30 more!

To my girl gang - Lizzie, Sarah and Adriann - you ladies keep me sane, keep me on track, listen to me whinge and still want to talk to me! You are all amazing people, your writing awes and inspires me and I cannot wait to see what you come out with next.

To my editor, Charlotte Black - just wow. You embraced my insane and thrived on it. Your work is top calibre, speedy and you put up with my crazy. THANK YOU. Your encouragement uplifts me and keeps me focussed and your attention to detail is phenomenal. In you I have found not only an amazing editor but a friend for life.

To my street team, my ARC team and my Beta readers - these women help share the word, keep me going and allow me time to keep on writing so that I can share more of the strange worlds in my head. You watch over my shoulder as I write and your positivity helps keep my "darkness" at bay. Thank you for everything.

To Jaime - aka Jme or my "Misery" fan - you, dear lady are a godsend. Every writer should have someone like you. One day we will meet, and I know that my world will never be the same again. (I'll probably be locked in your attic, but oddly enough I'm ok with that - as long as I can write ;)).

To Tash Will - cover designer extraordinaire, you lady, took my request for a "non-traditional academy" cover and raised it to the next level. You are kind, talented and so giving. You are more than my designer, you're an inspiration and a friend.

Finally, Sara Guthman PA - lady, I don't even know where to start. Kind, thoughtful, inspired, insightful, organised, helpful, gracious, forgiving - and a whole other pile of positive adjectives - you are them all, my love. This lady has been invaluable. Her knowledge of marketing, branding and her (frankly terrifying) degree of organisation, has taken me from the hot mess that I was, to a fully functioning author. But it is her kindness and her generosity of spirit that I will forever be grateful for.

Happy reading

Jade
xoxo

PROLOGUE

Melody, aged 4.

"Melody, darling, come here."

"Yes Mamma?"

"No, closer darling. I can't reach you. Come here, Mamma's tired."

She got up and walked towards her mamma who was sitting on the floor against the door. She had spilled her wine, it was on the floor all around her, a great big red puddle that kept spreading. She didn't want to get too close to her; she was wearing her favourite slippers and she didn't want to get them mucky.

"Closer Melody, I want to tell you a secret." Mamma gave her a funny smile. She looked tired and sad, and Melody wanted to hug her and make it all better.

"But Mamma, my slippers will get dirty," she wailed.

"It's okay baby, I won't get cross, I promise."

Reluctantly, she tiptoed as best she could through the red puddle. Mamma smiled and pulled Melody onto her lap, lifting her feet so that they were clear of the mess. She curled in on herself and Mamma's arms wrapped around her, Melody's head rested on her chest. Did Mamma's perfume always smell so metallic? Her mother's perfume wrapped her in familiar comfort, but it was overlaid with something else. Melody wasn't sure what it was, but it reminded her of the time she accidentally bit her tongue. It hurt so much, and the taste in her mouth was like the smell in the air.

"Baby, Mamma has to go away. A long way away. I need to give you something to help you to be strong, and I need you to be a big brave girl for me, okay?"

Melody's lip wobbled. She didn't like the sound of this. Mamma was her whole world. She couldn't go away and leave her, it wasn't fair. Aunt Georgia would have to babysit her, and she wasn't nice. She told Mamma so.

"Now, Melody, Aunt Georgia is going to lead the coven for me because I can't anymore. I'm sick. But you must promise to be a good girl for me. You know in your heart what is right and wrong. People will ask you to do things that are wrong, and you must find a way to not do them, without them knowing. There are bad people in the world, baby, and you need to be careful of them. Don't become them. Promise me that you will always be a good girl."

"Yes Mamma." She sniffled.

"I know it's scary, baby. Some of the bad people have hurt me and now I have to go away." Mamma's face had gone so white, and she struggled to keep her eyes open.

"Now, no more tears. This is the part where you must be brave. I want you to give me a big smile, and then open your heart. Remember how I showed you? Open your heart for me baby, let me see what a big strong girl you are!"

She was so scared. Bad people had hurt Mamma? But Mamma was looking at her with her ice-blue eyes; so much like Melody's own, filled with love but waiting for her to do something. Oh yes, open her heart for her, and smile. Mamma was smiling at her, so it was easy to do it back.

Mamma placed her hand on Melody's chest, and it began to grow warm. They had practiced this, gifting their magic back and forth between each other. But Mamma kept going. Usually Mamma just gave her a little bit, and then Melody would open her heart and give it back. But Mamma didn't stop. This was so much more than she normally gave. She gave and gave and gave until Melody thought she would burst from the light that she could feel shining brightly inside of her.

She started to panic. Any moment now she was going to burst from it all, it would pour through holes in her skin, but she didn't burst, and Mamma kept giving Melody more magic.

"Stop, Mamma. I'm full, it hurts," she begged.

"I know baby, but you have to. Just a bit more. It will sting for a day or so, but then you'll be so much stronger – forever!"

Mamma gave until the heat emanating from her hand flickered and then stopped. Melody was so full of their combined light that she could barely move.

"My big, brave, girl. I am so proud of you. Always remember to be strong, and to be good, and to listen to your heart. Promise me baby."

"I promise Mamma."

"Good girl. I love you."

"I love you too, Mamma!"

She waited for her to say something else. She waited and waited, and then waited some more. But it was silent. Mamma's hands slid from around her shoulders where she had cuddled Melody to her chest. They landed in the wine, which was still spreading across the floor, even though there was no glass. It seemed strange because Mamma only drank wine with her dinner anyway.

"Mamma?"

Mamma did not move.

"Mamma?" She patted her face gently, and her head slid to the side. What was going on? Why wouldn't she answer?

The door behind Mamma shuddered, the handle twisting back and forth.

"Adelaide? Open this door at once!"

It was her Aunt Georgia, she shuddered, but maybe Aunt Georgia could help Mamma. Mamma had said she was sick and hurt.

"Aunt Georgia, help! Mamma won't talk to me," she cried.

"Open the door Melody!"

"I can't, Aunt Georgia. Mamma is in the way."

"Very well then, go and sit on the bed."

She didn't want to leave Mamma, but she didn't want to make Aunt Georgia mad. She did mean things when she was mad. Reluctantly she got up, trying to avoid stepping in the red puddle and went back to Mamma's bed. She sat, her slippered feet dripping wine down the duvet to the floor. There was a pause, a moment of silence so absolute that for a second she thought that her ears had broken, and then the door opened, pushing Mamma across the floor and into the wall.

"Mamma!" she screamed, jumping down and rushing to her.

"Silence, brat!" said Aunt Georgia. She bent down over Mamma, slapping her much harder than Melody's gentle taps, earlier. "Adelaide? Wake up?"

Mamma didn't move. Aunt Georgia touched her neck and sighed, straightening up.

"Gwendoline, Adele, get in here and clean this mess up. I want this room stripped and refitted by the end of tomorrow. The ceremony will be tomorrow night. Ambrosia, contact the council, and inform them of the change in leadership."

Melody sat on the bed, agog, watching as members of the coven gathered at the door. They were all reluctant to step in the wine. Mamma stayed slumped on the floor as

Aunt Georgia left, and Melody started to cry, great heaving sobs.

"And for goodness sake, someone shut that brat up and get her out of my room. Move her down to the cellars, she'd best get used to staying down there anyway." Aunt Georgia laughed, but it didn't sound happy. It didn't sound nice either, but that was Aunt Georgia.

Melody looked at her aunt with tear-filled eyes, it was almost like she had never seen her before. She wanted her mamma. She supposed that Aunt Georgia looked a little like her mamma, they had the same nose and eyes, although Aunt Georgia's were a dark brown. But her mouth was pinched, not the beautiful smile that her Mamma had, and where Mamma's dark curls tumbled down her shoulders, her aunt had dull, mousy coloured hair that hung limply to her shoulders. It was like her hair hated being attached to her.

Where Mamma looked like a queen, Aunt Georgia looked like a wicked witch. Her mamma had scolded her for saying that once, telling her that real beauty was found within. Melody thought that Aunt Georgia was probably just as ugly on the inside as she was on the outside. She didn't want to peel back her skin to find out either.

Melody hiccupped a sob. Mamma wasn't going to be there to teach her these things anymore. She didn't understand why her mamma had to leave her, but she knew that her mamma was already gone.

"Now, that's enough of that Melody," said Gwendoline as she reached for her hand. "Your Mamma has gone now, and

Aunt Georgia will be looking after the coven. So we need to clean her new room. You'll be sleeping in the cellars, near the shifters. You remember them? You like the shifters." Her hand clasped Melody's, but she let it go with a startled shriek.

"Oh Goddess," she cried. "Adelaide, what have you done?"

There was the thud of her aunt's high heels coming back down the hall. "What was that? What is going on here?"

"It's the child, Georgia, Adelaide has tampered with the child. Why, her light is so strong I can barely stand to touch her."

"Rubbish," snorted Aunt Georgia. "You were always the fanciful one, Gwendoline. Here, Brat, give me your hand."

Melody dutifully held her hand up to Aunt Georgia, but her reaction was like Gwendoline's. She held it and dropped it with a loud wail. "Adelaide, you fucking bitch!" she screamed, marching over to Mamma and kicking her until Melody started to cry again in response. "You had no right to do that, that power was mine, do you hear me? It was mine!"

Furious, Aunt Georgia stormed to Melody and slapped her hard across the cheek. Then she loomed over her, placing her hand on Melody's forehead as she started casting a spell. Melody froze in terror. Her aunt's bony hand was icy, and her magic, instead of flowing smoothly over her, scratched at her skin, clawing its way down to her heart. When she was done, she looked at Melody, eyes narrowed. "Swear your fealty, Brat. Swear it now."

Melody was terrified. She didn't know what to do, it

didn't feel right to do this, but Mamma wasn't here, and her aunt was always mean if she did the wrong thing. She wasn't sure what the exact words were, but she had an idea. "I swear fealty to Coven Bestia. I vow to give my magic, my service and my life. Under the light of the Goddess, so do I swear."

Melody felt the spell descend on her, sliding across her skin, tightening around her. For a moment or two, she struggled to breathe as it slowly strangled her, but then it sank into her skin, into her heart and into her soul. For better or worse, she now belonged to the coven.

1. MELODY

PRESENT DAY

"Psst, Melody, wake up, they're coming," someone hissed.

In an instant she was awake. She'd long since learned to sleep lightly, it didn't bode well to be found asleep in her cage when one of the members of her coven came to get her. She sat up, rubbing the sleep from her eyes and pulling her hair into some semblance of neatness.

"Do I have time to get dressed?" she quietly asked the room in general.

The room was set up like a prison. Melody's cage was in the center, it was larger than the cages the shifters were kept in, but it was still a cage. Men and women with various levels of health ringed the room, all kept separate but close enough that they could reach around the dividers and hold hands for comfort when needed. Not one of them could reach across the aisle and hold her hand. That was deliberate.

Unlike the shifters, Melody's cage wasn't locked. She could get up and leave it at any time she chose, however the spells laid upon her were tighter than any chain. During the day, she was not allowed to leave her cage unless she had been summoned by someone in her coven. Melody knew the wording of that particular geas by heart. Aunt Georgia had laid so many geasan upon her, that she had become lazy. The one confining her said that in the morning, she couldn't leave her cage unless someone from the coven had come to fetch her.

It didn't say anything about the afternoon, evening or night. Melody had tested it. It was the only thing that had saved several of these shifters; her ability to leave her cage and sneakily give them food or water or even first aid. Ironically, although their lives were hell, nobody in the room wanted to die. Even Melody.

"Yes, but be quick," Sasha told her, her head cocked to the side, listening.

Melody threw off her ragged nightgown, splashing some water from the bucket under her arms and between her legs before drying herself with a scrap of fabric she used as a towel. Then she pulled on some clean underpants, a pair of jeans and a T-shirt. The days were getting cooler, but it was still warm enough for sandals, so she put them on instead of the ratty trainers and holey socks she had. She needed them to last as long as possible this winter.

When Ambrosia entered the basement, Melody was calmly making her bed, as though she hadn't just woken. Aside from avoiding a punishment, it thrilled Melody to be able to thwart the old cow from causing her more trouble.

"Come on you lazy bitch, we're hungry. We don't have all day while you sit down here lollygagging, some of us have important business to be about. And you're needed in the courtyard afterward." Ambrosia's piggy little eyes shone with a dark glee.

Melody froze for a second, before pulling up the threadbare blanket over the cardboard pallet that she'd managed to steal to use as a mattress when they'd had a new fridge delivered. The courtyard. That meant that her aunt had a new shifter.

Her stomach tightened into a ball. Today was going to be a horrific day.

Quietly, she followed the fat witch in front of her to the kitchen where she began making breakfast for the thirty witches who lived in the main house of their compound. Once the porridge was underway, she started working on the bacon and eggs while laying out milk, fruit, and sugar on the trolley where she had set up the cereals the night before.

As Melody wheeled the cumbersome cold breakfast into the dining room, she caught sight of her aunt in the courtyard talking to a man in the prime of his life. Aunt Georgia was laughing and flirting with him, putting on a show, enticing him in.

Bile rushed up the back of her throat, burning. She

wanted to open the window and scream at him to run, to get away from there as fast as he could, but her aunt would simply kill him and punish her to within an inch of her life. If she didn't need Melody's power, she would kill Melody too.

No, she was just as much a prisoner here as the shifters were, as this vibrant man would soon be. Aunt Georgia was a cruel and violent mistress, and Melody was her favourite tool.

"Stop your dawdling you lazy little bitch," Ambrosia growled from up ahead, and Melody jumped.

She quickly trundled the cereals into the large dining room before hurrying back up the corridor to stir the porridge and turn the bacon. Ruining either would see her birched, on top of what she was about to face after they had eaten. Although she needed the sustenance, Melody wouldn't eat this morning. She would only bring it up in the courtyard.

Her heart thumped harder in anticipation.

Once the meal was served, she worked to clean the kitchen. Not only did she have to do the washing up, but she had to sterilise all the surfaces and mop the floor. By then, the dirty dishes from breakfast had been returned. They would have to be cleaned, dried, and put away before she could report to the courtyard, and the longer she made Aunt Georgia wait, the more she would be punished.

Her anxiety was so high that her hands trembled as she dried the dishes, and several times she nearly dropped them.

Breaking crockery was also worthy of punishment. Melody's aunt and her cronies didn't stint on punishment, if she had earned one, then they would do their damndest to make sure that she cried, and because Melody was determined to never cry, the whipping for breaking a mug could go on for hours.

Melody rushed to put away the last bowls, hung up her apron, tidied her appearance and hurried toward the courtyard. As much as she dreaded going there, this was something unavoidable.

"My, my, Melody, you took your sweet time coming," Aunt Georgia said cheerfully.

Her heart sank. As soon as this shifter swore his fealty to her aunt, all pretence would be over. Aunt Georgia was simply letting her know that she was going to be punished. No excuse would be acceptable, so she didn't even try to defend herself.

"I'm sorry, Mistress, I came as quickly as I could." Melody could see the shifter examining her closely. It was likely that her aunt had primed him, telling him that he would be given to a fertile young witch. She would suggest any number of things to get a shifter to swear fealty, and then she would rip the rug from under them. This man thought he was getting something wonderful, but like so many things in life, if it sounded too good to be true, it probably was.

"Greetings, Melody. Your Aunt speaks highly of your ability. I have to say I agree. From what I can see and smell, you are indeed a very powerful witch. I'm Craig, my puma and I are pleased to meet you."

He reached out for her hand, bowing over it and kissing the back when she gave it to him. Like a gallant gentleman of old. The fact that he was such a charmer made what was about to happen all the more horrific.

Craig straightened and began to remove his clothing in preparation of his shift.

"Uh, uh, uh," her aunt sing-songed. "First you must swear fealty to me."

"To you, not the coven?" Craig queried.

Melody almost moaned, it was the worst thing he could have done, questioning Aunt Georgia's authority.

"My dear Craig," her aunt replied. "I don't know what you have seen in other covens, but Bestia has its own way of doing things. You told me that you travelled a lot to visit all of the beast magic covens. I have assured you that Bestia is not only the oldest but the strongest. If, however, you do not wish to join us, then please cease wasting my time. I have things to do and Melody must continue her studies."

Melody wanted to laugh. Continue her studies? The only things she had learned from her coven was how to duck, hide, and lie very well. She'd learned to endure pain, to clean something to within an inch of its existence, and never to grow attached to anything. She had learned to survive starvation, to exist in the shadows and to fear everything to do with her coven. But most of all, she'd learned to hate bonding shifters. She couldn't call them her familiars, for they weren't hers. Not in any way that would protect them.

Craig hesitated for a moment; his eyes were feverish as

they raked over her. She could hear his puma purring. He thought he was going to get the chance to take her, to tame *her*. He would quickly discover that she was even more a slave than he was about to become.

He dropped to his knees. "I swear fealty to Georgia Bestia. I vow to give my beast, my service, and my life. Under the light of the Goddess, so do I swear."

Melody felt her aunt's magic surge, binding the promise into him, even as a shudder of dread passed through her. His enslavement had only just begun. Indeed, when she looked, Aunt Georgia's face had lost any pretence of friendliness.

"Craig, I command you to strip and challenge her," Aunt Georgia ordered.

"My pleasure," he murmured, quickly divesting his lithe body of his clothes. Like many of the male shifters presented to her when she was an adult, he was already half hard as he stood naked in front of her. "Melody Bestia, I challenge you," he announced.

A moment later, jade green eyes looked up at her. He was a magnificent beast, long and lean with a sheen to his tawny fur. He was obviously in peak physical condition. Melody hoped that it would be enough to save him.

He had just begun to advance on her when Melody called out her reply. "Craig, I accept your challenge, now, shift."

She raised her hand, sending her magic forth in a controlled burst. She'd learned not to hit them too hard, nor to waste any more magic than necessary. Sadly, she had this down to a fine art.

Instantly Craig sat on his human haunches. "That was a fucking blast."

"I'm so glad you enjoyed it, shall we do it again?" Aunt Georgia asked brightly.

Craig looked at her in confusion. "What do…" That was all he got out before her aunt ripped their bond in half.

Melody grunted, while Craig let out a cat-like yowl.

"Again, Craig, I command you," her aunt shrieked.

Faced with a command after having magically vowed his fealty to her, Craig was compelled to obey.

"Melody Bestia, I challenge you," he said, confused. Then he dropped once again into his puma form.

"I accept your challenge, now, shift," Melody responded.

Again, he shifted back. "What's going on? Why on earth did you break our bond, Mistress? Am I not to be given to Melody?" His eyes roved over her body again, the heat in them banked, but the interest still there.

"Why? You're asking me why?" her aunt said in a dangerously quiet voice.

Fuck. Something had stirred her aunt's temper before this had begun, Melody could tell. This breaking was going to be even more brutal than usual. She fought the urge to vomit.

"Melody, for the good of the coven, remove your shirt."

Her aunt had learned how to manipulate Melody's oath to the coven as opposed to herself a long time ago. She too had it down to a fine art form. The sad thing was, what her aunt said was true. For Craig to be broken, Melody would also be made to suffer, and the coven needed him broken so that a weaker witch could defeat him.

Melody didn't hesitate, keeping her eyes down, she removed her shirt and turned around, presenting her back to Craig. Her aunt didn't even have to command it, she knew what was about to be done to her.

"Craig, you will not question me ever again. Or *she* will suffer for it." Three strokes of fire against her back later, her aunt snapped their bond. "Challenge her again."

Melody turned back to face him, her shirt discarded at her feet. She would not be permitted to put it back on again until her aunt indicated, nor would she be allowed to cover herself up. She knew that Craig was looking at her more closely now, noting the myriad scars that covered not only her back but her front, the gauntness of her body where her ribs showed clearly, and the tremble in her limbs. The trouble was, he was looking too long.

A fresh welt appeared on her torso. Her breath hitched, but she didn't cry out. She simply waited calmly for him to comply. Melody wasn't permitted to talk to him, other than to accept his challenge and defeat him, over and over. Soon enough he would understand what was happening today.

"Melody Bestia, I challenge you," he said hoarsely.

She looked up at him, then, seeing the fear and anguish on his face tore at her. This was only the beginning of the horrors to be forced upon them both this day.

Again, she forced his shift.

And again.

And again.

But still, her aunt wasn't satisfied.

Her magic lashed at Melody over and over. When Craig begged to take on the wounds on her behalf, she got two. If tears were on his face, she got another, if he took a fraction of a second too long, locked eyes with Melody, held out a hand in supplication. Every emotional response he made, was answered with another lash upon Melody.

Eventually he got it. He stopped talking other than to issue a challenge, he didn't look at her, and his cock was no longer hard – it hadn't been since the first wound. His voice grew hoarse, his puma learned not to growl, both of them learned to keep their gaze on the ground.

Sweat poured off Craig's brow, but still he managed shift after shift. His puma's coat was starting to dull, a sign that soon he wouldn't be able to. It was a fine line now, between when they had gone too far and they would have to wait for him to regenerate, and when he was weak enough to be taken by anyone. She prayed that her aunt didn't take it too far. She didn't want to go through this again with him.

The sun was overhead before her aunt called a halt. Craig practically collapsed on the spot. Melody was covered in blood, it poured from her arms, her legs, her belly and her back. The only place the wounds did not touch were her head, hands and feet. After all, she would be expected to continue to work even as she healed. Her aunt wasn't stupid enough to disable her hardest worker.

2. MELODY

"Run and fetch Claudia," Aunt Georgia ordered.

Running was beyond her, but she was able to walk at a fast clip into the main building and up to Claudia's room. She tapped on the door and waited with her head bowed. Claudia was a piece of work, she loved to play games, her favourite was to make Melody's life harder.

She wasn't permitted to knock again. She had to stand there, dripping blood while she waited. There would be a punishment for making a mess on the floor. Fresh pain lancing across her back indicated that she was taking too long, but she didn't cry out, even this far away.

Besides, Claudia would take too much delight in it on the other side of the door. She knew that was where the woman was standing, waiting. Melody could sense her magic simmering just inches away.

There was a sudden yelp and the door was yanked open. It seemed that Aunt Georgia had grown impatient with Claudia's games too.

"Look at this mess!" Claudia exclaimed, adding her own lashes to the bloody mess that was Melody's back. "How many times have I told you not to bleed on the floor. You will come back and clean this up afterward." She huffed, taking an exaggerated step over the small red puddle, before rounding on Melody again.

"You'd better have broken him for me, I'm ovulating, the mistress has said I'm to bring us another daughter. I don't have time to waste while you play at taming him."

Claudia grabbed her by the arm to drag her down the hall, squealing in disgust when she realised it was bloody. Another welt joined the others on her back, as if it were her fault that she was bleeding, or as if she had deliberately put her blood on Claudia.

Part of her hoped that Craig would be too strong for the nasty witch, she wouldn't wish Claudia on any shifter, especially if she was supposed to be breeding for the coven again. The consequences for both her and Craig, however, were far too great. It would be better for them all if Claudia got her way the first time.

"What took you so long, Melody? I swear you want to be beaten some more," her aunt groused, adding another five lashes to her.

She wasn't expected to answer, her aunt knew very well what had happened.

"She bled all over the floor again, mistress. I've ordered her to clean it up when you are finished with her." Claudia looked at her spitefully. "Maybe I should make her lick it up. Or maybe she should have to stand outside of my room until she's healed. Then clean it up."

While Craig would not understand, the three women did. Claudia wanted Melody to listen as she made the man fuck her. It took everything Melody had not to react. To do so would only have goaded the spiteful witch into doing it.

"Craig, challenge Claudia," Aunt Georgia commanded.

Stupidly, he looked up. Melody's flinch making him hurriedly look down again.

"Claudia Bestia," he said hoarsely. "I challenge you."

Claudia tittered and clapped her hands. "Why Craig, you sweet-talker. I accept."

Craig shifted into his beast one more time, but he wasn't looking at the ground, he was looking at Melody's feet. She had been afraid that this would happen. The bond forming and breaking so many times, so quickly, had meant that some breaks weren't complete. It was almost impossible to sense, and it usually took a few days of observation to be sure. Only now it meant that Craig had the strength to fight Claudia.

"Wait," Melody cried, fearing the consequences.

Immediately both women lashed her until she was a pile on the ground, although no sound escaped her, and no tear was shed.

"Bond isn't quite broken," she managed to whisper. Craig

sighed above her. So, he knew as well. "It's better this way. I ended up in a coma the last time the bond lingered."

The puma stood suddenly and vomited. The first real sign of his distress all day.

"Craig, you will bond Melody again, and this time I will make sure it is broken," Aunt Georgia decreed.

The puma yowled but didn't resist.

"I accept your challenge," said Melody, unable to rise. "Shift."

She was barely able to raise her hand and direct her magic at him. Despite being in a heap beside him, she still had plenty of magic within her. He could hardly hold himself up when he shifted back.

Instead of a simple tear, Aunt Georgia hacked at the bond, shredding it to pieces. It was bad enough to have it broken, but to have it destroyed in such a way was agonising. It drew the process out, chafing at raw nerve endings and guaranteeing that neither wanted to go through the process again.

"Now, challenge Claudia again," her aunt commanded him.

Craig sat there panting. She knew that he had almost hit his limit, it was doubtful that he'd be able to shift back unless defeated by a witch. He didn't stand a chance against Claudia, even as weak a witch as she was. Claudia's father, however, had been an alpha wolf, the only reason that Bestia Coven kept her, as Aunt Georgia made sure everybody knew. Claudia's value lay in the possibility of her having inherited the alpha gene from her father. When bred with a shifter, it was hoped that she would either produce an alpha son or a daughter strong in beast taming. Anything else was … unacceptable.

A puff of breath hissed from her mouth, and Melody was surprised to feel it escape her. Why had she … oh! It had taken a moment for the pain to register, but it seemed that she was being punished for Craig's delay, despite the fact that he was too weak to shift.

The pain began to crescendo and she was glad. It wouldn't be long now before it overwhelmed her and she passed out. Two, maybe three minutes. After all these years in Bestia Coven, Melody was a connoisseur of pain. She knew exactly how much it would take.

Craig, of course, knew none of this, just that she was hurting because of him. She could feel him call his beast forward, but it hunkered down inside, refusing to come out. If Claudia didn't get him today, didn't fall pregnant this cycle, then they would both pay for it until she did. Reluctantly, Melody sent a wisp of her magic to him, encouraging his beast to come out. This was permitted. It was certainly something that the other two women wouldn't stoop to. Of course, she would be punished for using magic without permission, but not until after she had done what was needed.

With a low moan, the puma emerged. She'd never seen a shift take so long. Bronzed fur, no longer shiny and golden, grew from his skin. His bones popped and cracked, and his breath hitched as the slower pace made the shift an agonising one. Eventually the cat sat there, panting with the effort the shift had taken. Craig gave her one last glance before looking at the ground.

For the next few days, he would pity her as he adjusted to his new situation. Depending on how he acted, he could be treated fairly decently while he shared Claudia's bed, but as soon as she got pregnant, he'd be down in the basement with the rest of them. At that point, he would hate her. This would last for several months until he realised how she was as much a slave as him, more so in fact.

He could at least look forward to death.

As the powerhouse of the coven, Melody wouldn't be permitted to die for a very long time. There were times, however, when she almost broke. When she almost wished she could. The memory of her mother was the only thing that kept her going. Melody had promised to be brave, but she wondered if her mother would have had any inkling what that promise would mean in the years following her death.

"Shift!" Claudia called, triumphantly.

For three seconds, Craig sat there as a human, and then he collapsed, unconscious.

He was now the property of Claudia.

The witch in question turned and delivered a sharp kick to Melody's ribs. "Juice him up. I can't stand here in the sun all day, it will ruin my complexion."

Despite being more powerful and uninjured, neither of

the women standing would lower themselves to help a shifter. It was beneath them to do so. Melody, however, was beneath contempt, so to give him some of her magic to heal would be a step up for her in their eyes.

She flung an arm across until it hit his flank and allowed her energy to pass into him. A minute or so later, he stirred, sitting up, but she kept her hand pressed to his ribs until he realised what she was doing and pulled away from her. That was proof enough for the two women that he was fit enough to stand.

"Get up," Claudia shouted at him. "Follow me and bring the filthy little bitch with you."

Craig staggered to his feet. Melody tried to drag herself up, but she could barely lift her head.

"Stop being a drama queen, you may heal yourself enough to stand. I have better things to do than stand watch over you."

Melody allowed her magic to trickle through her body, strengthening herself only enough to get to her feet. Her aunt's instructions had been very specific. She didn't dare try for more.

Getting upright was one thing, staying upright was another. Her head swam from blood loss and fatigue. Craig moved forward, grabbing her in a fireman's carry over his shoulder, before following his new mistress.

Claudia led them not to the upper halls where her room was, but to the basement, where Craig was instructed to lower her to the cardboard pallet on the floor. He looked around, his eyes wide, able to do so because Melody had fed him a steady stream of healing magic all the way back.

In cages all around the walls, shifter men and women stared at him in silence. Not one of them would say a word while Claudia was there.

"Be thankful that the mistress didn't let Melody keep you. You get to sleep in my bed tonight instead of hers," sneered Claudia. "Now come on, I'm ovulating, we will not be wasting this egg."

The spiteful witch turned and swept out of the room, a stunned Craig staggering after her. Not because he was weak, but because he was shocked. Melody suspected that he was finally beginning to understand the horror that was Bestia Coven.

When their footsteps finally faded back upstairs, voices called out to her from around the room.

"Melody, are you alright?" asked Malcolm, the head shifter. His wolf growled through his voice.

"No, but I will be," she whispered, confident that their shifter hearing would pick it up. "I need to sleep. Don't let them sneak up on me."

It was all she could do to drag the ragged blanket over her before she passed out.

3. MELODY

Bolts of ice peppered her skin, frightening her before she realised it was only a bucket of water. If Ambrosia had caught her sleeping, it would only be because the shifters had been unable to wake her. A bucket of ice-cold water was one of the better ways to wake, so she was grateful for that small mercy.

"Get up, you lazy bitch, you've got work to do," Ambrosia growled before stomping off.

Melody lay there panting with the shock of it all before she gingerly rolled over onto her hands and knees. She was still in the same position ten minutes later when Craig brought her some gruel.

There were some hushed whispers around her, the shifters talking about the new addition and she had no doubt that his keen hearing picked up every word. Still, he ignored them, putting the gruel on the ground near her hands.

"I'm to help you today," he said simply, before squatting outside her cage. The floor around her was wet, the water had penetrated everything, including the few spare sets of clothing, but she'd spent her remaining energy healing herself overnight, she didn't have enough left to dry them. Her magic was strong, her body wasn't.

"Why do you put up with it?" Finally, he'd asked the question that they all did.

Even though she had anticipated it, had heard and answered it before, hundreds of times, it was the question that Melody dreaded. Usually, she would try to ease them into their situation, but new shifters weren't normally brought down to the pens so soon. They were taken to the barracks for *training*, and only once they had been beaten and bloodied did the witches drag them down to their new accommodations to heal.

For once, she decided to spell things out quickly. Besides, she didn't have the strength for more.

"Do you know what a geas is?" she finally asked him, and he nodded. "Well, I don't have a choice. I have hundreds on me. They started after my mother died. Sometimes as many as a dozen a day, from the age of four."

Craig gasped. "But they're not supposed to be used on children!"

Melody laughed bitterly. "Tell me, Craig, from what you've seen so far, do you think that's a concern here?"

"I'm called the zookeeper; I'm expected to take care of the needs of the shifters. I empty their waste buckets, ensure they're washed once a week – I even heat the water with my magic, and I keep the floors clean."

Her own area was a small cage in the center of all of the others, so that the beasts could look upon her whenever they so wished. It was meant to be psychological torture, but for Melody, it was reassuring. They were lighter sleepers than she was, so she was never awoken by a member of her coven. The shifters made sure that she was awake when they sensed anyone approaching.

The stone floors were cool, no matter what time of the year. In the summer, the cellar was a blissful place to stay, which was why her coven made sure that she spent as little time as possible there when it was pleasant. The opposite, of course, applied for winter. The shifters didn't get sick, but she often had a cold from sleeping on the stone floor with only a single blanket. It was just another way for her aunt to ensure that she was too weak to challenge her.

With massive effort, she finally managed to push herself upright, sitting on her heels.

"Mel, honey. You need to eat, they're going to be back soon, I can hear them talking about you in the kitchen," Sonia called out. Her cage was the closest to the entry, she was often able to pick up gossip. "They're talking about getting you some new clothes, at least that's something to look forward to."

Melody wasn't so sure. Although hardly warm, the

clothes she had were quite serviceable when dry. If her aunt was talking about getting her some more, then it meant she was up to something. Melody wasn't so sure that she wanted to find out what her plans were.

Twice she reached forward for the bowl, only to discover that it was just out of her reach. Melody wasn't sure that she could lean over further without falling. After her third failed attempt, Craig grunted, got up and held it to her lips.

"You'd better just drink it, I don't think you've got time to eat it, I can hear them coming," he growled.

Gratefully, Melody opened her mouth and allowed the watery porridge to run down her parched throat. She had barely finished when Ambrosia and Marjorie swept into the basement.

"Are you still not fucking dressed?" Ambrosia snapped.

Magic wrapped around her, hauling her into the air. She'd managed to pull on her nightgown last night, despite the friction of the fabric against her wounds, but it was now torn down the middle by magic and discarded. She almost cried out with the loss, it meant that now she would have to sleep naked, like many of the shifters around her.

It helped her to remember how fortunate she was. Up until then, she'd had something to sleep in, a luxury that others didn't have. Like shifters, she'd long ago abandoned any fears of nudity in this place, although shifters were much more casual about it than witches were.

"Goddess, you're pathetic. You haven't even finished healing yet. Well, if you get blood on your new clothes, don't think we're cleaning them, or getting you any more. You'll have to either wander around naked or covered in blood. Either way, don't you dare disgrace your coven in front of others." Marjorie's voice was full of disdain.

Melody sent her magic across her skin, checking it for leaking wounds, but all of them were scabbed over. She pushed a little healing magic into those that were likely to tear open again, and even that made her eyelids droop. Healing didn't just take magic, it took strength as well. The double hit to her system was almost more than she could manage.

"What others?" she asked aloud, knowing it was what Marjorie wanted. The callous witch wanted her to beg for the information, and she'd still leave Melody in the dark. The lesser evil was to cater to Marjorie's hunger for power over her for the meantime.

Marjorie sneered, her thin face pinched even more than usual, as though she had sucked on something sour and it had drawn all the moisture from her mouth. It seemed that whatever was going on, did not meet her approval, although she would never speak against Aunt Georgia.

Ambrosia practically vibrated with anger. "The other witches of course, you stupid bitch." She rounded on Craig. "You there, fill up that bucket with water, the filthy brat will need to be washed. Marjorie, you deal with her, I have better things to do." Ambrosia swept from the room, oblivious to the murderous glare that Marjorie sent her way.

Yes, there was a definite hierarchy in their coven, and not

all of them were happy with their place. Marjorie and Ambrosia were the closest to her aunt in power, and they constantly vied for rank over each other.

Craig grabbed the bucket and headed over to a tap in the corner. It was better that he saw and understood the living conditions here now, because it was likely to become his reality in the very near future. Unless he could convince Claudia to keep him around, he would only stay in her bed until she was pregnant.

When he returned, Marjorie stood there waiting, one foot tapping. Hurriedly, Melody used the rag that was normally her towel, dipping it in the frigid water and using it to wipe the worst of the blood from her skin. She was unable to reach her back though. This was the bit she hated, because the newly bonded shifter suffered as much as she did.

Melody rinsed the rag, squeezed it out and then held it out to Craig. "Could you do my back, please?"

Reluctantly he took it from her, and she turned her back. Gingerly, Craig wiped at the wounds that were given in response to his actions the day before. It was yet another mindfuck that her coven had perfected.

The shifters would see the damage to Melody, know that they had played a part of it, and would blame themselves instead of the bitches responsible. No witch in Bestia gave a fuck whether she hurt or not, but the shifters would. Their beasts urged them to protect the witches that helped with their shifts. These wounds hurt all three of them, Melody, Craig and his puma.

"Hurry up, I haven't got all day, just scrub her down and be done with it," Marjorie snapped.

Melody felt his puma growl, and before he could lash out, she sent her magic to him, soothing the cat. If Craig lashed out at Marjorie, they would both be punished. Claudia wouldn't care that he was wounded, not as long as his cock still worked for her. All she was interested in was getting pregnant, and if Craig couldn't control his temper, then he'd be down in the basement with the rest of them as soon as she was done.

Marjorie would feel even that slight trickle of magic, but hopefully she would put it down to healing.

Behind her, Craig's breath stuttered as she settled his beast. "Why?" he whispered, low enough that only she could hear.

"That will have to do, dry yourself," Marjorie commanded before Melody could contrive to reply to him.

Melody didn't have a towel, and the nightgown that had been ripped from her was lying in the water on the floor. She had no other option than to use her magic and hope that she didn't pass out in the process.

Craig's hand landed discreetly on her hip. "Take from me," he whispered, again daring to ignite Marjorie's wrath.

As reluctant as she was to do so, as it would rekindle some of their bond, Melody took energy from him, not enough to be noticeable, but enough to dry herself and no more. Anything else and Marjorie might suspect, and it was possible that Claudia would feel it too.

"Thank you," she said, under her breath, knowing that his superior hearing would pick it up.

His hand squeezed her for a moment before stepping back and dropping the bloodied rag in the bucket of water.

"Follow me." Marjorie turned and stomped out of the room, confident that they would obey.

Naked and shivering, Melody walked past the cages of her friends, several of them reaching out a hand to touch her, all of them offering her strength. She didn't take from any of them, they were all rake-thin as it was. They would need it themselves, besides which, Marjorie would feel it.

Malcom, however, didn't just brush a hand over her, he jerked her to a halt, Craig stopping abruptly beside her in response, ready to defend her.

"Change is coming, stay strong," he said quietly, before releasing her arm.

Thankfully, Marjorie didn't hear anything over the clatter of her own high heels. Malcolm had taken a risk reaching out to her like that. Still, she nodded her thanks before rushing to catch up.

"Where is she?" Her aunt's strident voice made Melody wince as they climbed the stairs.

"Right behind me," Marjorie replied, turning and glaring over her shoulder at Melody.

Craig had to hold her up by the time they reached the top, the effort of climbing even one flight of stairs too much for her fatigued body.

"Still snivelling about her punishment?" The catty voice

was Claudia's, still out of view, but somewhere in the kitchen.

"Her what?" shrieked her aunt. Then, "Oh yes, I suppose breaking Craig in was a little taxing on her. Very well, you're spared, Marjorie. I will not tolerate her laziness."

If her aunt was irritated enough that she was willing to punish Marjorie, then things were grim indeed. Melody knew that she had to tread lightly. Another punishment like yesterday's and she probably wouldn't survive. As tempting as it was to take the easier path, she knew that she mustn't. Somehow, she had to outlive her aunt and try to restore her coven to the powerhouse that it was under her mother. A much better and safer place for shifters.

Melody shuffled into the kitchen, still leaning heavily on Craig, and all eyes turned to them. Aunt Georgia stood on the far side, her gaze as critical as ever.

"It's time you started repaying your debt to us," her aunt said with a sneer, almost as if she was daring Melody to protest. "Since you have now reached your majority, you're being sent to Adolphus Academy, the finest beast magic school in the country. Of course, you will excel, you will not shame us after all the time and effort that we put into your training."

Melody wanted to snort. Her training? Her coven had trained her to clean out the cages where the shifters were kept, to be their scullery maid and general dogsbody and to make herself very small so that she wouldn't be noticed. All the magic that she had learned, came from her own secret trips to the coven's library, where she studied in the small hours of the night, in the hopes that one day she would escape this miserable place.

"There are powerful shifters at that school who have been left to waste, as no witch has ever been able to defeat them. You will bring all five of them to our coven. It is time to step up our breeding program, and they will make excellent additions to our stock."

The witches around her smiled, their expressions filled with a cruel glee. Their eagerness for more powerful shifters made Melody sick, especially when her aunt referred to them as stock. Of course they would see them as that, rather than as people. Most witches were not much better, seeing them as lower-class citizens, but at Bestia, they were little more than animals to be trained for the coven's purposes.

"It is time, sisters," her aunt said, speaking to the witches around her that formed her inner cadre. "Bestia will rise and all will see our true worth." She turned pinning Melody with a glare. "The American council will tremble before our might, and after that, the world council. Bestia is destined to lead witches into a new era. Where humans will be enslaved and harvested for the paltry natural magic that they hold. We will rule the world."

There were cries of delight from the other witches, but Ambrosia's voice cut across them all. "Mistress, we can't trust her to do this for us, she's too soft on the shifters."

The cheering died away, her aunt's giddy expression

turning dark with hatred for Melody as she turned to face her again.

"You will not disappoint us. Ambrosia is right, I can see the defiance in your eyes. No, no, that will not do. Sisters, prepare her and the room. We must take precautions so this ungrateful trollop doesn't let us down right on the cusp of our victory."

Aunt Georgia swept from the room and the others either followed her or descended upon Melody. It seemed that her aunt was determined to lay one of the strong geasan upon her again. She had to resist.

Melody had heard of Adolphus, any witch with beast taming magic had. It was the premier academy, mostly because of the powerful shifters it had there, awaiting their witch. Two dragons. Two! When no young dragon shifters had come forth in a century to any of the schools. A couple of alpha wolves and she thought there was someone else. At least four strong shifters, and Melody was to defeat them?

She had no doubt that she could do so, but how on Earth was she meant to bring them back here and keep them safe. She couldn't allow her aunt to get a hold of them. The Goddess only knew what she had planned, but Melody had known for a while that her aunt had ambition. If Aunt Georgia couldn't rule her own coven with the matriarchal power, then she would gain enough power to make it a moot point. She would rule them all.

She had no chance to protest. Eager hands grasped at her, dragging her back down to the basement. She had only a glimpse of clothing laid out on the small dining table in the kitchen before she was whisked down the stairs. What they were going to do to prepare her, she had no idea, but she knew that it couldn't be good. She had to resist them. She had to, for everyone's sake.

Her aunt's lackeys laughed as they talked about how to ensure that Melody was not only weak enough, but stayed weak enough to participate in the spell casting. At the foot of the stairs, she could hear the murmur of voices as the shifters there asked for details before the witches began to emerge into the basement room.

Melody was thrown back into her cage, and for the first time that she could remember, it was locked, not just with a padlock like the shifter cages, but with magic. She wasn't strong enough to heal herself and undo the spell, so she was stuck there for the meantime.

"Well, starving her is the first obvious step," Claudia said with a smirk. "Withhold her breakfast gruel."

"She's already had it," Marjorie told them, scowling at her mistake. "I thought she was being brought up to work, I had to give her enough to keep going."

Claudia's pretty face turned ugly in her anger. "Well, that was stupid."

Ambrosia pushed between them, her mean eyes fixed on Melody. "She's already weak after yesterday, give her another beating, don't let her heal the wounds. If we keep her weak enough, she'll be ready before tomorrow."

Behind her, the other witches agreed. Magic, thick and

cloying, lifted her from the ground, holding her by her wrists. She was still naked, so they began straight away. Melody was too exhausted to care. She withdrew her mind into the dark corner where she kept herself sane during such a beating and tried to ignore the pain that licked up and down her body like fire. Eventually, everything faded away, until there was only Melody, sitting in a corner of her mind with the darkness for company.

4. MELODY

"Melody," a voice whispered harshly. Her shoulders were being held in a tight grip and she was being shaken.

No! She didn't want to wake up yet. She knew how bad it was going to hurt. If she had passed out, then it was bad. Likely the worst beating she had ever had.

"Melody, they're coming, quickly, take some power from me, or you're going to die from your injuries, please," the voice begged.

Despite her wishes, power was already being fed into her, great swathes of it. If her body was accepting it from this shifter, without her consciously drawing on it, then it was one of the shifters she was close to, one who she had befriended. Not all of the shifters in the cages had forgiven her for being their downfall, but they at least knew that she wasn't entirely to blame.

Somehow, several had become her friends, and they carefully gave her power whenever they could, forming a small secondary bond to the one they were held captive by. It was one of these bonds that was feeding life into her now. Despite her mind not wanting to, her body drank deeply.

Already Melody could feel her organs repairing themselves, her marrow pumping out more blood, her limbs straightening, and her bones realigning and connecting. Once again, her coven, grasping and lazy, had taken the simplest option. Instead of beating her daily until they were ready, they'd given her the beating of a lifetime that she wouldn't recover from. They'd been stupid. She could feel by how weak she was now – as her brain started processing the sensations coming from her extremities – that they had indeed pushed her too close to death.

The power flowing into her ceased, and it took Melody a moment to register that the shifter had collapsed and fallen out of her reach. What had she done?

She tried to open her eyes, but they were glued shut with grit. The ground was still wet around her, so she patted her hand in the closest puddle and brought the meagre moisture to her eyes, trying to get them open. It took several attempts before she could scrape away enough to blink, and even then her vision was blurred.

Had she cried? Had she finally given in and cried when they had beaten her? Melody's heart sank. She scratched away at more of the gunk around her eyes until she realised that it was coming away black. No, not black, dark brown, red. It wasn't dried tears encrusting her eyes, it was dried blood. Goddess, what had they done to her?

Melody rolled onto her side. In front of her, Malcolm lay on the floor, his breathing shallow. Of course, who else could give her so much strength in one boost? Still, she needed to give some of it back to him, he needed to make his own way back to his cage before anyone else came down. Aside from Melody, he was the only one with limited freedom in the basement. Melody's cage was left unlocked, Malcolm had simply learned how to unlock his with a sliver of chicken bone.

Uncoordinated, Melody's arm swung towards his outstretched hand until they connected, and she pushed his power back into him until he groaned and opened his eyes. By then, she was panting.

Dark, soulful eyes looked into her own ice-blue ones. "You mustn't claim the dragons," he whispered. "She's deranged. With a dragon at her beck and call she'd have the beginnings of a real army." He blinked slowly, pulling his hand from hers. "They've got magic, you know. Not like you, but their own magic nonetheless."

"I know," Melody told him. "They're not mine to claim, none of you are. I just have to make sure they don't try to challenge me. It's a decent sized college, I can make myself scarce, they won't know I'm there." She patted his hand, both of them lying in the water and filth, neither of them able to get up.

"I need you to do something for me," he said, after a pause.

"Anything that I can, you know that."

He nodded. "Take the rest. Take my life force, put it to good use. It's my time."

Melody was horrified. She couldn't do that, Malcolm, although not an alpha, was the cornerstone of the shifters here. Without him, many of them would lose hope and die, much, much faster. "I can't," she gasped. "Of all the things, how can you possibly ask me to do this?"

Malcolm shuddered. "My wolf died yesterday. I don't know what spell they were trying out on me, but I felt him shatter inside, felt him leave me. I can't shift anymore, he's not there. I don't want…" His voice cracked and a tear rolled across the bridge of his nose before dropping to the damp floor, lost amongst the dirty water. In a way, it was joining the thousands of tears, the millions, that had already been shed in this horrifying place.

"I can't live like this, a shadow. Please, Melody," he begged.

"Do they know?" she asked him. "Sonia, and Charlie and the others, do they know?" The other shifters would never trust her again if they thought she had killed him.

"Yes," he whispered.

Melody sighed. She really didn't want to do this, but after all he'd done for her, she couldn't deny him. "Tell me about your pack, where you grew up," she told him, taking his hand.

Malcolm smiled, closing his eyes. He'd had a good childhood, she knew that. They all had spent many nights talking together, telling Melody about the outside world, giving her hope, sharing stories of happier times to keep their spirits up. There was always the hope that they would escape. One way or another, they all hoped to leave.

"My parents were farmers. We grew corn, the witches that bonded to them lived in a small town nearby. Our house was surrounded by fields; wheat, corn, sorghum, oats. It was so quiet, so peaceful. You would have liked it there, Cub. Lots and lots of room for little legs to run around. We used to play hide and seek in the wheat, shifting and slinking between the stalks like water running down a hill," he said, quietly. His voice got softer and softer as she drew from him, until the last word left his lips with his last breath.

His chest stilled, the pulse at his neck jumped, and then stopped, but on his face, a small smile lingered. On the floor, in dirty water, Malcolm was happy and at peace. He'd died quietly with his memories of running as his wolf. In a way, she felt, they were reunited in his last moments.

Around them, there was only silence. Nobody wept, although she could hear their beasts howling and roaring inside their chests. Melody levered herself up onto her elbow, reaching out to stroke a hand down his cheek, her own farewell to Malcolm and his wolf. Already his skin was beginning to cool.

Outwardly, they would not mourn him, they didn't dare show affection to one another in front of the witches – aside from Melody. It wasn't safe, emotions were weapons to be used against them. Melody's heart hammered in her chest. Unable to express her grief, she turned it inward.

Somehow, she had to stop this. Her aunt's ambition was too much too far, and too many would suffer for it. Melody was the linchpin in Aunt Georgia's plan. She would have to prevent these geasan and circumvent whatever it was that she was being sent to do at the academy. Then and there, she swore it to Malcolm. This could not be allowed to happen anymore.

The shifters down here were good people, noble of spirit, brave, kind and any number of other wonderful things. This academy was a new opportunity. Her aunt would see it as the next step in her plan, but if Melody had anything to do with it, it would be the first step in Aunt Georgia's downfall.

5. MELODY

As desperate as she was, as hard as she tried, there was no way that Melody could have fought them off. Over the last week they had penned her in a cage with no food and hardly any water, until she was barely able to sit up.

Yesterday they had drawn a huge circle of salt around her and started chalking in various runes of containment and obedience.

She'd known what they were doing, and initially, Melody had used her remaining magic to blow the chalk away, smear it, or wash it off, until they got tired of repairing the thing. They had called down her aunt who simply laid another geas on her, demanding that she didn't interfere with the chalk marks, before ordering one of them to birch her. Aunt

Georgia had then swept out of the cellars and back to whatever she had been doing above.

In the cages around her, several shifters had winced. They hadn't voiced any complaints, they knew better than that. Any protests or signs of emotion would have led to both parties being punished anyway, so they watched in sullen silence as the women continued their preparations.

After some careful thought, Melody had realised that her aunt had done a very poor job of wording her geas. She hadn't been able to interfere with the chalk marks on the floor, but she'd said nothing about the chalk itself. It'd been satisfying to hear those bitches curse in frustration as all the chalk sticks in the cellar disappeared. Of course, it only meant they were twice as thorough in her birching, and that it started sooner, but anything she could do to delay the final geas was worth it. She had to stop it, somehow.

Ambrosia, the old bat, had used her magic to grip Melody's wrists and hoist her into the air so that her feet didn't touch the ground, her dark curls sticking to her temples with sweat. Despite her desire to fight, she hung there limply, conserving her energy. Her major battle would be with tears, something she refused to shed, no matter how bad it got.

Marjorie used her magic to give her welts from the nape of her neck, down to the balls of her feet. Each stroke was like fire on her skin, but she'd learned at a young age to internalise the pain. Her aunt was nowhere in sight. She never hung around for the punishments, it was like Melody's pain was beneath her, although it could also be the fact that Melody never cried. She knew that rankled her aunt.

Melody was beaten, but never completely broken.

The day her mother had transferred her the power was the worst pain she'd ever experienced, and she'd survived that. It had also made her the most powerful beast tamer their coven had ever seen, a power Aunt Georgia wanted, but must never have.

To get through all their punishments, all she had to do was hide in her mind — find a small dark corner and take refuge there while they did what they wanted to her body. That memory of her mother, however, had sustained her through a lifetime of abuse. She could handle another switching; she had the scars to prove that she was tougher than that.

When they felt her back was thoroughly striped with welts, Ambrosia had turned her around and Marjorie striped her front. Melody was proud to say that she hadn't cried. She never had, not since the day her mamma was murdered. It drove them all nuts, but she'd promised Mamma that she would be brave, and so she was. She'd simply withdrawn into her mind and let them do as they wanted. When they were like that, there was no point in fighting, and she'd been in no condition to do so, anyway.

Melody had landed in a heap, not even trying to prevent herself from being hurt. If she'd been incapacitated, they would have had to heal her before they could commence with the ritual, and with the amount of magic that this spell would need, they wouldn't have wanted to do that. It would have delayed the inevitable for a few more days while they recharged. Any delay tactic was worth it while she tried to work a way out.

Before her skull could hit the stone floor, there'd been a cushioning presence. One of them had cast something to prevent any damage to her head. Her body didn't have to be intact, but her mind did. A broken arm was nothing, bruised ribs, dislocated hip – pfft. Who cared? But a concussion was a no-no. Bitches.

Her head had bounced a second time on the spelled cushion, before the device disappeared. The resulting whack on the ground was enough to stun her, but not enough to cause lasting damage. She'd closed her eyes in pain, finally dragged from her safe place by the impact. She'd reset her mental barriers quickly, before the screaming of her body could overwhelm her. Then she rested – as much as she could.

Now it was a new day, the preparations had been made, and she'd been left limp in the circle overnight until they were ready for her. She almost smirked that she wouldn't be the only one hungry this morning. Without her to cook their breakfasts, they had been taking turns, and none of them were any good at it. If the food wasn't burnt, then there wasn't enough, or they forgot one of the dishes. It was Claudia this morning, she could hear the other witches berating her for not cooking enough again. It was a small thing to be thankful for, a petty thing, but it was what she had been reduced to.

The entire coven arrived, watching as the final runes were scrawled in place. Once the bitches were done, they all joined hands in a ring around the outside, their gowns swishing over the dusty floor as they moved into place. Melody could feel them gathering their power, before it swirled through the physical connection and into Aunt Georgia, who then fed it into the runed circle. As one, they chanted the words of binding in sonorous voices until the runes glowed with power.

The chanting went on and on, longer than was usual for a single geas. When they were finally done, the weight of the magic pinned her to the ground in a sweaty heap, she could hardly breathe with the pressure. This wasn't even the worst bit. The amount of power was telling her these weren't simple laws being laid upon her. Normally, the punishment would be a stinging slap on her face or rump, the weight of these told her that whatever was about to be placed on her was meant to harm, to maim. It was going to make stopping her aunt much harder, and if she disobeyed them all, it would likely kill her.

These geasan would form her, mould her behaviour for the rest of her life, forcing her to do things that she would never consent to otherwise. The hundreds already upon her were like a weight that hung on her, and these new ones simply added to the panoply of pain that was her soul. When the weight nearly crushed the breath from her entirely, the chanting stopped, and her aunt began to speak.

"Melody, I lay this geas upon you, you will accept every

challenge from every strong shifter at that school. Alphas and dragons, they are what we seek. You will bind them to you, and then you will bring them to the coven, where they will swear their fealty to us." Aunt Georgia smirked at her, knowing that any chance of Melody asking them to swear fealty to herself was now gone.

That was what her aunt had tried to do to her when Melody was a child, get her to swear to Aunt Georgia, personally, but her childish mind had sworn her to the coven instead. As long as her aunt was head of that coven, then the oath bound Melody to her indirectly, but if she should be replaced, or the coven disbanded, then Melody would be free of her.

Around her, the magic in the circle flared, and she screamed as it clawed its way into her skin. This was worse than anything else they had done to her, and even retreating into her head offered her no protection. This magic bound to her soul.

Before she had even drawn in a breath to scream again, Aunt Georgia laid another one upon her. "Melody, I lay this geas upon you: you will tell nobody about any geas upon you."

Melody threw her head back to scream again, but the sound was cut off by her body convulsing, trembling and shaking as the new magic burrowed into her, fighting its way even deeper into her flesh. With this restriction, Melody wouldn't even be able to explain any odd behaviour and she wouldn't be able to warn the shifters that she was sent after them, if she indeed sought them out. They would soon understand if she brought them home, but that would be the beginning of the end for everyone if she did.

Everything hurt so much, even her hair felt like it was on fire. There was, however, no respite before her aunt spoke for a third time.

"Melody, I lay this geas upon you, you will be loyal to your coven. So mote it be." And with those four words Aunt Georgia sealed Melody's fate.

Repeated by every witch joined there, they bound tighter. Liquid ran from her eyes, her nose and her ears, and a copper scent filled her nose. She knew that smell. It was the scent that had surrounded her Mamma as she bled to death in front of her. The blood that had dripped from her over the years in beating after beating, the precursor of death, a smell that she would never be rid of.

She had always suspected that Mamma's death had been caused by a spell from Aunt Georgia, but Melody had never been able to prove it. It didn't matter so much now, her aunt had proven herself more than capable over and over again.

For now, Aunt Georgia ruled the coven with an iron grip, and she had her sights fixed on gaining the two dragons that were at Adolphus Academy. That was where Melody was being sent. She would go there to learn and improve her powers, and to ensnare every poor damn dominant shifter that challenged her. She would bring them back here, and they would be stripped from her to form the core of her aunt's new army.

Her aunt would make the American council tremble before their might, and after that, the world council. Their coven was destined to lead the witches into a new era. Where humans would be enslaved and harvested for the little natural magic that they held. Her Aunt wanted to rule the world, and if Melody didn't find a way to stop her, then her Aunt would use Melody's powers to do it.

6. MELODY

Her departure was a rushed affair, thrust upon her like so many other things. She was never sure of dates or events, why did she need to know when Christmas was, when she would never celebrate it?

She dreaded leaving the shifters behind. Being ranked so low in her coven meant that the other members often ignored or forgot that she was there. It meant that she could sneak into the kitchen and get extra food, clean bandages, and water, and other luxury items like soap. Without her there to supply those extra things for them, their miserable lives would be that much harder.

The witches in her coven sometimes forced the shifters to hold their beast forms for weeks inside their small cages. The animals going insane with the lack of space to move and run. At those times, Melody would sit outside their bars and sing to them, stroking their fur and offering what comfort she could. Many of them had told her that she had saved their sanity. In short, the shifters loved her, despite her role in their downfall. Most of them loved her, but even those who didn't realised that she was caged far more effectively than they were behind their iron bars.

Several days after Melody had been bound by the stricter geasan, two of the less important coven members, Gwendoline and Martha, had appeared with a suitcase. They packed up all of her clothes and spell textbooks that she was required to have, books that she'd technically never had access to before. It was just as well she had spent so many nights sneaking in the library, otherwise she would have been too far behind the other students. It was ironic that her aunt demanded that she not embarrass her coven, yet at the same time denied her any formal training.

She had never seen any of the clothing before, it seemed that her usual rags were not to be included. That was a relief, there would have been no easy way to explain the level of poverty that they would represent. It would have been impossible to hide the abuse she had suffered as she was required to.

Melody was stripped, washed, dressed and groomed in front of all of the shifters. Given the amount of times that she had seen them naked, and the close bonds that they shared, she wasn't anywhere near as embarrassed as the two cruel witches had obviously hoped for. The older shifter women, Sasha and Sonia, had long ago explained the shifter mentality regarding nudity, and once she had adopted it, her embarrassment disappeared. It was just a different skin to them, and she was neither less or more, whether she was dressed or not.

She was called a bitch, a whore, and slapped and birched for her lack of modesty. Mentally, Melody shrugged it off. If she had complained and tried to cover herself, the punishment would likely have been worse. There was no way to win, so she no longer tried.

The two witches bustled out with as little warning as they had arrived, the suitcase disappearing with them. They had not told her to follow them, so she remained where she was, her eyes circling the area that she had called home for most of her life.

The cellars were cold and poorly lit, even in the daytime. No issue for the shifters with their excellent night vision, but it was sometimes a hazard for Melody. The witches liked to leave unexpected obstacles out for her, so that she would trip on them as she completed her duties down there.

Looking around now at the only home that she'd ever known, Melody felt a pang of loss. Even as miserable as most of her existence had been, there had been small, quiet moments of joy. It was the people that she would miss here, the familiars, not her coven. For as long as she could remember, Melody had wanted to escape this house of horrors, but now that she was, she didn't want to leave.

With only a small amount of time where nobody was about, Melody went from cage to cage, farewelling her friends. They were her real family, and she would miss them terribly, but she refused to cry. They offered her words of advice for dealing with shifters, and some stroked her hair, told her she was beautiful, and said all the right and loving things that they could in the little time that they all had left together.

She was hugging Sonia, one of the two women who had taken her under their wing, when Martha appeared with a sneer on her face. "We just washed you, you dirty little cow. Now you're probably covered in filth again. I'm not washing you a second time, let's go." She shoved a hand into Melody's hair and tugged, pulling her from Sonia's embrace and pushing her up the stairs.

The light was harsh on her eyes when they reached the top. Spring was on its way, and the cellars were finally pleasantly cool. It was just as well that she was leaving now because she wouldn't have been allowed to stay much longer. Her aunt would have probably made her sleep on the flagstone floor in the kitchen again.

Outside the gates to their compound, stood her aunt and two other witches. Ambrosia and Marjorie sneered as they each took one of her arms, holding her in place while her aunt opened a portal. It was impossible to portal directly into the grounds, but there was an area just outside the main gates where witches could arrive safely. Without a word of farewell or best wishes from her coven, she was frogmarched through the portal and into even cooler air on the other side.

Melody looked around in awe, although she had heard of

it, she'd never seen a picture of the place where she would be spending the next few years, and the sight filled her with both excitement and dread. The gates to Adolphus Academy were sturdy and practical looking, with small embellishments. Two large black shields were decorated with the academy's coat of arms. On either side, a tall sandstone wall stretched off into the distance, embracing the grounds and guarding them in one.

Marjorie pulled her along the drive, while Ambrosia dragged the suitcase along behind her. She didn't waste her magic to lift it, Melody knew that the nasty witch was saving that for the shifters as soon as she got back. Besides, what did the old bat care if Melody's bag arrived dusty and dented? It was just another example of the mindfucks that her coven liked to give her. What they failed to realise was, they had only succeeded in desensitising her.

The three of them made their way to the administration building where she was registered and assigned a room. Melody was shunted to the side as the two women took over filling in any paperwork and signing where indicated. There was a brief elevation of voices at one point, making her look away from her examination of the grounds through the window, but it was quickly silenced. It seemed that even the staff were afraid of her aunt's cronies.

They were handed a key and a map and then they moved on to inspect her dorm room, the two bitches pleased that she would not be spoiled by having a space to herself. However, they were disappointed that it was not a case of all the girls sharing one large space. Apparently, the word dormitory had stimulated visions of a lack of privacy, and a generally unpleasant place to be. Frankly, Melody was elated, it was far better than anything she remembered having. Melody was to share a room with just one other person.

Neither Marjorie nor Ambrosia were impressed. Melody couldn't care less, not even trying to hide her smile.

After the dormitory, she was escorted back to the central courtyard, told in no uncertain terms not to embarrass her coven, and left standing there like a dog waiting upon its master. Melody took a deep breath in, and let it out again. Was the air here cleaner or did the freedom just make it seem that way?

There were a few students lounging in the courtyard around her, but nobody who looked new or out of place like she did. Was this where she was meant to be?

She pulled her map out and looked at it again but could see nothing to indicate that she was due elsewhere. The main part of the academy was built around a series of corridors that looked like an asterisk, although on second thought, it was more like a rather unusual snowflake. As she folded it back up again, she saw that it had a short line of writing on the back in a neat cursive script.

Welcome lecture and orientation held in Gymnasium 1.

She flicked the map open again; the door should be just across the courtyard from her. That was handy. She hoped, however, that the gymnasium served some other purpose, because she had no intention of sweating through some arbitrary exercise class like a teenager. This was meant to be an academy for witches who had come into their majority, not a mockery of highschool experience. Not that she had attended human schools, but she had no intention of emulating them now.

From a central and sizable courtyard, long spokes of classrooms, storage areas and facilities spread out in all directions. These were bisected by a series of concentric rings. The corridors were covered, although not enclosed on the ends, so the breeze would flow along them. While it was pleasant now, she was sure that it would be horrible in the following winter.

7. MELODY

Towards the other side of the courtyard, between Melody and her destination, was a picnic table under a tree. Several men lounged on and around it, ignoring everyone else and talking amongst themselves. Other than that, there were a few clusters of students who were obviously second and third years. One or two had their familiars at their sides in human form, but many, especially the women, watched the shifters under the tree.

Even from where she stood, Melody could feel the power radiating from them. They were shifters, and powerful ones at that. Her heart thudded in shock. It seemed like she had found the alphas already. She took careful note of their faces. These were men that she needed to avoid.

When one looked in her general direction, her heart pounded in fear. The last thing she needed right now was to be noticed on the first day. Her body froze as his gaze swept past her, searching for something else, her breath releasing in a huff when it didn't return to her. It wasn't Melody that he was seeking, but that was far too close.

Turning carefully, she looked around, trying to work out what it was that he was searching for, but his attention continued to pan across everyone. Standing alone and looking as vulnerable as she did, she was painting a big target on her back, almost begging the predators to look at her, to see her as prey. But there was nowhere else for her to be until the lecture started. She could only hope that her anonymity lasted. If these men had been trapped at the academy for as long as she'd heard, they would be looking for a way out with a need born of desperation.

A subtle chime sounded, and from seemingly nowhere, a horde of students flooded the courtyard, talking and laughing as they crossed it into other corridors. The men on the table, however, didn't move, watching everyone with a predatory stare. Didn't they have to go to class too?

There was a slower stream of people moving into the gymnasium where she was meant to go, so she crossed the courtyard, carefully avoiding the table of alpha shifters. One of them turned to watch her pass, his eyes flickering golden before becoming human again. She heard a lion rumble with interest in his chest and hurried her steps. One of the others laughed, slapping the shifter on the shoulder, but his gaze never left her, burning the back of her neck with its intensity as she hurried towards the other students.

Several students gazed around with eyes filled with wonder as they walked. Even though no-one could attend before the age of twenty-five, Melody was struck by how young they looked. How innocent. They were definitely new enrollments like herself. Had they truly reached their majority? Or was this the first time they had left the confines of their coven too?

That made more sense, young witches who had grown up in healthy covens, stable environments wouldn't have reason to search for where the exits were, who the threats were, or even consider who was weaker than them. It was only Melody who was highly strung at being in a crush of bodies where there was nobody to protect her, to watch her back. She had no friends here, no allies, no help. These fresh-faced students wore a startling lack of caution. She could only hope that it was because it wasn't generally needed.

The students had filed into a large room filled with chairs, however, Melody could see markings on the floor that indicated basketball was often played here. There were also a few scorch marks high up on the walls and even one on the ceiling.

Defensive magic was one of the classes that was offered here, could that be the cause of the damage? It was the most logical conclusion. At least it wasn't sports and fitness tests. Still, defensive magic wouldn't be her strength. Although Melody had managed to find some texts on it, she'd never had the opportunity to practice. There was a good chance that the gymnasium would be a different kind of hell.

There were approximately a hundred other bodies packed in there with her, aside from the staff on the dais up the front. Melody quickly found a chair at the back of the room on the end of a row. Moments later, two burly men came up to her, predatory gazes pinning her in place.

They were like chalk and cheese, one blonde with dark eyes, the other with black hair and blue eyes. Yet there was something about their bone structure that hinted of shared ancestry. Were they brothers? Cousins? It didn't matter. Their attention was focussed on her, and she didn't like the level of threat they seemed to be projecting.

"Would you mind moving along one?" one of them asked. "If we sit side by side, we won't have enough room, but you're small enough that we could fit around you and not crush you if you were between us." He smiled down at her, his teeth unusually sharp. He was a shifter then. Her heart stuttered for a moment until she realised that they weren't that strong. Well, at least not compared to the shifters in the courtyard. They certainly would have given Malcolm a run for his money. Just the thought of him had her heart sinking again.

"Uh, ok," she stammered, moving down a seat. Immediately, the one who spoke jumped the row of connected chairs, sliding into the one on her left, and the other one fell into the chair beside her with a grunt.

"Aiden," said the chatty one, "that's my twin, Adam. We're hoping to be bonded by the same witch."

"I wish you luck with that, twins are very rarely bonded

by the same witch, in fact, witches rarely bond more than one shifter," she told him, and immediately he scowled.

"We know, we're just putting the word out there, because any witch who wants one of us has to take us both. It saves a lot of drama if they know what they're getting from the start," he explained.

"Oh, well, that's good thinking, I'll be sure and tell anyone who asks about you," she mumbled, but knew that he would hear it.

Aiden put an arm around her shoulders and leaned in toward her, caging her against his twin. "You looking for a matched pair?" he asked her, slyly.

Melody froze. "Uh, no. No, I'm not. I think the pair of you would be more than I could handle, you're huge!"

Aiden smirked, and she felt Adam lean towards her on the other side. "You know, we're not just big, we're proportional, all over." He leered at her. "All. Over." He ran his nose along the outside of her ear, making her shiver. "You smell good enough to eat," he husked, and there was a low growl from the other side of her. She wasn't sure if it was in agreement or not.

Suddenly, the pair of them leaned back, wincing, and Melody caught a glimpse of fine-boned hands gripping each of them by an ear.

"Aiden, Adam, what have I told the two of you about bothering the first-year students? And about ganging up on young women, and on attending lectures that aren't your own?" The authoritative voice grew sterner with each word, and as she spoke, she twisted their ears until they were standing and bent over to her height. The woman's magic flared, wrapping around the two shifters, binding their arms to their sides and lifting them over the seats to stand either side of her.

Melody wanted to giggle, it was rather funny to see the two overbearing males lugged around like that, especially when she knew that they weren't going to be beaten. At least she hoped not. From what she remembered of her coven before her mother's death, and from the little that she'd been able to garner, while shifters were often treated as second class citizens, the familiar bond was sacred to most of those who could hold one. The men might be chastised, but nothing like what would happen back at her coven.

"Sorry Mrs H," growled Adam. So, he *could* talk then!

"Really, we're sorry. It won't happen again, cat's honour. But you can't blame us for trying her, she's a right tasty smelling morsel," he said, then yelped as his ear was twisted even harder.

"Come with me, right now, the pair of you!" spat the witch, dragging them away. "Fucking pumas, think they're the Goddess' gift to all witches," she muttered, but loud enough for Melody to hear.

They made a hilarious sight, the two giant shifter males bent double and at the mercy of a much smaller witch. The jerked to a stop, frantically pulling against the woman when a stern looking man stepped through the door.

"Toby, please take these two out and have them chop firewood for a few hours. Maybe some good physical labour will get them back in control of their beasts. I've never seen a pair of shifters who think with their cocks as much as you two do, and that's saying something!"

Melody was stunned. This foul-mouthed woman was obviously a member of staff, but she was earthy and real, her idea of punishment much more benign than what Melody was used to. The men couldn't be allowed to continue to behave in such a way, especially given how much younger the other women seemed to be, and the boundless energy of healthy shifters would certainly be curtailed by some physical labour, but she wasn't so sure about the man taking them away. He looked a little frightening and she wasn't sure that his version of punishment was as benign and the woman's.

Toby growled down at the two shifters, but they didn't seem overly worried, more resigned. It was only then, however, that Melody realised he was a shifter himself, and from the way he looked at the woman, he was bonded to her.

Aiden glanced her way, and gave her a saucy wink, but before Melody could respond, he jumped a foot in the air and glowered at the witch beside him.

"You straighten your face young man, and you start thinking with the right head, or by the Goddess I'll make you bloody howl like a wolf pup stung by a bee!"

"Cat's don't howl," he said, confused.

"You fucking will when I'm done with you!" she snapped, and gave them a shove out the door.

Melody froze, memories of her own beatings flashing

through her mind. Immediately all three shifters turned and looked back at her, their noses lifted, scenting the air.

Toby grunted, looking at Mrs H and then jerking his chin at Melody. The witch spun, and whatever she saw on Melody's face had her own expression softening. She looked at Melody for a moment, her gaze roaming over her before she nodded to herself.

"There, there, dear. As frustrating as this pair are, I wouldn't actually hurt them." She turned and waved the three shifters out of the room. "Until they're bonded, they're often like overgrown children. Well, at least the male ones are. The females seem to be much more practical than their brothers. Either way, I need to take a firm hand with them. They'll be fine, you'll see."

Melody found herself liking the woman a little better. She didn't have much experience with shifters as young as that pair, but it seemed that the older woman had them well in hand.

The woman turned around to the students who had paused in their movements, shooing them off to find seats before she walked up to the front of the dais, standing in front of the other staff assembled there. There was one chair left on the small stage, and Melody presumed that it must belong to her.

"Good morning ladies and gentlemen, my name is Mrs Hardinger, and I am the student counsellor for witches and shifters alike. It is my great honour to introduce to you the head of Adolphus Academy, Provost Aer-Canticum." The witch who came forward to stand at the front of the dais was tall and shapely, despite her academic robes swirling loosely about her. Her hair had a hint of honey that looked like it had once been a deep auburn. Something about the way she carried herself struck Melody, until she realised that the woman moved a little like the faint memories she had of her mother.

"Goddess' blessings on you all, and welcome to Adolphus Academy, the oldest of the academies specialising in beast taming magic in the United States. We have a proud tradition here of working with witches *and* shifters to facilitate the best of all possible matches between magic and familiar. Here you will learn to work together for the good of both witch and shifter. We aim to improve upon your already impressive skills to raise you to being the best that you can be."

Grey eyes scanned across the room. "Unusually, this year we have more witches than shifters, something that should please most of the shifters, but do not fret, overall the academy has a greater proportion of shifters than witches, so as far as the witches go, if you are indeed talented enough to be able to manage a shifter bond, then you have come to the right place."

There were murmurs in the crowd of students, and Melody's heart was with them. It was all well and good for the witches, but for the shifters knowing that they were stuck here until they found their witch, and now discovering that the witches were outnumbered and their own chances reduced, it must have been a rude awakening.

The provost must have understood this as well because she raised her hands in a calming motion. "Do not let this deter you, shifters. This means that we attract stronger witches here, so anyone that you do challenge will have a greater chance of being able to make your beast submit. This academy specialises in finding the right bond, rather than just any bond. Mrs Hardinger is an excellent counsellor, and I would recommend speaking to her before you decide to challenge, or to accept a challenge. She's our secret weapon – Mrs Hardinger has a good nose for knowing who will work together well."

There were groans around the room. A shifter's sense of smell was supposed to play a part in choosing witches to challenge. Nobody knew the exact science of it, but they were usually able to scent witches who were strong enough to defeat their beasts. Melody wasn't surprised that the twin puma shifters had homed in on her. She was strong enough to defeat any shifter in the room from what she could sense of their power. She would have to work at hiding her scent somehow, or she would be inundated with challenges.

"Some of you have the goal of finding a familiar as soon as possible, so that you can begin shaping your relationship under the tutelage of the staff here. Please, let me disabuse you of that notion. I have seen many witches and shifters regret a hasty bonding in my years here, and it is never a pleasant experience to have to sever a bond."

There were gasps around the room. The bond between a witch and her familiar was a sacred thing, supposedly a gift from the Goddess herself, and they weren't severed lightly.

"You think me cold-hearted for agreeing to sever those bonds, but if you had seen the suffering of those involved, you would think me heartless for not agreeing to do it." She paused and looked at them all again. "Yes, suffering. Shifters, imagine agreeing to bond a witch who seemed ok, and then down the track, finding another witch who not only lived up to all of your dreams, but turned out to be your mate!"

Around the room, shifters stilled. The only thing more sacred to them than the familiar bond, was the mate bond.

"Witches; imagine finding out that your familiar was fated for another witch and losing control of their shifting. Or feeling them pine until the point of death. Imagine bonding a shifter who hadn't found their mate but had been unknowingly weakened at the time of the challenge, and then later finding that you could never repeat the feat of that first challenge. That your shifter was growing wilder and more out of control because your magic wasn't quite up to helping them." She paused again to let that sink in.

"So, yes, I have severed bonds. I really cannot emphasise enough the need for careful thought and consideration when seeking a bond. I also cannot emphasise enough the help that Mrs Hardinger can be. I have never, in all my years, seen her steer a bond wrong."

The witch in question inclined her head graciously when

the provost looked at her. "I like to joke that she is the best matchmaker in the country—"

Her speech was interrupted by chuckles. Many witches, male and female alike, had been subject to scrutiny by matchmakers who claimed to have an uncanny knack for making good marriages between covens.

"And that she has been the midwife to many successful bindings, so I do encourage you to seek her advice. Finally, I'd like to warn you about her earthy approach to things. I've tried, unsuccessfully over the years, to get Mrs Hardinger to conform to shall we say, more politically correct language, but it has been an exercise in futility. The woman swears like a trooper, tells it how it is, and frankly, is one of the funniest people I've ever met. I count it as a sign of growth on my part that I have realised that she is perfect as is."

This time everyone laughed, and behind the provost, Mrs Hardinger poked her tongue out. It was obvious that the two of them were good friends. Their easygoing relationship gave Melody a sense of hope that maybe they would be able to help her. She didn't know how, because she couldn't talk about it, but somehow, if anyone could help her out of her mess, it would be those two women.

From there, the speeches moved on to more practical matters. Warnings to the shifters not to test the wards that marked the boundaries of the academy, that not even the dragon shifters could defeat them. There were concerned murmurs at that.

Notices were given out about dormitory protocols,

timetables were handed out, and information on meal times and where condoms could be procured from was dispensed. There were again ripples of uncomfortable laughter about the last item, until Mrs Hardinger stood up and addressed them again, talking on the practicalities of living with a bunch of hormone driven shifters and often inexperienced witches.

"At the end of the day, you're adults. We expect you to behave accordingly and responsibly. While it may be fun to fuck like rabbits, let me tell you from experience, it is certainly no joy to breed like them."

There was a moment of shocked silence, and then the entire room erupted in laughter.

"Mrs Hardinger," the provost chuckled, "I do believe that is one of the best warnings you have ever delivered. I suggest you write that down and use it every year from here on out." Mrs Hardinger flapped a dismissive hand at her, but Melody noticed that she did indeed write it down in a notebook that she procured from her pocket. At the side of the room, the shifter that had accompanied her earlier shook his head with a rueful smile on his face.

"On that note," the provost chuckled at her own pun, "you are dismissed to your first class. Good luck everyone, and again, welcome to Adolphus."

There was scattered applause from the gathered students before everyone got up and began to file out again. It was certainly an interesting start to her time here. Melody wondered if everything would be as much fun.

8. DEAN

"Hey, hey. First-years, one o'clock!" Ryan nudged him. Dean looked up in interest. He couldn't help it. He watched as the new students spilled out into the courtyard for a break after the morning orientation session. The males he dismissed outright, and his lion snorted in amusement at him. It was his bloody lion that insisted he only challenge a female anyway, so he didn't know what was so funny about it.

Looking across the female population, he was pleased to see several that he found attractive. While not essential when finding your witch, one that was pleasing to the eye was certainly a bonus.

"Who's up?" he asked, looking around at his friends. The five of them lounged on a wooden table and chair set under one of the trees in the courtyard. It was *their* spot, none of the other students ever sat there. It was on a slight rise due to the roots of the tree above them which gave them a slight advantage when looking across the other students. His lion was rather pleased that he could survey *his* kingdom.

"All yours," muttered Justin, from where his head rested on his arms on the table. He was dozing in the dappled light. They had all been up late the night before, talking, laughing and drinking. While they couldn't get drunk with their shifter metabolisms, the lack of sleep could still affect them.

Dean sighed, he should have kept his mouth shut. If he had, it would be Ryan making his way over to the first-years now. The new students all watched him approach, a little fearful of his predatory grace and reputation, so he put on his warmest smile. If a witch did manage to defeat his beast, then it would be best to start off their partnership with a positive image.

He looked over the assembled witches. They were all whispering amongst themselves, and without trying, he could hear the word *Apex* filtering amongst them. Good, it was always better when he didn't have to properly introduce himself.

The Apex, that was what their little group was known as. Two dragons, two alpha wolves and an alpha lion, they were the apex predators at Adolphus Academy – hence the name. Dean was the latest addition to the group, but it hadn't all been smooth sailing. Now that he knew them better, he could see them for what they were, but right at the start he thought that they were a bunch of elitist cunts.

The Apex held themselves apart from the other shifters. It wasn't about superiority, it was about survival. The dragons had been here for over half a millennia. It was a long time to be away from your people, a long time to be stuck at this bloody school, waiting for their witch to turn up. The school held them in a kind of stasis, so despite being almost a thousand years old themselves, the two of them only looked eighteen.

When everyone you know either moves on with their witch, or dies, it's sensible to only spend time with people in the same boat as you. As Apex shifters, they all knew that they would be there for a long time, and it was better to suffer as few losses as possible. If you didn't get to know someone, then you couldn't really miss them. It had taken Dean ten years before he really began to understand. The others congratulated him, it had taken some of them two to three times that long.

Dean scanned the students, looking for one that would meet his eyes. Failing that, the one that cringed the most would do. The choice was made for him. An attractive young witch strode right up to him, her eyes scanned him up and down and a low hum of approval sounded under her breath, easily audible to his enhanced hearing.

"Well, aren't you a snack? I gather you're one of the Apex shifters." Avarice was plain on her face and it disgusted him. He hoped that she wouldn't defeat his lion. The beast inside him growled in his head, this bitch would be no match for *him*. Dean appreciated his confidence, but he didn't share it. It only made his beast growl more.

He didn't bother responding to her statement, simply going through the motions. "I challenge you for mastery of my beast," he said without fanfare. She looked disappointed, and he smirked. If she wanted drama — a show, she wasn't going to get one from the Apex. Some of the other shifters liked to make a production of it, and in the early days, he had been one of them, but when you've challenged over a thousand witches, it loses its appeal. He just wanted to get this over with and get away from her as fast as he could.

"You're not very excited about it, are you? Never mind, sweetling, I'll make sure you get plenty of excitement after," she purred, and he shuddered in response.

Yeah, now he was going to put everything into defeating her. His lion concurred.

"Very well, I accept. It's about time someone tamed you."

He gave her a feral grin. "Do you even know which one I am?"

"It doesn't matter. I'll claim as many of you as I want." She took a few steps back from him. "Well? What are you waiting for, the sooner I claim you, the sooner we can begin your overdue training." She smirked and flicked a hand in his direction, indicating he should shift.

Rather than giving her the satisfaction of stripping in front of her before he shifted, Dean exploded through his clothing, fabric spraying in shreds around him. She frowned in annoyance which pleased him even more, he knew that she would have enjoyed seeing him naked, he really did have a reputation as eye candy for the spank bank.

His lion preened at the admiring glances of the other witches, the cat knew that he was worth chasing, his mane was long and an unusually bright-golden colour that had fingers twitching around it. Women loved to stroke it. His lion stretched, flexing both sets of claws before letting out a roar, indicating just how irritated he was by this pathetic witch. Pathetic bitch more like it, snorted Dean in the lion's brain, and his lion roared again in agreement.

To their mutual satisfaction, the witch paled and took several more steps back. There were snickers behind her, and suddenly her retreat stopped. She stood taller, raised a hand dramatically in front of her and shouted, "Shift, you feral feline!"

If Dean had been in his human form, he would have laughed out loud at her. Instead, his beast prowled forward until he was standing right in front of her, then, with a gentle nudge of one paw, he knocked her on her ass. He was tempted to turn and lift his tail and give her a spray but thought better of it. She wasn't worth the effort. He did, however, kick dust onto her with his back feet.

Dean prowled back to the hillock where the others sat and jumped up onto the table, knocking Justin off his perch on the edge as his lion stretched out along the top. The others snickered and slapped his shoulders. Dean didn't even turn to watch the witch, but he felt the moment when Nick raised a shield around them, the hex that the humiliated witch threw, bounced right off it.

There were gasps from the other students, and instantly a teacher materialised beside the stunned witch. Attacking shifters was grounds for expulsion. The teacher clapped a hand on her arm, and just like that the two of them disappeared. The girl would be off campus before the dust of their departure had settled.

"One down, sixty odd to go," Nick murmured with a snicker.

The dragons' magic was what made them such a prize. That and their strength, and probably their sheer size. Unlike any other shifter, dragons had their own magic, although they still needed to bond to a witch to manage their shifts. They didn't breed often and were rare, so having two at this school had made it a target for those who wanted a strong shifter.

The boys had seen it all time and again. Witches that were strong in their coven were raised with the belief of their own importance. Their egos were fed, pumped up, primped and then packed off to tame one of the stronger beasts there. These girls were big fish from small ponds until they arrived at the academy, then they realised they were just the minnows. The Apex were the sharks. They ate little fish for breakfast.

"Well, none of the others will come near us for a while, anyway. What do you want to do? Chase them or just lounge around. I don't feel like repeating rune history again." Austin looked around at them all.

"But I thought runes was your favourite class, Oz?" Ryan teased. The others chuckled. "We couldn't keep you out of that class when that witch was teaching it. What was her name again? Miss…"

"O'Connor," Nick supplied, with a smirk. They all roared with laughter.

"Miss O'Connor," sighed Ryan. "Fuck she was hot. You didn't seem to mind being stuck here for fucking eternity when she was teaching."

They all laughed again, but there was a slightly harder edge to it. It was the other side of being stuck within the academy boundaries. Once here, the shifters couldn't leave until they had been bonded to a witch. The five of them had completed their three years of classes, and then done so again. Dean had only been there ten years, but the others had been here long enough to complete it multiple times.

Realistically, the dragons could teach the subjects better than the teachers could, but because they were unbonded – although more likely because they were shifters and therefore inferior – they would never be allowed to teach. Still, nobody bothered them when they skipped class, it wasn't like they could justify making them attend. It did have the advantage of making them look even more badass to the other students, which kept the usual clingers away.

"I feel like a hunt, come on Ry, Dean, let's go play." Oz got up, waiting for the two of them.

"I suppose you want me to facilitate this?" sighed Nick.

"You could play along?" suggested Oz.

Nick snorted. "No thanks. No point, but we'll take note of the ones that you knock off the list."

"How very kind of you," said Ryan, mirroring Nick's snort.

Dean knew all three of them felt it, the moment that Nick's magic combined their minds together so that they could speak to each other as though they had a pack link. The two alpha wolves, Oz and Ryan could manage that easily, but with the species difference between them and Dean, it was impossible. Instead, Nick cast some spell that made it possible for the three of them to talk, mind to mind, whether in their beast or human forms.

You going to get dressed, or are you going to prowl for a bit? asked Oz in his head.

I hunt, he simply told the wolf, before stalking off towards one of the corridors that left the courtyard.

I'm going to up the ante, boys, Justin said in their link, surprising them all. They knew that the dragons listened, but it was rare that they participated. *I'm going to scent one, and then give you that scent. You have an hour to find her and get her to challenge one of you.*

The three of them laughed mentally. *Game on,* said Dean. It certainly was, this had just become much more fun.

Justin got up and casually sauntered over to where all the first-years had initially paused when emerging from their lecture. Everywhere, students stopped what they were doing and watched him. He walked in circles for a bit, inhaling deeply here and there, but doing nothing really interesting. A discreet chime sounded, and everyone rose to their feet and split up amongst the many corridors, heading off to their classes.

Justin kicked up some dust, Dean knew he was making a mess of the scents where he stood, to confuse matters a little for them. While he was messing around, the two wolves stripped and shifted, catching the attention of anyone still lingering. Finally, ten minutes after the chime had sounded, Justin walked back to them with a smirk.

"Here you go, gentlemen." He passed the memory of the scent to their minds.

"Huh, I thought you were going to go for that other one, she smelled amazing," commented Nick, thoughtfully.

Justin looked at him for a moment. "No. That would be too easy. They would be too attracted to the scent. Their beasts would insist on finding her. Instead, they're going to have to ignore her as they scour for this one. She's now the ultimate distraction for them."

You fucker. What's the good one smell like then? asked Dean

"Nah, if I give that to you directly, you won't be able to resist. She's like fucking catnip for me, and I'm much more used to ignoring scents than you are. Just go with the one I gave you, I'll be watching to see if you cheat."

Dean's lion snarled, but he trotted over to the starting point with the two wolves. His lion rumbled at the closeness of the others, but Dean told him to settle down. They had a witch to track. She may even be *their* witch. The lion snorted, doubtful, but played along, opening his mouth to scent the air better.

This way, Ryan had already found her. He trotted across the courtyard towards the far corridor.

I'll take the right flank, said Oz, *you take the left.*

Dean's lion did not like being ordered about by the wolves, but he took the corridor that was indicated. The three of them would come at her from all sides, she wouldn't know what hit her. This first one was easy. They knew, however, that Justin had picked up several scents for them to chase. The next hunt would commence from wherever they were, whether it was near the new target or not. Justin would have them running around the school and causing havoc all day.

The teachers and the other students would ignore it, it wasn't a new thing, but the first-years would be both thrilled and terrified to have the three huge beasts prowling amongst them all day. Inside his lion, Dean smiled. Today was going to be a lot of fun. The hunt was on!

9. MELODY

The first time one of the giant wolves barged into her classroom, Melody was surprised. It had lifted its nose, giving a little whimper, before it slowly turned and left. The teacher continued his lecture on the intricacies of portal dynamics as though nothing had happened, but the students were all astir. What on earth was that about?

In her next class, it was the lion who entered for a moment, sniffing deeply and then turning to leave before he froze on the spot. Slowly, he turned and scented the air again, his gaze seeming to fix right upon her. He took a hesitant step forward, but in the corridor, a wolf howled. The lion growled, lowering his head and leaving. Again, the teacher acted as though nothing had happened.

For the rest of the day, beasts wandered in and out of the classrooms, distracting the students and thrilling everyone.

It wasn't until her last class, however, that she got to see what the fuss was truly about.

This time, all three beasts prowled in, sniffing deeply before aiming for a girl toward the back. Silently they approached her, one wolf head-on, the other and the lion on either side of her.

"Really gentlemen?" huffed the teacher, "must we do this now? I would have thought that this game had worn out long ago."

The collective attention went from the drama in front of them, to the teacher and back. Everyone waited with bated breath to see what would happen next. It seemed that whatever game they were playing, would continue.

The girl looked frantically at the beasts, the wolf in front of her snarling and getting ever closer, before turning frightened eyes back to the teacher. "What do I do?"

"Oh, for goddess' sake. Tell him you accept the challenge, and then tell him to shift. Let's get this farce over with so that we can get on with our day," snapped the teacher.

"Oh, oh, okay," stammered the poor girl. "I accept your challenge?" Somehow, she made it into a question. The wolf stopped growling and sat down in front of her, waiting. When she said nothing else, he gave a little growl again and stood.

"Fucking change him back, you stupid bitch," snapped one of the guys in the class, and she flushed scarlet.

"Oh, yes, of course!" She held her hand up in front of her and Melody could feel the intense focus of her powers as they gathered. "Shift!" she commanded, as she released her magic into the wolf. The wolf sat there, sighed, and then the three beasts turned to leave.

As he passed Melody, the lion paused, sitting for a moment beside her. He huffed at her, and her papers scattered across her desk and onto the floor. The other students laughed, and the teacher sighed.

"Dean, please, we really need to get on with this semester. The three of you have caused enough disruption for one day, have you not?"

The lion pondered this for a moment, then he stood and turned to her. He licked her from jaw to temple before she could even blink, giving a satisfied sounding huff when he turned to leave. The class laughed again, and Melody was left with a great deal of slobber running down her face and dripping from her chin.

What a jerk!

A hanky appeared in front of her, and Melody looked over to see the boy sitting next to her holding it out. Hazel eyes regarded her steadily as she took it and wiped down her face.

"Thank you," she said, quietly. He nodded, a dimple puckered his dark skin when he smiled briefly at her, before returning to his notes.

The lecture resumed as soon as the lion had left. It was just so bizarre. She'd known that Adolphus Academy was going to be different to what she had imagined but this was a little ridiculous. The chime sounded to signal the end of the class and the teacher sighed.

"I want you to read the first five chapters of your text tonight, we'll be discussing them in class tomorrow. Failure to participate will result in an outright fail."

There were groans around the classroom as everyone packed up and headed out. Melody gathered her things and, to her surprise, found the boy who had passed her the hanky waiting for her.

"Oh, um, I'll wash it and get it back to you," she stammered.

"Keep it." He held out a hand to her. "I'm Quinn, I'm a shifter."

"Oh, um, Melody. I'm a witch."

He chuckled. "Yeah, we can smell who is what here."

Melody blushed crimson. Yeah, that wasn't creepy at all, but she had forgotten that fact. With all her knowledge and experience working with the shifters back in her coven, how could she have forgotten?

"Of course you can, sorry. I guess I'm a little distracted." Melody continued to wipe the gunk from her face as they walked toward the courtyard. "What kind of shifter are you?"

"Wolf. But don't worry, I won't be challenging you. Not after the lion staked his claim, anyway."

Melody looked at him, startled. "Staked his claim? Licking me was staking his claim?"

Quinn laughed. "No, the scent he released when he did. It let every shifter in the room know that he was interested in you. He's one of the Apex, word will get around fast and nobody will bother you for a while. It sucks, because I can feel how powerful you are, I wouldn't mind challenging you myself."

Melody shuddered. "Yeah, about that. I don't want a familiar until my final year. I was kind of hoping to fly under the radar for a bit. I put a mask on my power, I thought that it would be enough to deter most shifters."

Quinn looked at her in askance for a moment, and then seeing she wasn't going to say more, he looked thoughtful. "The mask works for a bit, until you get up close, then there's no hiding it. You know that not all shifters want to fuck their witches, right? Some of them can hardly stand who they've ended up bonded to. You can still have a familiar without it getting messy." He looked at her hopefully.

"It's not that, it's complicated really, I can't talk about it, but for now, I just want to get on with my studies. If I can graduate early, even better."

"You came here, the premier shifter academy, the one with the Apex, and you don't want a shifter, and hope to graduate early? Melody, you're quite an unusual woman."

She flushed. Well, put like that, she did sound kind of nuts. "I promise, it's for the best. There's other stuff going on at home. I just … I need to do it like this, ok?"

Quinn moved suddenly, pinning her shoulders against the wall. "Are you alright? Do you need protecting? Bond me, and nobody will lay a hand on you again."

From behind him there was a roar, and then suddenly

Quinn was gone. Melody looked for him, finding him sprawled on his back with a naked man sitting on his chest and pounding away at Quinn's face. Furious, she stormed toward him, but two equally naked men beat her to it, pulling the man away by the arms, even as he kicked and struggled to get back to his quarry.

Melody ran to him. "Quinn, are you alright?" She laid her hands on his head when he didn't answer and delved deep within him.

"Move back from him this instant, young woman. His shifter healing will put things to right in moments, and if he wakes up with his beast in control, he'll rip you to shreds!" commanded one of the teachers behind her, as he strode up, his robes billowing behind him.

I'd like to see him try it, thought Melody, but she wisely said nothing aloud as she took two steps back.

The teacher stood guard over Quinn, and moments later he sat up, shaking his head. Even as she watched, his cuts sealed themselves and his bruises faded from purple to green to yellow and then disappeared. His eyes, when she finally looked at him, were golden. His wolf was in control. She had to help him find his balance again, and quickly before he attacked someone.

Melody stepped toward him again and the teacher reached out to grab her, but Quinn moved faster. Thankfully, Melody was close enough to intercept his clawed hand, and she caught it both with her own and her magic before he could rake the teacher.

"Enough!" she snarled at him, and immediately he subsided. There was a hush across the courtyard. She had made his beast submit, she knew now that it was only a matter of time before he challenged her whether the lion had indicated his interest or not, so she took the initiative, speaking quietly to him. "Go sit with your friends and calm down. I'll talk with you later when you're more reasonable."

The shifter nodded curtly and walked off. If he challenged her now, his heightened emotional state would have him at a disadvantage. She knew that he respected her for not using that against him while he was vulnerable. The only thing was, it meant her time was limited before he challenged her. Well, she would just have to do her best to avoid him. Him and the lion. It was a pity, because she thought Quinn might have turned out to be the first friend she'd ever had.

10. RYAN

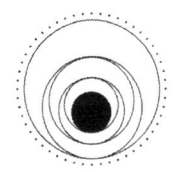

Ryan watched the witch as she spoke to the other wolf, instantly forcing him to back down. Yeah, those two would be bonded by the end of the day. Pity, he would have liked to challenge that one himself.

He held on tighter to Dean as he struggled to get his shit together. They had all seen the wolf shifter pin the witch to the wall. At first he thought it was a challenge, but when it didn't pan out, it looked more like an attack. Either way, Dean's lion went nuts and leapt from the table where he had been standing, growling. He shifted midair – something Ryan didn't even know that Dean could do – and hit the ground running. Still naked, he grabbed the wolf and tore him away from the witch.

The look of fury on Dean's face was startling to say the least. Ryan had never seen his friend so angry. By the time the third blow landed, however, he knew that Dean was going to kill the wolf. Ryan wasn't sure if it was his loyalty to his species, given that the guy on the ground was another wolf, or to his friend that made him move as fast as he did, giving him the strength needed to get there in time. Together with Oz, he managed to pull the rabid lion shifter away and hold him at a distance until Dean got his shit under control.

To be safe, they dragged Dean back to the table where one of the dragons threw a pair of sweats at him. Dean continued to growl even as he pulled his pants on, his eyes never leaving the witch.

"I told you," chuckled Justin.

"Told us what?" Ryan asked, taking the bait.

"If you smelled her, you wouldn't be able to resist!"

Nick's head jerked around at that. "Wait, she's the one that smelled so good?"

"Yep, and the cat has it bad for her," said Justin with a snicker.

"Too bad that wolf got there first then," Ryan said, frowning. "She quelled him with just one word. There's no way he won't challenge her now. Sporting of her to give him time to calm down first. His wolf will respect her more for that."

"There's nothing stopping you from going after her first, pup," said Nick. "You're an alpha, you outrank that fucker. Go make your claim."

Dean turned and snarled. "She is mine to challenge."

Justin roared with laughter. "Fucking told you, his beast is smitten."

Dean said nothing, he just turned and punched the dragon in the jaw. Justin shook it off and laughed even harder, holding up his hands in surrender when Dean raised his fist to swing again.

"Easy dude, easy. She's your catnip, literally. I get it. I smelled her first, remember? It's why I kicked up so much dust, I wanted to give the rest of you time to encounter her scent when it wasn't so strong. I thought it might help you build a resistance or something. Even my dragon took notice, and I can't remember the last time he looked at a witch."

Dean's snarls subsided, his lion's golden eyes gradually receding to reveal his usual tawny ones, but he didn't relax. "Where is she?"

They all looked around, but she wasn't anywhere in the courtyard. "Relax, man. We'll hunt her next and you can challenge her, ok? Your beast will calm down once she fails. Jus and I have seen this before. Fuck, we've done this before, right dude?" soothed Nick, running a hand through his honey coloured hair.

"Yeah man. About my fifth year, there was this witch, fuck, her scent almost made me shift on the spot. Turned out later on that she was using some sort of spell on her scent." Justin shook his head at the memory. "This witch smells just as good, I'm willing to bet that she's doing the same. We've been here for ages, they're all keen to nab one of us by fair means or foul. We just need to be patient and wait for the right one to come along."

"We'll give her a sporting chance, we'll wait for ten minutes after the bell again, and then we'll hunt her." Ryan slung an arm around Dean's tense shoulders. "It'll be over soon, dude, but you know if you don't let your cat hunt her, he'll grumble about it for weeks."

Dean sighed and nodded, his flaxen locks falling over his face, finally relaxing enough to sit down with them. "Sorry Dude," he growled softly at Justin, who just waved it off.

WTF was that? Ryan asked Oz on their pack link. *Is she his fucking mate or something? I mean, I smelled her the other day, and I wanted to stay with her, but I was able to walk away.*

No idea, man, Oz sent back. *I've never seen him like that, but then the dragons said they've seen this kind of thing before, so I'm just going along with what they're saying. They're probably right. There are a lot of covens out there who would want any one of us. I'm surprised that we haven't seen more efforts like this to get us.*

No way, Oz. The academy screens them pretty carefully. I'm surprised that the other one got through; she must have cast the scent thing after she arrived. Ryan ran his hands through his short brown hair and yawned. *Don't stress, the teachers will pick up on this one too, and then she'll be expelled like the other bitch. Let's just keep an eye on Dean and see how this pans out. Yeah?*

Yeah. It's not like she'll beat him or anything, although he'll probably piss on her now, just to settle the score, sent Oz.

Fuck yeah! Ryan laughed. *I totally thought he was going to do it to that bitch this morning. That would have been hilarious!*

Oz snickered both in his head and out loud. The others

turned and looked at them expectantly, knowing that the pair had been talking silently again.

"Oz and I were wishing that you had pissed on that bitch this morning," he explained.

"Not worthy of the honour," grunted Dean, and they all cracked up. Ryan slapped the surly lion on the back.

This hunt would be epic!

11. MELODY

*D*eciding that her absence was the best course, Melody spent her lunch break in the library. The librarian had given her an odd look before pointing her in the direction of the reserved section. It wasn't that these books contained anything special, it was just the fact that they were the only copies the school had.

While searching the neatly handwritten catalogue of books she'd found several references to secret passages in the school. All she had been looking for was alternative routes from her dormitory to her classroom, but the prospect of secret passages had her heart beating rapidly. If Melody could use them, she could get to and from her classes and avoid the lion, and poor Quinn, until she could sort out something better.

Melody was only onto the third book when she struck

gold. Nestled between the pages was a rough map of the grounds with pencil lines tracking back and forth across the campus. Each line had been given a number at either end, and when Melody looked at the text, corresponding numbers had been written in the margins next to descriptions of part of the school. It was a key to what went where. The book hadn't specifically listed secret passages, it was a history of the construction of the school. But someone else had obviously put things together. Whomever it was, she was grateful.

She couldn't justify stealing the map, so she hurriedly got out a notebook and copied it, along with the descriptive list of where the entry points were. Melody was so invested in her task, that she didn't hear the chime sound for the final class of the day. Nor did she hear the chime that ended the school day entirely. It was the silence of the library, when she was finally done, that clued her into the fact that something was different. There were no hushed voices, no whisper of pages turning, no sign of human life at all. Except the lights were being turned off bank by bank.

"Hold on!" she called out to whoever was turning off the lights. She'd never make her way between all the tables and shelves and return bins in the dark. She gathered her things together, shoving them haphazardly into her bag, and shelved the three books again. She didn't want to risk anyone else finding the map while the returns were being sorted.

"Who's there?" called the librarian. It sounded like the stern woman who had helped her earlier.

"It's Melody, I was in the reserved section. I must have lost track of time."

"Well, that will be dealt with later. Right now, you must return your things to your room and freshen up. They will begin serving dinner soon."

Dinner! She had completely forgotten that meals were served communally. It was pointless sneaking around the school if all they had to do was stake out the mealtimes!

Melody sighed in defeat, rounding the corner and almost falling over a largish wolf that was lying across her path. It sat up and growled at her, and she stepped back.

"I'm sorry if I disturbed your nap, but you do know that you're lying down in a totally ridiculous place." What an idiot.

The wolf, however, wasn't interested in what she had to say. It lowered its head, bared its teeth and advanced on her. Instantly, she knew what this was, just as she knew it wasn't one of the alpha wolves. She could feel it in her magic.

"Quinn?" she asked softly, and the wolf paused and nodded. She could see a pile of clothes folded neatly behind him. He had obviously followed her here and then waited for her to come out. "Oh Quinn, I'm so sorry for this."

Taking a deep breath, she held out her hand in the same manner she would if she were accepting his challenge. "In the light of the Goddess, I deny your challenge." She put a surge of magic into her words and felt it pass into him.

Quinn shuddered, whimpered, and finally sat down on the ground, pawing at one of his ears. Denying a challenge disoriented shifted beasts. If he were in human form, it would have knocked him on his ass. Either way, the spell allowed the witch time to get away.

Melody knew, however, that she had to face this. The geas that her Aunt had put on her had specifically said Alphas and Dragons were what they sought along with strong shifters, so she was free to refuse his challenge without punishment. Quinn was not a weak wolf, but he wasn't up to the standards of the shifters kept caged at Bestia. At least this was now out of the way, and it was only the lion that she had to worry about. Well, she hoped that Quinn's wolf would give up now.

A sigh came from in front of her, and when she looked up, Quinn sat there, naked. "Did you really have to refuse me?" he asked her softly.

"Yes, Quinn. I did. Trust me, you do not want to be dragged into what I face at home. You would not have been respected and cherished as you deserve to be." Melody grunted as a pain slashed across her back. It felt exactly like the birch stick that Gwendoline liked to use magically on her. She had been disloyal when talking about her coven!

"What was that?" asked Quinn, rushing to her.

"Nothing more than I deserved," Melody told him, pushing him away. "But something you would be subject to if you were mine." Again, the sting appeared on her skin. She wondered if it was because she was disloyal, or because she had come close to telling him about all the geasen upon her. It didn't really matter either way, Melody was skirting trouble and she knew it.

"Stop it, whatever you are doing, stop it. I can smell your pain." Quinn growled at her, his hazel eyes becoming more golden as his wolf pushed forward.

What? She hadn't known that. That would mean Melody had to be much more careful. She wondered if her Aunt had known, and whether it had been a deciding factor in putting the more powerful ones on her. She was willing to bet that it had.

"It's alright, you don't need to worry about it," she said, trying to soothe him before his wolf pushed all the way forward.

"You're a sitting duck, Mel, and you don't even know it."

Melody liked his nickname for her.

"If you really want to dodge all the shifters here, why don't you just say no to them?"

"I can't." Melody braced, waiting for the punishment, but it seemed that this didn't break any of the rules.

"What do you mean, you can't?" Quinn's confusion was plain on his face. "You just refused me!"

"I know. I can refuse most of you, just not all of you."

"That makes even less sense!"

"I know," she said, miserably. "It's the truth, however."

"I can smell it. I still don't understand, and I know that you're not telling me everything, but I do know that what you are telling me is the truth."

"Wow, your senses have been trained well!" she told him.

"Yeah, my family are truthfinders and they thought that by training me, I would be more attractive to a witch." He shrugged like it didn't matter to him, but she knew that it did. All shifters were required to attend one of the academies that dealt with familiars, and all of them feared being stuck there until someone finally claimed them. Just like the Apex were.

"Under different circumstances, I would snatch you up in a heartbeat," she told him, and she knew that he could smell her honesty.

"So, you need to hide from a certain few?" he guessed.

She didn't dare confirm it. To say aloud that she was going to avoid a bonding may just trigger the geas. Melody looked at him but said nothing. If Quinn were half as bright as she thought he was, he would work it out.

"Well, there's a couple of things that you're going to need. Scent masking for starters. Do you know how to do that spell?"

Of course! Melody had been so fixed on hiding from them physically, that she hadn't thought about hiding from their senses. Of course, they would find her, all they would have to do is follow their senses and soon enough they would find her entrance and exit points. Dammit!

"Yes, yes, I can do that!" She had learned the spell in secret a long time ago, back when she had higher hopes of escaping her coven. Melody knew that if she simply ran, her aunt would use the shifters they had to track her down. So she had memorised the spell when she'd come across it in the course of her studies. She couldn't practice it, not even in secret, because the shifters would have told her aunt the next time they were punished — whether they wanted to or not. Still, it wasn't a difficult spell, there shouldn't be any problem.

Hastily, Melody drew her power around her and then chanted the necessary words, folding her will into the spell and then releasing it around her. She looked up at Quinn, who watched her with an open mouth. "Did it work?"

"You're fucking powerful, aren't you? It's part of why you need to hide, because everyone here is going to come for you, aren't they?"

"Yes, and yes," she whispered. "Please, Quinn, did it work?"

He walked up to her, inhaling deeply as he circled her.

"All I can smell is the remainder of the scent trail that would lead me here from the library. There's no fresh scent. Anyone else would track you here and then stop because it seems that you disappeared."

"Oh, thank fuck! That's one load off my mind. Now to work out meals."

"What do you mean?"

"Well, I can hide me, and I can hide my scent, but I do have to eat. All they have to do is wait in the dining hall. I'll turn up there sooner or later, and bam, challenge."

"They, so there's someone specific that you're hiding from?"

Again, Melody didn't dare answer that. "How am I going to eat?" She asked him.

"Pretend I'm yours?" he offered.

"What?"

"Well, if you walk in there, with me at your side, and you order me around, sit here, fetch me this, be a real brat, it's going to make everyone think one of two things. First, that I challenged you and lost, bonding to you. Or second, that you're a real bitch and not worth knowing."

Melody thought about it for a moment, and then dismissed it. "It would last until bedtime," she told him. "Students with a familiar are immediately moved to one of the cottages rather than one of the dormitories. If we go back to our rooms, it's proof that I haven't bonded you."

"Well, just walk in with me tonight. Don't order me around, but we'll sit together away from everyone else. You were missing in the last class today, so they'll wonder if it was because I challenged you and we had to move rooms. It might not last forever, but at least it will give us tonight to work something else out."

She looked at him in wonder. "That might actually work! And maybe in the morning, you wouldn't mind filching some food and bringing it to me somewhere, so I've got breakfast too."

"Sure, I can do it for lunch as well. I won't say that this is a permanent solution, I'm willing to bet they catch on really quickly, but it should get us through a couple of meals. At least until we find another answer."

"Oh Quinn, you're a genius!" Melody rushed forward and hugged him. He held her tightly against him, and she wondered how soon it would be before he challenged her again. His wolf would continue to push him to challenge her as long as she didn't have a familiar.

"Come on then, put on your game face and let's go face the music." Quinn nudged her and she smiled, linking her arm through his.

"Ooh, nice touch there." He laughed, and she joined in.

Melody knew that when they walked through the door to the dining room, they would look like a couple, linked together and laughing like that, but she couldn't help but feel happy. She had made her first friend ever, and now she had a chance at avoiding the worst fate.

It was rather anticlimactic when they walked in, for her to realise that none of the Apex were there. The coast was clear for now. Melody hurried to the buffet, scooping up some rice and stir fry onto her plate. It didn't surprise her that Quinn walked straight to the carvery and loaded up his plate with as much as he could, most predator shifters ate a lot of protein to help their beasts – it didn't hurt their human forms either, she thought as she watched his muscles move under his shirt.

"You know, your wolf might not like vegetables, but your human side needs them," she chided, laughing.

"True, but this is only the first course. I'll do the vegetables on my next plate."

Melody's heart sank at the memory of the underfed

shifters back at her coven. She'd heard of shifters' near-insatiable appetites, but she'd never had the chance to see it in person. Her aunt had kept all the shifters underfed to help control them. The more loyal they were, the more meat they were given, but never enough for them to be at full strength. No, the way her Aunt treated the shifters in their care, meant the coven could never fully trust them. Except for her of course. Once they had forgiven her for trapping them.

Quinn was watching her curiously. "Did I say something wrong?"

"No, you just reminded me of someone back in my coven."

"That's a half truth," he scolded her gently.

"Yes. Yes, it is." He hadn't reminded her of anyone specific, but of all the starving shifters in her coven's enormous compound.

Quinn got the message not to ask more, and let it drop. Instead he regaled her with stories of growing up. The mischief he and his siblings got into, the fights he had seen, the pairings and matings. His family sounded beautiful, she wished she could have met them.

Melody must have said this last out loud, because he answered her. "You can. Two of my older brothers are here. They've been bonded, but you can still meet them." In a quieter tone he added, "It will look more authentic if I start introducing you to my family."

Melody smiled and rested her hand on his, "You are too good to me, I wish I could be yours."

Quinn's head snapped up, but then he sighed. "You're going to have to watch your wording, Melody. My wolf hasn't given up."

She blushed. "I'm sorry, Quinn, that was thoughtless of me."

He shrugged it off, but she knew she had hurt him, that the whole situation hurt him.

"Eat up," he said, suddenly stiff. "Don't turn around, either. They're working their way through all the new students, if you want to hold off on getting a familiar, then we need to go sooner rather than later."

It took all of her willpower not to turn and see what had caught his attention, but she had a fair idea of what it was, or rather, who *they* were. She took his advice and started shoveling food into her mouth, eating as quickly as she could. This was going to repeat on her later, eating so much, but if she wanted a meal, then this was what she had to do. At least here she had the option of eating regular meals. Back at her coven, all her meals – if you could call them that – were hurriedly consumed for fear of having them taken away.

Within minutes she was scraping the last of it onto her spoon, while Quinn ate just as quickly. At first glance, he appeared to be casual, chatting to her about nothing and looking around in general, but she knew what he was doing. He was eyeing up where the exits were, and who would likely get in their way.

"There's a door about five feet behind you," she said quietly. "I don't know where it leads."

"Fuck, ok, um, I think it goes to the north corridor from the main courtyard. If that's the case, we can cut along there and then through the east one out to the dormitories," he stammered, his composure diminishing.

"Oh! I can go one better, if I can find the right tapestry and activate it, I think I know where there's a secret tunnel!"

Quinn looked at her, astounded, and she shrugged. "It's what I was doing in the library. Hunting for alternative routes, when I found a map with all these apparent secret tunnels marked out. It was my plan for avoiding them. I can skip in and around the school without ever coming across them in person. If they can't find me, they can't challenge me."

As soon as she said it, pain flared across her back and she realised her mistake. She grunted and Quinn stiffened, his wide eyes conveying that other shifters around them could smell her pain as well. A ripple of reaction was spreading out from them, and it was only a matter of time before it reached the Apex boys where they were sitting several tables over.

"It's time to test your theory then, Mel, because we need to go."

In full agreement, she slowly pushed her chair back, ignoring the pain across her shoulders. This was stronger than the welts from earlier, but she was pretty sure that it hadn't broken the skin. This time.

Melody took her plate to the end of the row and casually stacked it and her cutlery in the dishwasher stands. Beside her, Quinn scraped his leftovers from his plate. They moved at a normal pace, Quinn looking quickly over his shoulder, once, before huffing a laugh.

"It's ok, they've seen you, but they're not chasing you. I'm betting they figure they can follow your scent later."

Melody relaxed a little. "I can mask my scent, but I don't know if I can mask yours. We would need another shifter to confirm it for us." She looked at him helplessly. "We're going to have to split up as soon as we reach the corridor, or else they're going to follow your scent straight to me."

Quinn cursed under his breath but nodded. "Yeah, good thinking."

12. MELODY

They reached the door without hindrance from any party, and Quinn opened it for her. It was much darker in the corridor. Something that wouldn't be a problem for him, but for her it was a definite trip hazard on the uneven stone, so she opened her hand and raised a witchlight on it. Now that she could see a little better, she could discern something hanging on the wall further along to her left.

"I'm going to go this way, hopefully it's the right tapestry."

"What's it supposed to have on it?" he asked her.

"A white wolf and a black wolf, howling at the moon." She grinned when he grimaced. "Don't roll your eyes at me, I didn't make the darn thing, and for all I know, the tapestries could have been switched around since this map was made."

"Ok, well, I'll go in the opposite direction. If I see what I think you're looking for, I'll double back and get you, ok?" Quinn frowned. "I don't want to leave you here to face them alone. What if they come out before you're in the tunnel? You'll have nobody to defend you."

She swallowed hard, that was exactly what she was trying not to think about. "Technically, I don't have anyone to defend me anyway, Quinn," she said gently, but he tensed anyway, his hazel pupils flashing golden.

"And if you shift, even if you managed to stop them, what is the first thing your wolf is going to do?"

"Challenge you," Quinn said with more growl than voice. His wolf was obviously close to the surface.

"You have to go, Quinn. Either way, you're putting me at risk."

Quinn's shoulders dropped, the faint golden glow of his eyes, dimming. Melody smiled and hugged him before they parted ways – Quinn holding on for a little longer than necessary – and then she walked up to where the deviation in the smooth wall was.

She had wondered why there was a tapestry in a corridor, that although long, would be exposed to a certain amount of the elements, certainly whatever the wind brought along it. Now that she was close, however, Melody could see that it had been carefully mounted in a clear Perspex frame and attached quite solidly to the wall behind it.

The picture was indeed a pair of howling wolves, so she pulled out her notes with her other hand and read the description for the door.

"The darkness points the way,
Light gazes in counterpoint,
An intersection of movement,
With blood you must anoint."

She read it through three times, aware that the Apex would be finishing their meal soon and seeking her out. Melody was pretty sure they would split up, one group following Quinn's scent, and the other taking the most direct route to the dormitories. She only had a few minutes to work it out.

The last line of the riddle was clear, once Melody found the right spot, she had to smear it with blood, although how that would remain secret for long she didn't know. 'An intersection of movement' took her a few minutes. Movement implied something that moved, like a button, or a block. Hastily she ran her hands across the blocks on either side of the tapestry, but none of them seemed to budge.

Intersection, well, that was the meeting of two lines. But what were the two lines? Then it hit her that there were two lines of the odd poem above that. One pointed the way, the other moved in counterpoint. Melody had read once in an old book about music, that counterpoint didn't necessarily mean parallel. Because that would then deny the possibility of an intersection. No. In music, the counterpoint melody could sometimes rise above the theme music, crossing over it, weaving in and around it. So, somehow, the picture would give her two lines.

Melody's heart beat faster, any minute now, the Apex

would come through the door, looking for one of the witches they hadn't challenged yet. If she didn't work this out soon, then she was out of time. She tried to calm her jangling nerves with a few deep breaths, but it wasn't working. The more anxious she became, the harder it was to think, she really needed to solve this now.

Closing her eyes, Melody thought through the little rhyme again. It was obviously a means of stopping just anyone from using the tunnel, so she had to think beyond the literal meaning of the words. She opened her eyes and tried again.

Looking more closely at the picture, Melody saw that although both wolves faced the same direction, and both howled at the moon, their snouts were at different angles. Darkness – the black wolf. Light – the white wolf. When she traced the paths of their snouts, however, the two lines diverged until they were nearly at right angles. Somehow, Melody didn't think she should be tracing those lines back in the opposite direction until they converged. For starters, that would be behind the center of the tapestry, and completely out of reach. So, it wasn't the direction that their faces were pointed in.

But the poem specifically said *gaze*. Melody couldn't see their eyes, the Perspex was a little crazed, so she had to squint and tilt and move until she could give her best guess. This time, she ended up at a block that was two to the right of the top right-hand corner of the frame. She couldn't see any other marks there, but it was worth a try. Otherwise she would have to start running. From the sounds in the dining hall, people were moving. Someone would come out that door any minute, she needed to be inside the tunnel before they saw her.

Melody put her thumb in her mouth and bit it, wincing as the skin tore, before smearing her blood across the corner of the stone. She had been given a boline knife by her coven just before she left, as she would need it for any potion work, but it was lying uselessly back in her room. From now on, she would carry it with her.

Melody's blood soaked into the rock and disappeared. There was a quiet rustle, and part of the wall folded in on itself.

Holy shit!

She had found it, the first tunnel entrance. She stepped inside, quickly lighting her witchlight again. Before she could figure out how to close it, the door closed itself with a quiet snick. The darkness spread off into the distance, so instead of holding her witchlight in her palm, something that required little concentration, she set it free to float above her. This took a bit more effort, but it left her hands free to get out her map. At this point, she had no idea where the tunnel led, just that it was a safe space to hide from the Apex.

Melody took a brief look around her. She expected the tunnel to be full of dead insects, spiderwebs and lots of dust, but it was actually immaculate. Magic, of course. It was rather narrow, barely enough room for her to walk without twisting her shoulders to the side, which made sense seeing she was walking inside a wall. If it were too thick, it would be obvious to anyone who stopped to think about it.

Looking around made things easier too. There was only one direction that she could go, so Melody took it, being careful to keep her witchlight close to her in case it shone through cracks in the walls beside her, but she wasn't seeing any light coming in, so she had hope that at least on the dining room side, it was sealed.

The only sounds she could hear were her soft footfalls and the pounding of her heart, although the latter was easing somewhat, and her rapid breathing. It was funny, in a space small enough to cause some people to freak out, Melody actually felt quite safe. It reminded her a little of the stone basement where she had been kept along with the shifters back at the coven, but there were subtle differences.

The air was dry and a little stale, although free from the stench of unwashed bodies and buckets full of bodily waste. It was cool, but not as cold as the basement got, something she was thankful for. It was likely that the tunnel would become bitter in the winter, unless it went deep underground, where the temperature might be a little more constant. Still, it was eerie, the rustle of her clothing echoing oddly in the confined space.

Within a few minutes, Melody reached a set of stairs. They were steep, with short treads, and the corridor was even narrower because of the railing on her left side. Whoever had built this, had tiny feet!

Gripping the rail tightly, she made her way down, finding

that the tunnel floor continued to slope when she reached the bottom, stretching off into the dark.

Eventually, she felt the floor was rising again, confirmed by the fact that a puddle of water had settled right where she thought the angle changed. She couldn't see any seepage, but the water must have been coming from somewhere. Melody made a note to herself to be careful if it had been raining, although there was no sign of flowing water on the stones, she would hate to be caught there in a flash flood.

Not far past the puddle was another set of tiny-tread stairs. This time, before she climbed them and risked her light being seen through any cracks in the mortar, Melody consulted her map. What she found was better than she could have hoped. Not only did this tunnel lead toward the dormitories, but it ended in an apparently disused janitorial closet in the dormitory kitchenette.

She hadn't been in the kitchenette since she arrived that morning, but given that each room had a small one anyway, she couldn't imagine that it got used a lot. Not unless people were relaxing in the common room nearby. Still, she would need to be careful.

Melody folded her map and tucked it back into the small pocket on her skirt. Then she pulled her witchlight back to her palm and dimmed it as much as she possibly could. It was time to climb the stairs and see what was at the top.

It was a stone door, of course. This one had a very humble handle on the inside of it, and when she pulled the lever down, it opened silently toward her. One hurdle down!

On the other side was a rather musty smelling storage space filled with various cleaning supplies and mops that should have been put out of their misery generations ago.

The welcome brochure had explained that students would need to keep their dormitories clean and that inspections would be carried out weekly. The use of magic to keep them clean was not only permitted, but highly encouraged. So it was unlikely that the things in this room would ever be required. Still, she would need to be careful about entering a space that was supposed to be obsolete.

And that was something else to worry about. She could travel from the dining room to here in safety, but how would she get back again? There was no nifty little poem telling her how to open the door. Melody was reluctant to let it close behind her, but then, she could hardly leave it open either. In the end, the door made the choice for her, closing with barely a sound before she could do anything about it. She put her hand on the stones there and pushed, but nothing happened.

The other door had required blood, so maybe this one did too? She bit her thumb again, smearing the blood on the largest stone in the center. The door swung open. She wondered if it had to be that stone, or would any stone do? That was a question for another time, and another journey. Right now, she had to get from the closet to the kitchenette without being noticed, and then from there to her room, without anyone wondering where she had come from.

Melody put her ear to the door, listening carefully for

sounds of anyone on the other side. She couldn't hear anything, so she carefully turned the handle and allowed the door to open just a crack. From the limited view she had, there was no sign of anyone, but to be sure, she whispered a spell under her breath and released it into the room. There was nobody there, and there was nobody in the common room either. It seemed that everyone was either at dinner, or in their room tonight. What a relief!

Feeling more confident, Melody opened the door fully and stepped into the kitchenette proper. It was a sparse galley-style set up with a small microwave, kettle and sink. There were shelves with tea and coffee supplies, and under the bench was a small refrigerator. According to the map, she should be on the ground floor of her own dormitory with a nearby door leading outside.

With dinner almost over, people would be coming back soon, she wanted to get out of there. While they may think that she had come in the back door, she didn't want to be associated with the area, so nobody would think to search for her there in the future. She had no idea how long she was going to have to skulk around the academy like this.

On her right was a door that she hadn't been able to see from inside the cupboard, and when Melody opened it, she saw that it was the one that led outside. Not far away, there was a similar door on the other dormitory building, and she was willing to bet that it was a mirror image of this one. So, even if a student from the other building was using the maps, it wouldn't be hard for them to access this tunnel. Maybe there was a tunnel in the other building. She would have to study her map a bit more once she got to her room.

Melody hurried from the kitchenette to the common room. It was packed with lounges, armchairs and coffee tables, as well as being furnished with fireplaces on opposite sides. It really was a cosy and inviting space, one that she hoped she would be able to use down the track. Once she had worked out how to avoid the Apex permanently. Right now, it was a hodgepodge of furniture that she had to weave around to get to the stairs leading to her room.

The lash on her back ached as she trudged up the stairs. Along with the two weals from earlier, it made her quite uncomfortable. The smaller marks would probably be healed by the morning, but the larger one, she suspected, would be with her for several days. Her aunt would know that some of the geasan had been activated, but not which ones.

Melody had hundreds of them on her, from not speaking back, to cleaning behind her ears when she bathed. Things that people would normally chide their children for, Aunt Georgia simply set up a permanent punishment for. If she bit her nails, there would be a welt on her backside. It meant that her aunt had to do as little as possible to raise her. Any lesson that she wanted Melody to learn, she had simply turned into a geas. The cumulative effect held her permanently weakened, unlikely to be strong enough to challenge her aunt for the leadership of the coven.

Of course, it was all against witching law. A coven leader could use a geas to correct the behaviour of a member, but any witch worth their magic could break it within a few weeks. The things were never meant to be permanent. However, there was one odd quirk of the magic. If a second geas were laid upon the first, the first one wouldn't start to weaken until the second one had been broken. So, if someone were to continually apply them, then the person being held by them would never be free.

It was what had happened to her. Melody carried the weight of hundreds of them, if not a thousand. These new stronger ones meant that Melody could be left unattended for several months at a time without any of them starting to break down. The fact that her aunt had laid three strong ones on her before she left the compound meant that they could be apart for up to a year without her enslavement needing renewal.

For that was what Melody was, a slave.

To do something like that to a witch was a terrible thing, but to do it to a witch child was even more heinous. There was a risk that Melody would never come into her full power. But that was what she suspected her aunt wished. With her dying strength, her mother had passed the family's matriarchal power on to Melody. With Adelaide's death, it should have passed on to the next eldest sister, but her mother must have known how power-hungry Aunt Georgia was, so she had gifted it to Melody instead. This was something that Melody had worked out on her own much, much later.

Melody couldn't pass the family power on to anyone but

her own siblings or her own offspring. So, because Aunt Georgia was no longer able to inherit it, she controlled it by controlling Melody.

From her brief visit to the dormitories this morning, Melody knew that the third door on the left of the first floor was hers. She hadn't met her roommate, but there was light coming from under the door, so she supposed that the woman was there now. It would mean that she wouldn't be able to examine her map any further if she was. She could only hope for a little more alone time.

With more confidence than she actually felt, Melody put her key in the door and turned the handle. As soon as it opened, her hopes were dashed. There on the bed on the other side of the room from hers was a young woman with the most stunning deep brown skin. Her hair was a dark afro held in bunches on either side of her head, purple highlights twisting through them, and a pair of trendy-looking black rimmed glasses were perched on her nose.

"Hi, I'm Melody. I didn't get to meet you earlier." She held out her hand to the other girl, who took it and shook it vigorously.

"I'm Carla. It's good to finally meet you!" she replied, smiling up at her. "I'm from Coven Venenum, in South Carolina. Where are you from?"

"Bestia, in Virginia. My family has a large compound there for the shifters."

"Oh! My! Goddess! No wonder you're here. Are you

going after the Apex then? I heard the lion singled someone out this morning. Was that you?"

Melody laughed. "I'm here to study. I want to improve my knowledge in all things so that I can better serve my coven." There was no sting, and she was grateful. She hadn't been disloyal, and she hadn't refused to bond them, she had just avoided the question entirely.

"You're like the poster child of beast tamers then, huh?" She giggled.

"Oh Goddess, no. I'm more like the poor klutz who's finally been allowed to leave home for the first time. I have *so much* to learn." Melody tried to play down her strength. She didn't want to brag, she was sure it would get back to the Apex sooner or later and that would only make them keener to challenge her.

"Well, I can feel your strength, you're way stronger than me," Carla continued.

"Ugh, I wish that I wasn't. Every shifter is apparently going to sense it and want to challenge me, and I can't bond with them all. And I don't want other witches giving me a hard time because I'm stronger. I just wish I could hide it."

Carla snorted. "Then why don't you wear dampeners? Being as strong as you are, they would probably make you only average strength, and then you could walk incognito amongst us mere mortals."

Melody felt her heart thump. "What are dampeners? I've never heard of them."

"Well, they're spelled jewelry, rings, or pendants, cuffs,

that sort of thing. They absorb or muffle your magic so that it's not detectable. Only they're not that strong, so rather than making you appear human, it would make *you* seem average strength. You would have to wear lots of them to weaken yourself to the point of appearing human."

"Carla, you have to help me! Where can I get them?" Melody begged.

"Well, silly, if you have any jewelry with you, you can make them, right here, right now. I know I've seen the spell for them somewhere in our texts," Carla told her.

Melody dashed to the bookshelf on her side of the room, opening textbooks, scanning the indexes and then laying them aside to hit the next one. Of course, it was in the second to last book that she found it. Flipping to 'Enchanted Objects', she skimmed through it until she found a spell to enhance a witch's strength using a charmed object. At the foot of the spell, were the changes needed to make the object do the opposite, concealing or reducing the strength of the bearer.

Melody tipped out her bathroom bag until a small pouch fell out from the bottom. Inside it, were two matched bangles. The only possessions of her mother's that her aunt had allowed her to keep, and only because her aunt thought that they were ugly.

"Oh, they look perfect for this," murmured Carla in her ear, and Melody jumped a foot, causing Carla to squeak as she leapt back. They looked at each other for a moment, bewildered, and then Carla began to giggle.

"Well, shit, that was a dumb thing for me to do, you're obviously as jittery as a bird in a cage with the cat sitting on it. Sorry about that, roomie!" She chuckled.

Melody, still gasping for breath, gave a wan smile. "No problems. I'm sorry for overreacting, it's just that I've been really stressed about this. I've already had to turn down one shifter today, and it wasn't pleasant for either of us, although he's forgiven me. I don't want to have to do that several times a day."

Carla gave her a sympathetic look. "Yeah, ok, I get it. I can't imagine that would be fun. I'm just hoping that one of the shifters likes me enough to challenge me before I leave here."

Carla leaned over Melody's shoulder to look at the spell. "Uh-oh!" she said.

"What?" Melody frantically searched the spell for any words that were unfamiliar to her, but she couldn't see any issue with it.

"Well, it also says at the bottom that the spell can only be cast on the new moon. The one to enhance is the full moon, but the one to absorb is the new moon. That's still three weeks away. So, you're going to have to put up with all that shit for three weeks until we can spell them for you."

"We?" asked Melody, a faint hope stirring in her heart.

"Yeah, roomie, *we*. Of course I'm going to help you with this. We're going to be living together for the next few years, I think it's important to begin the way we mean to go on, right?" Carla held up her fist, but Melody just looked at it.

"Damn girl, you really have been let out for the first time, haven't you? Bump it with yours."

Melody raised her fist slowly, but before she could do anything, Carla bumped it with hers. "Fist-bump, roomie," she said, smiling.

On the spur of the moment, Melody decided to trust her. Carla was right, if they were indeed going to be living together for their time at the Academy, then they needed to bond, and she couldn't think of a better way.

Carefully, so that she didn't tear it, Melody removed the map and the key she had copied, laying them out flat on her bed. Carla looked at them, her head tilted to the side.

"Okay, I can see that it's a map of the campus, but what are all the lines? And what's with all the bad poetry?"

Melody looked at her somberly. "Carla, I'm trusting you with this, you can't tell anyone. But those lines, they're tunnels under the academy, and this is how I'm going to try and avoid the … shifters for a while." Damn, she had nearly said it. Apex.

"Holy shit, are you kidding me? This is so cool!" She bent eagerly over the map. "Which ones have you used?"

"Well, I only found this today, so I've only used the one leading from the dining room here," she pointed at the map, "to the kitchenette downstairs."

Carla stared at her wide eyed. "Roomie, we are going to have so much fun with this!"

"Well, we will, but not until you mask your scent. Once the shifters see you with me, they'll follow your scent to me, so you'll have to mask it well. I'll even get Quinn to check you out."

"Quinn? Is that the shifter you turned down?"

"Yeah, and he's the nicest guy. He's a truthfinder, and he's been so sweet to me," Melody told her.

"Seriously? A fucking truthfinder? Do you know how rare that is? And you turned him down, are you nuts?"

Melody frowned at her. "Well, I didn't find out about the truthfinding thing until after I turned him down, and I wouldn't bond him just because he has a skill." She knew she had to watch her words carefully. "I need more from my familiar than that." Melody let Carla think what she would, she couldn't afford to be any more specific about the requirements that she had.

"So, if he's your friend, does that mean I get to meet him?" Carla asked, with a speculative gleam in her eye.

Melody sighed. "Yeah, I guess."

"What's that about? Why don't you want me to meet him?"

"It's just, I grew up with shifters all around me, bound to witches that they weren't compatible with. They were miserable, and they were treated like commodities. I just want to see shifters happy with their matches." It was as close to the truth as she dared to get.

"But you know we're all here to bag a shifter, right?" asked Carla, confused.

"Yes, I understand that, but it doesn't mean that you go shopping for them like a pair of designer shoes. This is a person's life that you're talking about. These men and women will never leave this place unless they're bonded, and for some of them, those bonds they walk away with, will be worse than actually staying here."

Carla snorted. "Yeah, right. Tell that to the dragons who have been here for a few hundred. I'm sure they'll understand."

I wish I could, she thought.

Instead, she said aloud, "Well, I need a shower, and then some sleep. I don't know about you, but today has been a bit full-on."

"Yeah, I guess it must have been. I'm telling you, Roomie, we're going to have the best year here, this year!" Carla grinned at her, and Melody felt her spirits lighten a little.

If nothing else, she would have Carla to help her and watch her back. She could feel the certainty of it in her bones. Between Carla and Quinn, and the passages, and the dampeners, she was going to make it through this year intact. She would be perceived as an average witch, and she would honestly be able to tell her aunt that none of the Apex had challenged her. What could possibly go wrong?

13. DEAN

They had sat and joked around the dining hall table, lingering over their meal and watching in amusement as their quarry scuttled off with that fucking wolf. She had managed to avoid them all afternoon, and Dean certainly hadn't scented her when he'd entered the dining hall, but there she was, just a few tables away. He could have easily shifted and challenged her there on the spot, but it didn't feel right. It was the way she had treated the wolf earlier, a sporting chance. He could give her that.

When they followed her into the corridor, however, there was no sign of her, and so they had split into two groups, each one following a different direction. Dean could see a map of the grounds laid out in his head. He, Ryan and Oz went left, following the most direct route to the dormitories. If she had gone this way, they would catch her in no time.

The two dragons headed off in the opposite direction, following the scent of the wolf. If they found her first, they would reach out with their magic and speak to him in his head. It was a foolproof plan.

It failed spectacularly.

When they reached the dormitory without having encountered her, Dean swore profusely. His lion was growling with frustration as he paced up and down on the lawn outside.

"Why don't you shift and go for a run, take Oz with you. I'll shift and sit here in the shadows, and if she comes this way, I'll tell Oz and he can bring you back. I promise, I won't let her enter the building, okay?"

Dean was reluctant to walk away, but his lion was becoming frantic. Dean didn't understand why the big cat had such a thing for the witch, but he couldn't help but indulge it. His lion rarely asked him for anything.

He let out a huge sigh and nodded, starting to peel his clothes off. "We'll go and find the others, hopefully they've had better luck, and if they call me. I'll already be half way there."

"Well, well, girls. Now isn't this a welcome home?" purred a new voice, and Dean turned towards it, his heart shriveling in disgust.

Shawna and her clutch of bitches had emerged from the shadows and were eyeing him up and down appreciatively.

"If you wanted to challenge me baby, all you had to do was ask," she said, and the others tittered.

In her first year here, he had made the mistake of fucking her. He had never challenged her, and he never would. She made his skin crawl with her attitude toward shifters. She saw them as objects to be owned, much like pets, and she had no true respect for them at all. Word had gotten around the academy very quickly, and nobody had challenged her since, a sore point from what he'd heard.

He decided to ignore her. No matter what he said, she would twist it for her own purposes. Dean turned to Oz, "You coming? If we leave now, we might catch her ourselves." He grinned at the thought, pouncing on her and holding her there, and if she made him shift … well, he'd land on her completely naked. He had no problem with that at all!

Oz was shucking off his jeans. "Try and keep up, slow poke. Follow my lead," he said, obscurely referring to the fact that they couldn't communicate in their beast forms. Neither of them were comfortable with the bitches listening in to their every word.

"Eat my dust, fucker. My lion wants her bad, he's pulling out all the stops." He laughed with the sheer joy of it, and Oz snickered.

Ryan rolled his eyes at the pair of them. "Well, are you fuckers going to shift or—"

They shifted before he could finish, and sprinted off into the darkness, leaving him to deal with the bitches and the piles of their clothes. Oz had his nose to the ground, scenting everything, but Dean ran on ahead, eager for the chance to find the witch. His cock had been hard before he shifted, and his beast was keen to rut. Whoever this witch was, if she didn't own him with her magic, then he was going to make sure that he would own her with his body. Well, at least for a night or two. Or maybe three.

His lion let out a short bark of a laugh and raced off. Behind him, he could hear Oz rise to the challenge, the wolf huffing as he thudded faster and faster on the turf until he galloped along beside them. Their paws pounded against the ground, kicking up tufts of grass as they sprinted together, his lion exhilarated at the thought of chasing their prey.

At this speed, neither of them would scent anything on the ground, but they would be able to pick up her scent on the air if she had been through here recently. Of course, the further they moved from the dorms, the older her scent would be.

As they sped along the stone corridor, he caught nothing of her scent. Dean had hoped that he hadn't smelled her earlier because he was in his human form, and that the breeze had carried it away, but his beast couldn't catch a whiff of her either.

She had masked her scent.

Son-of-a-bitch!

And because the dragons hadn't linked their minds, he couldn't tell anyone until he shifted. He slowed to a trot and Oz doubled back to him, whining softly because he couldn't understand. He contemplated stopping and shifting on the spot, but there were still people leaving the dining hall and he didn't want them to see his distress, so he took off at a slower pace this time, using his other senses rather than relying on smell.

Dean felt an odd sense of pride. She had outwitted him at his own game. It was annoying as fuck, but smart as hell. He would give her this round. When he finally caught her, he'd give her a lot more than that. His lion chuffed in agreement, and Oz's wolf turned to him, wondering what was going on.

They smelled the dragons long before they caught the scent of the wolf that she had been with, so they followed them until they neared the shifter dorms on the other side of the campus – the wolf had taken a longer path and had probably been a decoy from the start. Yes, his witch was very smart. She had masked her own smell, then left his, sending him out as a decoy. This hunt was suddenly a lot more interesting. A prey that challenged him? That was hot as fuck.

I take it you didn't find her, sent Nick, standing just ahead of them. It was a relief to hear the dragon in his head.

Can you link us up? he asked them.

Done, sent Jus.

Hey guys, called Ryan. *Did you find her? Is Dean balls deep in her yet?*

Laughter rippled across the link.

No, in fact, she's outsmarted us, Dean told them. He couldn't hide the satisfaction in his voice.

Then how come you sound so smug? asked Ryan.

Because she just made this game way more interesting. She's masked her scent. And she sent the wolf out as a decoy.

Both of the dragons swore profusely.

Well, well, well. It seems that you've found us a better game than we thought, Dean. So, we could have run over the top of her and not realised. I like this witch already. I might even fuck her when you're done, murmured Nick, and they all paused in shock.

Nick hadn't shown interest in any of the witches for decades.

Don't hold your breath then, lizard lungs, I'm going to take my time taming her, Dean told them.

They all chuckled. He turned and trotted around the outside of the college, passing the teacher's cottages and heading for the female witch dormitory. The softer sound of Oz's paws skittered behind him and further back, the dragons loped along in a steady jog. Just because Nick and Justin didn't shift often, didn't mean that they weren't fit. They often ran with the others as a pack.

So, can we call tonight done then? Ryan asked, plaintively. *Shawna and her crew are here, and they're waiting for you to come and get your clothes.*

We're almost there, sent Oz. *In fact, I can smell her cheap perfume from here. What the fuck is that crap?*

I don't know. Dean sneezed. *But you're right, it smells awful.*

Stop! Nick sent urgently. *That's not perfume, it's a spell. She's trying to pull you in, Dean. Don't go any closer. If you give me a minute, I'll counter it.*

There was silence, and then Dean felt a wave of magic encompass him.

Ok, there are a few variations of the spell that she's trying, so rather than counter that, I've spelled all of us to resist them. She's going to pitch a fucking fit when she finds out it doesn't work, Nick chuckled as he sent his thoughts to them.

Awesome dude, thanks, sent Ryan.

Dean and Oz emerged from the shadows and walked up to Ryan. *Give us our clothes and we'll carry them in our mouths if you can get the shoes and open the door when we get back,* Dean sent.

"No problem, dude." Ryan said aloud.

The women watched them as they stalked forward and accepted the bundles of clothing, the presence of the two dragon shifters likely forestalling any attempt to coerce the three of them further. Ryan bent and grabbed their shoes. The dragons had already turned around, jogging back the way they had come.

Dean ignored the women and turned to leave, but Shawna's grating voice halted him.

"Aren't you even going to say hello, baby? I would have thought that as your future witch, I deserved a bit more than this."

Dean didn't hesitate, he swung his hind quarters towards them and lifted his tail, preparing to spray the lot of them.

"Don't dude," cried Ryan. "She'll just say you were marking your territory. She'll tell everyone that you're not listening to your lion, and the provost will get involved."

With a huff, Dean lowered his tail, and then stalked off into the dorm. Shawna was lucky to escape, he was quite amenable to soaking the entire lot of them in piss, but Ryan had a point. She would claim it as a mark of favour, even as she desperately tried to wash the stink off. His scent *was* quite pungent.

Jus and Nick snickered at him as he walked past. "No golden shower for your favourite girl then?" teased Jus.

Dean growled around a mouthful of clothing and sauntered past them on his way back to the shifter dorm, the laughter of his friends following him. It didn't bother him, he had more important things to think about. Like how to catch a witch as smart as his quarry.

14. MELODY

The morning following her first tunnel trip, Melody had taken Carla discretely to the entrance, and from there they had made it to the dining hall. There was no sign of the Apex, so she had grabbed a couple of slices of toast and left, heading in the opposite direction to the night before.

The north corridor brought them to another small courtyard which, according to her map, was just around the corner from her first class of the day. They sat down in a quiet corner and nibbled at their portable breakfast.

"We'll get better at this, I promise," she said, quietly.

Carla nudged her. "Girl, this is like a picnic breakfast. Stop worrying." She took a huge bite of her egg and bacon sandwich and moaned. "Damn, this food tastes good no matter where you're sitting. I'm gonna have to watch my hips."

Carla moaned before taking another big bite, and Melody joined her. It was only two slices of toast with some orange marmalade, and an essential amount of coffee in her favourite travel mug that she'd brought from home, but it was still bliss compared to the stale bread and dregs of tea that she usually had. The mug was one of the few possessions that she'd brought aside from her clothing and spellbooks, and she'd stolen that from the kitchen in the compound.

"Found you!" called a voice triumphantly across the way, and her heart stilled. No! Surely they hadn't found her already? It was too soon, she wasn't ready to deal with them.

Across the courtyard, Quinn waved merrily at her, oblivious to her panic. Even though part of her realised that she was still safe for now, her body still gasped, causing her to inhale her coffee rather than drink it. It took a few minutes and some hearty thumps between her shoulders from Quinn, before she was able to stop coughing.

"Sorry, Mel! I didn't mean to startle you," he apologised, eyeing her roommate. "Oh, hi, I'm Quinn!"

"Carla," her friend said distractedly, "Melody, are you ok?"

Melody flapped a hand in front of her face because there wasn't anything else to do. Quinn gave her one more solid tap on the back and then stood back when she pushed him away.

"Fine," she eventually husked. She sounded like a two pack a day smoker, on their last legs.

"So you made it through the tunnel ok?" Quinn asked.

Carla's head snapped up, "You know about the tunnels? Wait, are you the guy who challenged her yesterday?"

The question was out there before Melody could slap a hand across Carla's mouth, and Quinn visibly winced, scratching at the back of his neck sheepishly.

"Yeah, that was me. But I'll get her next time!" He winked at Melody to indicate that he was joking, but she knew that there *would* be a next time, his wolf wouldn't let it go.

"So, you're a truthfinder?" pushed Carla.

"Uh, yeah. Mel told you about that?" Quinn's hazel gaze met Melody's, before he looked back at Carla.

"Yeah, she was telling me how awesome you are. You sound like quite a catch." Carla smiled at him, and he blushed. She looked him up and down. "I don't mind being a second choice if it's ever a possibility."

It didn't seem possible, but his blush deepened, although he gave her a speculative look. "I'll keep that in mind," he told her, and she beamed at him.

Quinn turned to Melody. "They came looking for you, you know."

Carla's head whipped back and forth between them both.

"Two of them followed me all the way to the dorms, I sat in the common room and watched. One of them was standing in the snow holding clothes and ignoring this woman who kept trying to get him to challenge her, and the other two shifted and eventually joined the two with me. They must have gone in the opposite direction to me."

He looked shrewdly at her. "The lion, especially, was annoyed that he didn't find you. And you had better watch out for that woman, because she was pissed that they were all ignoring her. The guys were talking about tracking a witch and challenging her, if the bitchy one works out who you are, you're toast, because she's a third year."

Melody looked up at him and smiled. "We've got a long-term solution, I just need to get through the next three weeks and then I should be all set. I'll be free to do as *I* wish." There was no weal this time, because she hadn't exactly spoken against her coven, and she hadn't said that she would refuse the shifters. Melody was finding that there was a lot of leeway in these geasan if she was careful with her wording.

"What *you* wish, as opposed to what who wishes?" Carla's question underscored the very thing she was trying to avoid. Quinn's gaze snapped to Melody, but Carla continued on, oblivious.

"Why are you avoiding the lion? The Apex are going around and challenging all the first years, just get it over and done with. The more you hide from them, the harder they're going to search. It's not like you could defeat them."

Melody didn't answer, and Carla's jaw dropped.

"Holy fucking shit, are you strong enough to defeat him?"

Melody lurched to her feet. "We should get to class before anyone else turns up. I'm kind of a sitting duck out here in the open," she told them, heading across the small courtyard.

Her two new friends said nothing, but the silence weighed heavily.

There were no surprises waiting for her in her classes and there were no unwelcome visitors either, but several times throughout the day, Melody heard them searching. At lunch time, Melody remained in her classroom, and Carla went out and grabbed her something to eat, while Quinn stayed with her. They all knew that anyone looking for Melody by scent would follow him back to her. The searchers wouldn't know about Carla yet, and Quinn had affirmed for her earlier that Carla's scent was now well masked.

Still, by the time dinner came, Melody was wound up so tightly she could barely eat. "I don't know if I can do this for another three weeks," she told her friends, as they secretly ate in one of the courtyards together. "I keep waiting for the other shoe to drop."

"Don't be silly. You'll breeze through it." Carla wrapped an arm around Melody's shoulders in comfort. "Right Quinn? We're going to get her through it."

"Yeah, yeah. Of course. But why do you have to wait three weeks to be safe?"

Carla looked at her for permission, and Melody nodded. "Well, we've found a spell to make enchanted objects that can dull or hide a witch's powers. Melody has these cool bangles, so we're going to cast it on them, and when she wears them, she'll seem like an average witch, so the shifters will leave her alone."

"And the strongest of them won't be defeated by her, either, right?" Quinn asked.

Melody frowned at him. Between the two of them, they were going to make her trip up. "I don't know what you're talking about," she lied, and then poked out her tongue.

"Is that what this is really all about?" Carla demanded. "You're hiding from the lion?"

Melody's remaining appetite vanished. They had worked hard today, and earlier she had been ravenous, but this line of questioning was going to get her in so much trouble if she allowed it to continue.

"I'm full, and I'm exhausted. I'm heading off to bed. You coming Roomie?"

There was a beat's pause, and then Carla turned to her with a devious grin. "Nah, I'm not that tired yet, how about you Quinn? You up for a bit longer? We could get to know each other a little."

Quinn looked at her, eyes wide. "Uh, yeah, sure. That'd be great."

Melody glanced back and forth between them. Carla looked like the cat that got the canary, or in this case, the wolf shifter. While Quinn, well he looked conflicted. Part guilty, part hopeful. Melody hoped that the pair of them could come to some sort of agreement, because despite Carla's predatory comments the night before, Melody actually thought that they'd be good for each other.

Lost in thought, Melody wandered back to the dormitories, so the hand that appeared out of the bushes and grabbed her was completely unexpected. At first she feared it was one of the Apex, but she quickly found herself surrounded by a bunch of older women.

"You're the one that the lion licked?" asked one girl.

"Yes, and it was totally disgusting!" Melody told them, but that was all she managed to get out as a resounding smack deafened her, and it took her a moment to realise that it was the sound of a slap hitting her cheek. Dazed, she fell to her knees where she was pummelled with kicks and curses before she could get herself together and start defending herself.

Melody hadn't put up with twenty years of abuse without learning how to roll with the punches, and she certainly knew when to capitulate and when it was ok to strike back. This was an instance where fighting back was ok, and Melody had more than a few tricks up her sleeve.

She threw up a shield around herself, blocking all magical attacks, although the blows still rained down on her. Then she sent a breeze flying around them, lifting their skirts up above their waists, making them squeal and fight to get them back down. It was funny, she knew that most of them would be happy parading around in a bikini, but threaten to expose the same amount of skin without their permission, and most women would try to prevent it.

While they were distracted, Melody got to her feet and lashed out, her first hex making one woman's hair fall out completely. The woman's hands went from her flapping skirt to her head as she screamed out her horror. The others paused in shock, another distraction and another chance to get in a free shot.

Melody sent out a slew of minor hexes and curses. Around her, women swore, or fought futilely against eyes that were sealed shut, or mouths that simply disappeared. You couldn't throw a spell against something you couldn't see, not when there were so many others around whom you could hit. And you couldn't hex at all if you couldn't talk.

As Melody cast her hexes she had to let the breeze go, which meant they were no longer distracted by it, and once they realised what had happened, they were free to turn their physical anger on her. Well, those that could see her. But they forgot that Melody was no longer helpless and unarmed. The shifters at Bestia had taught her how to fight.

As quickly as she twisted one girl's arm, breaking it, she head-butted another, breaking her nose instead. With her mouth already sealed, this meant that breathing became incredibly difficult, and it was more important to labour at that than anything else.

Those who were blinded were shrieking up a storm instead of saying the simple counter-curse that would have returned their vision. Two women came at her at once, one wielding a large tree branch that she had picked up. This was going to be more complicated. They were the last two threats. Five of them were blind, one sat mute on the ground while she clutched her broken arm and wept, while another helped the woman who was struggling to breathe through her broken nose.

Ten of them, there had been ten of them, and she had taken out eight so far. It had all happened so quickly, but Melody knew that this last part was going to drag out, and it was going to hurt a lot.

Well, it would have, but she suddenly found herself frozen. Her and all the other women involved. Melody could only blink her eyes in frustration, but the rational part of her realised that at least the fight was over. Well, she hoped it was.

A stern woman walked toward them, fury on her face. "Just what is the meaning of this?" she shouted. But none of them answered – they couldn't, they were all still frozen. The woman seemed to realise her mistake, and Melody staggered forward as she was released.

"You," the woman pointed at her. "What happened here?"

"Well, Ma'am, I was walking back to my room after dinner, when these women attacked me. They wanted to know if I was the one that the lion licked, and when I said I was, they started hitting and hexing me, and there were a couple of curses too." She lifted her skirt to show where the spells had left deep cuts in her legs.

The woman scanned the group and then rounded on the ones who had led the attack. It seemed that the two knew each other well, because the woman sighed and released the leader. "Shawna, really? I had expected better of you, but I see now that I was mistaken. You and your cohort will report to the healers, and then you will report to the punishment hall. I cannot let this go, ten of you against a first-year is bad enough. Even worse though, that she managed to incapacitate eight of you and was still standing strong enough to face off with the final two."

Grey eyes turned and regarded her shrewdly. "I suggest, Miss Bestia, that you retire for the night. I will talk with you in the morning before class."

Melody looked at the older woman, then looked again. Holy shit! It was none other than the provost of the academy herself. Provost Aer-Canticum was renowned throughout the country for her weather spells – which was appropriate, seeing as her parents were strong witches from both the Aer and Canticum covens. One specialised in spellweaving, the other in elemental work.

"Yes Ma'am."

Melody wondered if she was going to survive the academy. She knew that no matter what action the provost took, this wouldn't be the end of the matter. The irony of it all was that she didn't even want the lion shifter. Well, no, that wasn't quite true. He was handsome and seemed alright when he wasn't smirking at her, or covering her in saliva. It was just that she didn't dare let him challenge her. She would be forced to accept him, and Melody knew that she was more than strong enough to make him submit.

As a matter of course, her coven would be notified when she gained a familiar, and during the next school holidays they would take him from her. He would be made to swear to the coven, and then their bond would be broken. She would be forced to capture him again and again until the frequent shifting had weakened him enough that his beast would submit to any of the witches in her coven. Then he would be bound to one of them, and his life of slavery would truly begin.

15. DEAN

Dean's lion was going insane. Word had spread through the academy like wildfire that Shawna and a large contingent of third-year students had attacked the witch that he was seeking, and that she had trounced them effortlessly.

Part of him wanted to roar from the rooftops at her triumph, while another part of him wanted to find every single one of those third-years and rip their throats out. Then there was the matter of finding her. None of them could, not even the dragons. The wolf's scent had simply disappeared on the third day, and the bastard walked around looking smug and sure of himself. Dean fretted that it was because the wolf was *with* the witch, but he wasn't sure.

The dragons had noticed another witch wandering

around with no scent, and Nick had called in Ryan to challenge her. Because they were so big, the dragons rarely challenged the witches. It needed to be in a wide open space so they would have enough room to shift. So usually, the wolves and Dean took care of it between them. Of course, the witch failed, but the wolf was watching from the sidelines, and when she walked away, he had put an arm around her. Or so Jus had said. Dean wasn't taking any chances.

He'd stopped playing the dragons' game, following the assigned scent until they found the hapless witch and crossed her off the list. Of course, the provost gave them a list of all the new female students. It made the process more streamlined if they could ensure that they had indeed vetted all of the new females. He also knew that it meant the whole process would be over sooner, so that there were fewer disruptions to class.

There were a few males who were interested in being challenged, but the dragons wouldn't permit it. Neither would any alpha beast. All of the Apex wanted their witch for a mate as well as for their bond. The dragons had even talked of sharing one, just for the chance to get out of there – they were desperate enough to agree to just about anything. Eventually Dean and the wolves had come on board with it too.

The five of them had been together for just over a decade, they'd had a long time to talk about it. While the alpha beasts were strong, the dragons were so much stronger. It stood to reason that any witch strong enough to take down one of the dragons would be strong enough to take down any one of the others.

The reverse, however, would not necessarily be true so they had all come to an agreement. Any likely candidate would be vetted by the dragons, then they would all challenge her if she passed. That way, the five of them would stay together. Adding a female to their midst wouldn't be as disruptive to their sense of *pack*, as adding five females!

But this witch was different. Dean had sat there, stiff and silent, while they discussed it. The others could see his increasing desperation to find her, his need to challenge and claim her as his own, and in turn be claimed by her. There was no doubt in his mind that she could do it. She had quelled Quinn's beast with a single spoken word, there wasn't even any magic behind it! He had no doubt that when he challenged her, his life would change. He was also starting to suspect that she was his mate. From the looks the others gave him, they suspected it too. Still, none of them talked about it.

Dean knew the wolves were torn – chances were that they too would end up being with her if they challenged her, but the likelihood of her defeating one of the dragons was slim. These men were his brothers. They had spent every single day together for the last ten years. The Apex had been his salvation when he had first arrived, giving Dean the tough love that he needed until he was as prepared as they were for year after year of failure to find a witch. The wolves had been with the dragons for almost a hundred years, and the dragons had been there way longer.

The four of them had stronger pack bonds than he did, but there was also the desperation to leave the academy. Shifters were delivered to one of the three academies set up to contain shifters when they turned eighteen. Unlike the witches, who had to wait until their twenty-fifth birthday to come into their majority, shifters were considered adults with their first shift.

Shifters attended classes relevant to their beast and abilities. Rarely were they in classes with the witches, so socialising between the two groups was very important at mealtimes and on the weekends.

Unlike the witches, the shifters weren't free to leave at the weekends, or even the holidays. The academy was a prison to them as much as it was an educational facility. They had to remain there until they had bonded to a witch. Only then would they have the ability to fully control their beast.

Ordinarily, Dean would have chosen his pack over a witch, but something about her was driving him insane. The pull to her was unmistakable, the problem was that it was also non-directional. Day after day she eluded them, slipping past their net to attend her classes. Well, at least they assumed she was. They'd had enough sightings of her turning a corner ahead to confirm that she hadn't been expelled, but upon turning the same corner, they were always faced with an empty corridor. It was like she could walk through the walls.

The dragons speculated that she was actually portalling around the academy, it was an interesting theory, except that it was unthinkable. Opening a portal within the academy grounds was impossible. The grounds were strongly warded to prevent the escape or abduction of any of the shifters present.

Witches around the country fought to be accepted to Adolphus because of the presence of the strongest shifters. Rumour had it that there was another alpha wolf shifter at one of the other two shifter academies, but he hadn't bothered to try to confirm it. The strongest witches came here, and so it would be from here that he would find his witch. Except, now, he thought he had.

Dean was torn in two. The chance to escape this place and start living a life again was appealing after so long. Most shifters barely made it the three years without being bonded, and as soon as they were, they could leave the grounds in the company of their witch. Ten years was a long time, although short compared to the other four Apex members, it was still four or five years longer than any other shifter in one of the academies. But Dean didn't want to leave his pack.

It was a strange concept for him. His beast would have been happy to be the only shifter in a coven full of witches, offering his *services* to all of them. But Dean had emotional bonds with these four men, they were brothers, and lions often hunted with their brothers before they settled down with their own pride. Indeed, some lions ruled in pairs. So to extend that into five males wasn't too much of a stretch. Only, something told him, if this witch was indeed his, then there would never be anyone else for him.

16. MELODY

Of course, Melody knew that it wasn't the end of things with Shawna and her friends. As if life wasn't complicated enough. Now she had ten women, some still sporting bruises, who went out of their way to make things difficult.

She was shoulder checked in the corridors when she did use them, and when she was courageous enough to show her face in the dining hall, Shawna and her gang would whisper and point. Although whisper was a relative term. When you could hear it from the other side of the room, it wasn't really a whisper.

"Look, that's her. That's the one who attacked us the other night. She's completely crazy. We were just walking back to the dorm after dinner and she sprung out of the bushes and attacked us. Apparently she's jealous because

Dean and I are together. She seems to think him licking her was like a claim. So pathetic!"

There were snickers at that, but from then on, the other students were wary of her. It hadn't helped that she had been isolated while in hiding either.

The morning after the incident, the provost had called her into her office to talk about it. The room was bright and airy, unlike many in the older parts of the academy. Melody suspected that the windows had been enlarged because she hadn't seen any others that were as big. Brilliant sunlight lit the room from one end to the other, illuminating bookshelves and cabinets crammed with treasures from around the globe.

It had taken her a moment or two to remember that there was a woman behind the desk who was waiting for her to sit down as she had been invited to when she entered after a timid knock. When Melody finally realised her faux pas, her gaze snapped to Provost Aer-Canticum, who wore an indulgent expression, as though she were used to being ignored in the presence of her admirable collection.

"Oh my goodness, I'm so sorry, it's just that, well, look at that, is that a dragon's tooth? And those stone bowls, are they basilisk eggshells? And over there …" she trailed off uncertainly. She had just apologised for ignoring the provost, and now she was doing it again.

The woman in question laughed. "Melody, do please come and sit down. On another day I would only be too happy to indulge your fascination, but this morning, however, we need to complete this interview in time for you to attend class."

"Of course, Provost. My apologies."

"Don't fret, it's a veritable Aladdin's cave in here. I see them all so often that I forget just how wondrous they are. It's nice to have my perspective refreshed from time to time." She shuffled some papers on her desk and then fixed Melody with a stern gaze.

"In the absence of a truthfinder on campus, I will be asking you a lot of questions today that may seem a little unusual. I ask that you bear with me. There may be wider consequences to the actions of last night that you are not aware of."

"I beg your pardon, Ma'am," interrupted Melody, "but are you aware that Quinn has been trained as a truthfinder?"

The provost's gaze sharpened. "No, I was not aware, but thank you for bringing this to my attention. It seems that Mr Brevors and I should have a little chat. Nothing fearful, it is just that I would like to avail myself of his services now that I know I have a truthfinder on campus again. Thank you for this knowledge, it is quite a gift!"

Melody faltered. Had it been a secret? Quinn had been surprised that she'd told Carla, and now the provost was saying that it was a gift to know. Melody would have to corner him and ask him, before she told him what she'd just done.

"Now, as to last night. Could you please tell me, in your own words, the sequence of events."

Melody recounted her version of what happened, the provost interrupting from time to time to ask questions that clarified certain things. Some of the questions indeed were unusual and not what she had expected. There was a whole line of questioning about her aunt that she felt had nothing to do with things, but as the information was general knowledge, she felt that answering was not betraying her coven. It seemed that the geas regarding her loyalty agreed.

"Well, I think that clears that up. I will be speaking quite firmly to Shawna. This sort of behaviour isn't tolerated at the academy, however, there are political consequences to expelling her," her shocked gaze swung to Melody from where she had been staring at a crystal on a shelf. "Well, it seems that the crystal of truth works both ways. I will have to remember that in future."

Melody's jaw dropped, no wonder she had been willing to go ahead with the interview without a truthfinder present.

"I ask that you keep everything that was said in this room between the two of us. I would also ask that you limit the knowledge of the hidden tunnels to yourself, Carla, and Quinn. I do not know why you insist on using them, but I will not forbid you. I would say, however, that if you are experiencing difficulties here at the academy, my door is always open. I am more than the provost of this school, more than the keeper of the keys. I am a good listener as well." Shrewd grey eyes watched her for a moment, before the chime sounded in the distance, indicating the first class of the day.

"I promise, Provost Aer-Canticum."

"Very good. I am also, Miss Bestia, a terrible enemy. Keep that in mind as well."

On that ominous note, she was ushered from the room and sent off to class. As she crossed the main courtyard, there was a shout from one of the corridors on the other side. Melody looked up to see one of the dragons pointing at her. There were scuffling sounds coming from behind him, indicating someone running in her direction. Terrified, she hurtled down the nearest corridor with a tunnel entrance and bolted inside.

She didn't dare move for fear of them hearing her footsteps, and she tried to calm her breathing and her galloping heart in case they could hear that too.

There was no sound for several moments, but then she could vaguely hear male voices. It sounded like they were arguing but she couldn't tell. Suddenly, there was a bang on the wall just to the right of her, hard enough that grit sprinkled down from above, coating her in a chalky white powder. What on earth was that?

There were more male voices, this time quieter, and then silence. Still, Melody didn't move. Too terrified to go out, too terrified to stay, her heart beat faster and faster until she thought she was going to pass out.

This was ridiculous! Thinking about it, Melody realised that they had been talking right outside where she stood, and most likely shouting. If that came through as muffled as it did, then it was unlikely that they would hear her walking.

With that logic arming her courage, she made a small witch-light in the palm of her hand and started walking down the tunnel. This one came out near the greenhouses on the far side of the academy. It would mean that she would miss the entire first class of the day, but it was better than exiting the corridor and revealing her means of hiding, especially if it meant she bumped into them straight away.

The whole incident clarified one thing for her. They knew that they hadn't challenged her in their ridiculous game, and they were looking for her!

17. MELODY

The next week had passed quickly in a blur of new classes, new people, and new tunnels and now tonight was the night she would make the dampeners. How she had lasted this long, Melody didn't know, but she suspected she was the only female witch left of the first-year students who hadn't been challenged.

She'd noticed that the dragons didn't challenge anyone, and it was understandable. Melody had never seen a dragon, but she'd read that they were large enough to devour an elephant in one sitting. She wondered how the academy managed to feed them. Indeed, how it managed to feed all the shifters.

Melody had seen an astounding number and variety of them. Only yesterday, she saw a beautiful woman shimmer and disappear into her clothing, a male witch stooping to help her out of them. She flew to his shoulder as a beautifully coloured lorikeet. Melody had thought that all shifters were predators because they were the only ones she had encountered in her coven. Certainly, none of the texts that she'd managed to sneak a peek at back at the compound mentioned anything other than strong predator shifters. Their selection must have been biased towards Aunt Georgia's tastes.

Coven Bestia were only interested in the strongest of shifters. And many were lost in their first year. Well, at least the male ones. The females were kept as broodmares and the males used as studs in between "lessons" that left them bleeding and exhausted.

Melody was never permitted to watch what was done to the shifters. For that, she was grateful. It was bad enough that she was unable to deny her aunt anything that she demanded, but it would have been far worse if Melody had actually seen the horrors that she was consigning them too. She was already near mad with grief for them.

She had contemplated her options when she came to Adolphus Academy. If worse came to worst and one of the dragons did challenge her, then Melody had decided to deny it, and curse the name of her coven in the same breath. With the geasan that her aunt had placed upon her before she left, there was a good chance that the punishments delivered would kill her. And then that option would be lost to her aunt forever.

Indeed, the matriarchal power of her coven would be

destroyed along with her. With no siblings and no heir, it would simply die within her. It was why the scion of the coven usually came into her power after she had completed her education. The sudden death of her mother – and the actions she had taken with her last breaths – ensured that Melody wouldn't face a similar death in her aunt's ascension to the role of coven leader.

When Melody had reached the age of twenty-five, she came into her majority, and would have been well within her rights to challenge for the leadership. She'd known that her aunt already had some sort of contingency plan for that, there was no way that she had waited all these years for Melody to approach the peak of her powers and not have some way to ensure that her cruelty was not the source of her own downfall. So for now, the geasen and the academy were effectively holding her back, but she was sure her aunt would have something else up her sleeve.

Tonight would be a step toward defeating her aunt in the interim. It wouldn't hold her back forever, but if Melody could get through college without bonding any of the stronger shifters, then her aunt would have to rethink her schemes.

Carla bounced into the room, full of excitement. She was looking forward to the spell and had been bugging Melody about it all week. When Carla hadn't been hanging off Quinn, something that still disturbed Melody for reasons she couldn't explain, she had been helping her explore the tunnels. They were surprisingly extensive, a rabbit's warren right under the academy buildings. Some even went to odd places, the middle of the field, the rear of the kitchens, and one went as far as the academy boundaries. As far as she could tell, though, it stopped just a bit short.

"Are you ready to go, Roomie?" asked Carla.

Melody laughed. "Yep. Just as ready as I was yesterday, the day before, and any other day in the last three weeks. We've got this, and tonight is the night!"

Carla started singing that song by the Black Eyed Peas about having a good night, and Melody joined in, the two of them giggling insanely. Tonight would mark a new era for Melody at the academy, no more sneaking around. She'd be able to be herself and finally get to mingle with the rest of the student body.

Of course, they still had to wait for the sun to set and the moon to rise, but that wasn't going to dim their excitement. If anything, it only stirred them up more. To be safe, they were going to follow one of the newer tunnels. It was the one that led toward the academy boundaries, but it apparently ended somewhere in the forest. Quinn had been down that one and said it came out between some rocks, that there was no actual door to it, although he hadn't tried to exit the tunnel. It could have been protected by a spell, and he didn't want to set it off without the witches there.

The item had to be placed in a silver bowl filled with lavender oil. It didn't matter if it was one, or two, or a hundred, as long as it was covered. However, the more items to be charmed, the more magic was required. Thankfully, that wasn't the problem, Melody wasn't short of magic, so bespelling two bangles at once would pose no issue for her.

Carla had managed to borrow a silver bowl from one of her teachers. She had produced a spell to make some moisturiser, one that also used lavender oil, and the teacher had laughed at her vanity and given the items over without question. Melody was thrilled, because there was no way that she would have been able to lie to a teacher.

"It's not a lie," Carla had told her, "the best manipulations are based in truth. This is a genuine spell, and I do intend to make the cream. In fact, I have to, the teacher wanted to see the results. It's an old spell of my grandmother's, and she had amazing skin. Now, the fact that I also need these things for your spell, well, that's a happy coincidence, and not something that the teacher needs to know."

So that was that. They were the only ingredients. The rest was up to Melody, her spell and her magic. It was the will that she put into the magic that would flavour the results. The more determined she was to make it work, the more likely it was that it would. Especially as she had the power to back up her will.

The path to the tunnel they wanted wasn't straightforward. She would have to use two others to get to the one she wanted. First, she would have to go down to the kitchenette and walk to the dining hall. Then they would carefully surface and walk from the north corridor to the next one to the right, on the other side of the dining hall. She didn't dare cut through the dining hall itself, it would be too easy to bump into the Apex there.

Once in the second corridor, there was another tunnel that started, this time after the third light bracket on the left. It led from there to just outside the library, where they would round the corner and find the start of the final tunnel in the woodshed. Melody had been a bit doubtful about that, but Quinn had assured her that one of the wood piles was fake and covered a trapdoor in the floor. There was no tricky little poem for that one, only those in the older parts of the academy had them. It was as if a second generation had added to them..

"What are you wool gathering about now, Mel?" Carla asked. She had adopted Quinn's nickname for Melody, and now even her teachers had started using it.

"Sorry, I was just thinking about the tunnels. I can't believe that I made it all this time, and that now we get to do this spell, and finally we'll all be safe."

"Safe from what?" asked Carla.

"The clustserfuck that is my life," sighed Melody, making Carla laugh.

"Girl, one day you are going to trust me enough to tell me everything that is going on," Carla said, wrapping an arm around her. "I'm willing to wait you out, you know. I don't know what's going on with you, but I know it's juicy, full of drama, and that I'll be able to help you."

Melody rested her head on Carla's shoulder for a minute,

before stepping away and grabbing her bag with the bowl, bangles, and bottles of lavender oil. "Let's go do this!"

Together, they walked down the stairs to the kitchenette, opening the broom closet as soon as they were sure the coast was clear. Melody cut her thumb, opened the tunnel door, and they were off. At the end of the first tunnel, Carla offered to step out first, but there was nobody there, so they carefully made their way to the next corridor over, activated the door there, and set off again in the dimly lit passageway.

One thing that Melody wanted to do when she had more freedom was work with Carla to see whether witchlight would show through any gaps or crevices. It would make things a bit easier if they could light the way without fear.

This time, when they emerged near the library, Melody went first. The likelihood of running into anyone out here this late at night was slim. The library had closed hours ago. Still, they doused their lights and carefully made their way across the lawn to the little woodshed. Once in there, they identified the false woodpile that Quinn had told them about, and then they were off again.

This third tunnel was different from the others, it seemed to be much, much older. The floor at the base was sandy, and Melody couldn't tell if there were stone pavers under it or not. It also sloped downward quite steeply. Knowing they were well underground, she sent her witchlight ahead, and brightened it significantly so that they could see where they were going.

Melody couldn't tell at what point they started to rise

again, but a breeze warned them to douse their lights and proceed more cautiously. Around the next bend, there was a cave, the floor here uneven and littered with rocks. They picked their way carefully to where the barest light filtered through, and sure enough, it was a crack in a giant boulder set into a slope. It was angled so that it was almost impossible to see.

Before she passed through it, Melody cast her magic forth to see if there was any sort of trap there, but all she sensed was a spell to discourage animals from entering. She wondered if it affected shifters as well.

Outside, the moon was a mere scar in the sky, so thin that at times when she looked at it, it didn't seem to be there at all. It was only when she looked away from it, that she could see it. This was as newly minted a moon as one could hope for.

"So, where are we going to do this?" Carla asked.

"Not at the door to the tunnel, that's for sure," Melody told her.

The two women started toward the treeline when something dark hurtled toward them. Melody barely had time to draw in a breath to scream when it hit her chest and knocked her to the ground. A large wet tongue licked her all over her face, and a weight settled on her chest. They'd found her. It was one of the wolves, the Apex had finally found her. Holy fucking Goddess!

"Shift!" commanded Carla, and immediately the weight on her chest changed. Quinn's tongue hung just an inch above her cheek where he was about to lean in and lick her again, and he quickly withdrew it, and looked up at Carla in shock. He wasn't the only one.

Melody threw him off, brushing off the dirt and leaves as she processed what had just happened. Carla had just defeated Quinn and bonded his wolf. It seemed that there was more going on between the two of them, because she stalked over to him, slapped him, and then pulled him in tight for a kiss, her hand unfalteringly finding his cock which rapidly grew hard at her touch.

Well, that was two things that she hadn't expected in less than two minutes! Feeling like an intruder, Melody quietly grabbed her bag and sneaked off into the trees.

"Wait." Quinn panted, moaning deeply. "I found the perfect clearing to do your spell. Oh fuck, Carla, fuck, fuck, fuck ..." His hips thrust forward into her hand which was pumping him expertly.

"We'll be with you in a few minutes, Melody. I don't think either of us are going to last long." Carla grabbed Quinn's neck and pulled his head down for a deep and lasting kiss.

Ok, this was beyond awkward. Melody turned and walked away. She was happy for her friends, but right now, she needed to focus on this spell and getting it done. Within minutes, she was lost. There was no sign of any clearing and she was sick of falling over things that she couldn't see. The fifth time she landed on her hands and knees, however, there was someone there to help her up.

Melody yelped in surprise as strong hands not only lifted

her to her feet, but into the air, before setting her down gently. "Sorry, Mel. Guess I'll have to remember to be careful of my increased strength."

She was startled to realise that Quinn had hauled her up while Carla was riding him piggy-back style. She shouldn't have been surprised though, Melody had seen the same thing over and over with shifters at her coven's compound. Once bonded, shifters received a boost in their strength, and witches received a boost in their powers. In a proper bond, there was a partnership, and in times of difficulty one could loan extra power to the other. It was part of why familiars were so popular.

Quinn's new strength meant that he was able to support her through the dense brush while still carrying his new mistress. It seemed that Carla wasn't opposed to it either. Melody liked them both, she just hoped that her roommate wouldn't take advantage of her new friend. She couldn't see Quinn doing the same, he was just too soft-hearted. On the up side, she didn't have to worry about him challenging her again!

Within minutes, Quinn with his superior senses, and having scouted the area already, led them to a clearing with a large area of exposed stone. He was right, it was a perfect place to perform the spell. Melody got out the bowl, filled it with the lavender oil and then placed the two bangles inside of it. She quickly chalked out the simple rune circle described in the book, and sat in it with the bowl.

Once she was satisfied that all was as it should be, and Carla had checked her runes, she chanted the spell.

"Let what is there,

be no more.

Let power be dulled,

and strength forbore.

The Goddess alone,

be the one to see.

Bind this to a charm,

so mote it be."

The oil began to glow a silvery blue, and Melody focused her will and her power on combining it with the bangles. The spell was a simple one, and she could feel the magic imbue first the oil, then the oil and the magic coated the bangles. When the light dimmed, Melody removed them and carefully put them on her wrists.

"Holy shit!" exclaimed Quinn. "I can barely feel you."

"Same, Roomie! You're barely stronger than me!"

Melody's eyes welled with tears. Here was the answer, right here in these bangles was the freedom that she sought. Now, nothing could stop her from walking the halls and corridors of the college. Now, she could finally join in and experience life for the first time!

18. MELODY

*I*n the morning, she woke with a renewed sense of vigour, despite having been up late celebrating with Quinn and Carla the night before.

"Come on, Roomie, get your arse in gear. Today, we eat breakfast in the dining hall – in public!" She nudged a groaning Carla who was still buried under her blankets.

"And you get to register Quinn as your familiar."

Melody laughed as Carla threw back her blankets with a squeal. "Oh my Goddess, yes!" she shouted. "Oh Melody, you should have seen him when we fucked. He was magnificent!" she crowed.

"Um, you forget, I nearly did!" said Melody.

Giggling, they got ready and then bounded out the doors together, eager to face a new day where the world held possibilities it hadn't the night before. They laughed and chatted the whole way to the dining room, gathering curious looks from the other students. Not many people were that cheerful so early.

When Melody walked in, she saw a guy look up at her in shock, and then run out of the door on the other side. She wondered if it was a coincidence, or if he was off to tell someone. It was probably the latter, but she hoped it was the Apex he was telling and not Shawna and her posse. Melody didn't need any more of their shit, not on the first day of the rest of her life.

Even with her newfound optimism, she didn't want to linger in the dining hall, it was too fabulous a day to spend inside anyway, so she had the same fast breakfast that she always did. Today, Melody wanted to spend as much time out of the tunnels as possible. It was time to reclaim the sunlight!

"You still in a rush?" asked Carla, confused. Her expression brightened, however, when Quinn walked in, his gaze zeroing in on her. He grabbed his usual breakfast roll, then thought about it and grabbed a second one, before heading to sit beside her.

"Have you eaten?" he asked, offering her the second bun, before eyeing the empty plate in front of her dubiously. "I mean, would you like seconds?"

Carla laughed. "No, I'm good thanks Quinn. I was just asking why Melody was still eating light." Their focus turned to her.

"I'm not in a rush per se, it's just that I've been hiding for weeks, and now I want sunlight. I *must* have *all* the sunlight!" She laughed, and they joined in.

"Fine with me, I can eat while I walk. Let's go." Quinn stood, pulling Carla's chair out for her, and she preened under his attention.

The three of them stepped outside and walked to the main courtyard where there was more than enough sun to satisfy Melody. They found a bench against a wall in the full light, and settled in to wait for the chime for first class.

Across the courtyard there was a disturbance, protests and shouts. Melody drowsily opened her eyes to see the Apex burst into the open, the lion's gaze fixed upon her before he barreled towards her. Hot on his heels were the other four shifters. Half way across he shifted, bursting from his clothing as he leapt toward her.

The other shifters laughed, but Melody could see his intent. He was going to force her to accept his challenge one way or another. If she stood there and did nothing, he'd maul her before he could rein his beast in. It was a risky gambit.

Melody stood and walked toward him, Quinn and Carla shouting at her to be careful from behind. It was ironic. On her first day of freedom, she was going to be killed by the very thing she was trying to avoid.

"Shift!" she yelled at him, throwing all her power at it, knowing that it wouldn't be enough, that finally she would be free from her aunt and all the drama that her power caused. Melody was dumbfounded when he fell to the ground in his human form, mid-leap. His sides heaved as he looked up at her in satisfaction.

Even with the dampeners, she had defeated his beast.

What the everloving fuck?

Time seemed to slow as everyone in the courtyard froze in shock. She'd done it, even with all her precautions, she was still strong enough to force his beast to submit.

No, no, no, no, no! This was not supposed to happen. Not now, not ever. She had just effectively killed this magnificent man. It wouldn't be today, but his days now had a number on them, an underscore, a full stop.

Time started moving again, as the rest of the Apex roused themselves and started running for her.

No! Fuck! No!

If she bonded one of those dragons, her aunt would pull her out of school faster than you could say stud services, and her plans would be fast tracked. Seeing no other alternative, Melody rounded on the lion shifter in front of her.

"Shift and defend me. Do not let any of them reach me!" She waited a split second longer for him to shudder as he turned to comply, compelled to protect her, even from his friends. Melody turned and ran for the nearest tunnel. Today was supposed to be the first day of her freedom, instead it was the worst day of her life.

19. DEAN

Fuck! It was ecstacy!

Never had Dean experienced a feeling anything remotely like it! He knelt there, his body trembling in shock as the magic bond coursed through him, strengthening his muscles, enhancing his senses and hardening his cock. As if his cock wasn't already hard at the thought of her finally being his.

And then she tore down his world.

He could hear his friends rushing towards them, see the hope in their faces that finally they would be free of this hell, only to have it dashed when she forced him to change and defend her. He didn't understand, but he also couldn't refuse her.

Dean let go and his beast roared forward, eager to obey, desperate to defend her. His friends drew up short in shock, not willing to fight him, but keen to find a way around him so that they could find his witch. She didn't want to be found, she had made that clear. He had been thinking of the pleasure of his hunt, how much he was enjoying chasing her around the campus. How thrilled he was that she had outwitted them all again and again. How much more satisfying it would be when he finally cornered her and ended their game.

Only now he could see that it wasn't a game for her. He had been too caught up in his own needs to see hers, and now he had forced this bond upon her, an unwilling witch. The look of horror and sheer desperation on her face when he shifted, would haunt him for the rest of his life. It had simply never occurred to him that a witch wouldn't want him.

Nick walked slowly toward him. "Come on, Dean. You can't deny us this. We have to see, we have to know. Fuck, it's all I can do to stop myself shifting right here and now, and just bypassing you. You know that I can fly to wherever she is and challenge her there. After what I just witnessed, I don't care if I knock down a building or two to get to her."

Dean felt Nick's magic wash over him, and he knew that the other shifter had opened him up in a link. He hoped that all of them were in it, because they needed to understand this.

I'm hers, he told them, and they all nodded.

She didn't want me. She doesn't want any *of us. She was horrified that she'd bonded me. You didn't see her face.* His lion moaned sadly, rejected. He agreed. He was a grown ass shifter, but he wanted to curl up and cry.

She's asked me to defend her from you all, and it is my duty to do so. I forced this upon her. I will not allow you to do the same thing. It's bad enough that I'm bound to an unwilling witch. I would not wish this pain on you all. And I will kill you if you try to reach her.

His friends looked at him in shock, the hurt and betrayal on the faces of the wolves was especially painful to witness. This was a clusterfuck, but he had to make them understand

We were all so focused on what we wanted, on the fact that every witch in the academy wanted us, that we failed to consider that there would be one who didn't. We were so focused on what we wanted, that we neglected to think about her. It's too late for me, my soul is hers, and I'll feel her hatred for me for the rest of my life. Don't let this pain be yours too.

"We can change that, we can convince her," begged Jus. The dragons had to be feeling this the most. They had waited centuries!

Then convince her, but do not challenge her before you do so. I will kill you before she accepts it.

He waited to see the defeated slump of their shoulders before he turned his back on them and went to find her. Now that he was bonded to her, it was no trouble at all to find her scent. The masking spell no longer affected him.

She smelled fucking amazing, just as wonderful as she did in his memory. He quietly stalked her across the campus until he found her shivering behind the library. Quietly he shifted before sitting beside her. Nudity was nothing to shifters, just a part of everyday life. For witches, however, it could be a bit of a hangup, so he was careful to sit in a way that covered his junk, no mean feat when it was slapping happily against his belly. She made him rock hard.

"You ok?" It was so lame, but it was all he could think to ask her. Dean could smell her tears and he was desperate to pull her into his arms, but something told him that she wouldn't accept that right now.

There was a soft snort from her before she lifted her head. "I thought it was ok, I thought I was safe, that you were safe. But it's all a joke. No matter what I do, I'm fucked, and I just can't take it anymore. I've lost too many of you."

He had no idea what she was talking about, but she sounded miserable.

"I'm just so sorry that I've consigned you to the same fate as the others. I was trying so hard to protect you all. I thought if I could avoid bonding you, then you'd be safe. Then I thought if I dampened my power, you could challenge me and I'd fail ..." She flinched and grunted. Dean could smell blood on her.

His lion roared in his head, pushing to be released so that he could take on whatever it was that had just wounded her. Dean looked around quickly, but he could neither see nor scent a witch close enough to hex her. He quelled his beast, telling him they needed answers first, but the smell of blood was growing stronger.

Frantic, Dean pulled her forward and ripped a hole down the center of the back of her shirt. There before him was an ugly wound, the skin split open like an overripe fruit, telling him it was deep. Blood poured down, and she was moaning in pain. It went from the bottom of her bra on the left side, to just above her hip on the right. It wouldn't kill her, but she needed a healer.

"I can't carry you like this. I'm going to shift into my lion, and then you can ride me to the healers." He took a step back from her, and was about to call upon his eager cat when she stopped him with a word.

"No," she told him.

"We'll make our way back to my room where you will help me dress the wound. Then together we will go to the admin block to register you as my familiar."

The deadness to her voice worried him, as did what she had said before.

"What are you afraid of?" he asked her gently.

"If I told you, it would be the death of me."

She pushed him away, rearranging her shirt so that the buttons went down the back, and the gaping hole was at the front. Then, with her hands clutching the two halves together, she started walking toward the dormitories. Dean had no choice but to follow her.

A shadow passed overhead, and he looked up to see Nick hovering as he watched them both. He wondered if the dragon could smell her blood or if it was covered just like the rest of her scent. It would probably drive him mad to sense it, he hoped that Nick was too high to notice. He should have known better.

You fucking clawed her? Nick roared in his mind, and there were protests from the others in the Apex.

No! It's witch made. She started babbling about dampening her power so that she couldn't bond us, so that she could keep us safe, and suddenly she's flinching and I can smell her blood. She won't tell me what she's afraid of either. She says it would kill her to do so. Somehow, I think she means that literally.

There were shouts and roars of beasts across the link, a sign of just how distressed his friends were, if their beasts were in control of their thoughts.

So why aren't you heading toward the healers? Jus growled.

She won't go. Flat out refused. She wants me to dress the wound. I have no fucking idea how to, it's not like I've seen anyone wounded that couldn't heal it with a shift. It's a fucking deep cut!

Where are you headed? asked Ryan, finally able to form a coherent thought.

To her room in the dorms. She's going to get cleaned up, then we're going to admin to register.

I'll meet you there. I know what to do. Don't tell her that I'm there, and let me tell her that I won't challenge her, no matter how much my wolf is pushing me to. We listened, Dean, we really did. I'll convince her before I challenge her.

Dean walked miserably beside her all the way back to the dorms. He could smell not only her blood, but her pain. She didn't say a word the whole way there, not until they got to the common room where Ryan was waiting for them.

"What the fuck? Dean, defend me!" she called.

"Wait, hear me out. I'm not here to challenge you!" Ryan held up his hands in supplication, bandages and gauze pads clearly visible in his hands. "I know first aid," he nodded his head in Dean's direction. "He doesn't. I just came to help, that's all."

The two men paused, waiting for her verdict. Eventually her shoulders slumped and she came out from behind Dean. "You'd better come up to my room then," she said in that dead voice again.

Dean and Ryan shared a look, but they followed her. It was killing him to see her so dejected like this. When Carlos had come to tell them earlier that he had seen her walk into the dining room, Dean had been elated. Finally he would have his chance to stake his claim. He knew she would defeat him, he hungered for it. His beast was riding him hard, finally they would have the chance to challenge her! The reality, however, was a nightmare.

When they reached her room, Melody put her key in the door and turned it, stepping in and waiting for them both to enter before she closed it behind her. She shrugged off the ruined remains of her shirt and opened another door into the bathroom she shared with the other witch.

Ryan followed her in with his supplies, and Dean lounged against the doorframe. He didn't want to crowd her, but there was no way that he was leaving her exposed and vulnerable with a wolf shifter who was bursting to challenge her.

"You'll need to take your bra off, it goes from top to bottom, I'm going to need access to your entire back."

She didn't say anything, and Ryan shot him a worried glance, but a second later her hands reached up behind her and undid the blood soaked clips. She allowed the straps to fall down her arms, and then the bra fell to the floor. Ryan guided her over to the sink, his hands never anything other than professional. He reached into his bag and threw a pair of sweats to Dean, who caught them and shoved his legs into them.

In the meantime, Ryan had produced a sterile cloth and was carefully cleaning her back. The bleeding seemed to have stopped for now, but the wound was a dark and ugly stripe across her skin. It was only as her skin was cleared that the two shifters caught a glimpse of a darker story written across her in scars and weals. There were two other recent marks, still red and raised, although they hadn't broken the skin.

"Have you been a bad girl, Melody?" Ryan asked her softly in her ear, and she shuddered, causing the wound to crack open again in several places. She did not, however, respond. Dean growled, and the wolf shifter shot him a mute look of apology.

Can you smell her blood? Her scent? Dean asked him across the bond.

Her scent in her blood, yes, but not on her skin. It seems that the masking spell is only skin deep.

Ryan continued to wash her skin, the two of them aghast

at the plethora of white stripes across her back. Finally he moved closer to examine the wound, poking gently at the flesh where it was bleeding again.

"Melody, it needs stitches," he finally told her. "We need to go to the healers."

"No," she sighed. "If you can't treat it, then I'll do it myself. I have before, it's just awkward."

That thought alone made Dean want to roar, but he clenched his teeth to keep his mouth shut.

"Why don't you just heal it?" Ryan asked her.

Melody froze.

"I'm ... I'm not good at it," she stammered.

They could both clearly tell she was lying, but when Ryan opened his mouth to call her out, Dean nudged him. He met Ryan's eyes in the mirror, shaking his head. Right now, they just needed to deal with this. There was obviously more at play. If Ryan pushed her now, she might tell him to leave, and Dean needed Ryan to do what he could for her wound.

Before either shifter could stop her, she bent down and opened the door under the sink, producing a first aid kit that she had obviously brought with her. What kind of witch travelled to a school with that fucking get-up in her possession? Dean was starting to get a very bad feeling about the coven that his witch was from.

"I can treat it, it's just going to take longer to heal," Ryan told her.

"I understand," was all she said, dully.

Her whole demeanour was beginning to freak Dean out.

There's something seriously wrong here, she's withdrawn, she's resigned, and she refuses to get stitches even though she needs them, Dean told the others.

Tell me exactly what happened, what she said, what she did, when she got hurt, Nick ordered.

So Dean did just that, he described every last detail, his lion helping him with the things that the cat had noticed about her scent changes. When he was done, both dragons growled across the bond.

It's a geas, sent Nick. *A fucking strong one at that. It won't heal until she's done whatever it was that she's being punished for not doing. That's why she can't heal it, and it's why she won't go to the healers. It sounds like she's being punished for avoiding bonding us. We need to tread very carefully here. None of us can challenge her now until this is cleared up. There's obviously something very wrong in her home life. I'll reach out to my father and see what he can find out about her coven.*

Thank you, Dean sent to him.

Ryan looked helplessly at him, his eyes sadder than ever. When he was done with the dressing, he leant forward, kissed her good shoulder gently, and then left without saying another word. Dean went into her room, rooted through the drawers and cupboard until he had gathered a bra and a shirt, and then came back to her in the bathroom.

He stopped short when he saw her. Her hand was pressed against where Ryan had kissed her, and tears poured freely down her face.

"It'll be ok, Melody. Whether we're bonded or not, you

have all of us on your side now. We'll help you work it out." Before she could protest, he dropped to his knees in front of her.

"Under the light of the Goddess, I swear my fealty to you, Melody Bestia. I vow to give my body, my service and my life. So do I swear."

The magic brushed across his skin like a silken cloth, before it cinched tight, causing him to fight for his breath for a moment or two. Then it settled into his skin, into his bones, and he felt it no more.

"I don't know whether to kiss you or slap you," she finally said. She reached out and took the clothing from him, and he helped her into it. He was careful not to press on her wound when he did up the bra for her, her arms struggling to reach behind her without ripping the wound open again.

He waited while she tugged and tucked until the thing sat comfortably on her, and then he held out her blouse. He'd taken the time to undo all of the buttons, so that all she had to do was raise her arms a little, and he could feed them into the sleeves. Then he turned her around and slowly did them up for her.

The whole time he felt her gaze on him, watching him, weighing him, judging him. When he was finally done, he looked her in the eye.

"I'm sorry for forcing the bonding on you, I see now how selfish my actions were. I have warned my friends, they won't challenge you unless you ask them to."

She said nothing, merely watching him.

"I'm not sorry for swearing fealty to you. Something tells me that you needed me to, but would never ask it of me. I give you everything, Melody. My life, my love, and my soul. I ask only for the chance to serve beside you."

Still those ice-blue eyes regarded him. Then she took a step forward, placed her hands on his face and pulled him down for a long, slow kiss.

Her lips against his brought his universe to a halt. He didn't dare touch her for fear of hurting her, but his lion was pushing him to grab her, spread her thighs and rut her until she didn't know her own name. Only the scent of her blood and pain held them both in check.

Finally she drew back from him. "I have been alone in the darkness for so long. Thank you for shining your light and finding me."

He wasn't sure if she forgave him, but he knew that with those words she was giving him a chance. A chance to prove himself useful to her, worthy of her. It was a chance he would grab with both hands and fulfil for the rest of his life.

20. MELODY

The paperwork to register a shifter was not complicated, so they were done much sooner than Melody had expected. Above her entry on the register were Carla and Quinn's names, and she smiled in happiness. At least they would come out of their time here alright. Knowing her hadn't hurt them at all. Even Quinn, despite their rocky start.

Dean hovered over her the entire time she was filling out the forms. He seemed to be reluctant to be further than a foot away from her, but rather than bugging her, she found his quiet presence comforting. Sebastian, her first familiar, had been like that. He hadn't been able to part from the tiny girl who had bested him, and he had been the closest thing to a father figure that she had ever had.

Bestia Coven was an all-female coven, an unusual thing in this day and age. But there was a reason for that. Their core power was matriarchal, only passed through the female line. The witches there used the shifters to get them pregnant. Male children were "adopted out" unless they were shifters, she suspected that the male witch babies were not allowed to survive. They might be a matriarchal coven, but they were not a maternal one.

Having a shifter for a father seemed to improve the beast control powers of the next generation of witches, and Bestia was well known for their beast taming powers. Melody had never known her own father, he had died long before she had been old enough to ask about him. From what she could tell, the coven had been quite different under her mamma's leadership, and had only taken a darker turn once Aunt Georgia had come to power.

The sound of keys slapping onto the counter in front of her, brought Melody back from her musings, startling her and making Dean growl.

"You need to move your things, clean your room, and return your old keys by the end of the day," the woman behind the counter told her.

"Pardon?"

"Well, you can't sleep with your shifter in the girls' dormitory, so you need to move into one of the bonded cottages. That's the keys to your new cottage, here's a map with the cottage marked on it. You need to move your things over and have your half of the room cleared and cleaned by tonight. You've got the day off classes to get yourself sorted, but you will be expected to keep up with your coursework."

Melody was stunned. She hadn't even thought of accommodations at the time of the challenge, of course they would have to move today, Dean's lion would be pushing to be near her.

She looked at him out of the corner of her eye. It wasn't hard, he was practically leaning up against her back as he looked over her shoulder. His large right hand came up and grabbed the keys and the map, while his left arm snagged her around the waist and pulled her away.

"We'll get it done," he called over his shoulder as they left.

The paperwork had been the easy part. The larger issue was moving all her gear, and then Dean's, before they cleaned the rooms. Thankfully, because the Apex no longer needed to attend classes compulsorily, they had help. Melody had nearly peed her pants on the spot when the two dragons and the two wolves showed up, but Dean had reassured her that they wouldn't bother her.

When they got to her room, they found it in a state of uproar already. It hadn't clicked with Melody that Carla would be going through the same process. In the space of a day, both women would be moving out. They had only shared a room for a few weeks, but Melody felt a connection to Carla. She'd only ever had her coven's shifters as her friends, people who were just as trapped as she was, they weren't exactly the healthiest of relationships, but they were the only positive ones she'd had.

"Roomie!" Carla cried when she spotted her. "I knew you'd be here soon …" Her voice trailed off when she saw the rest of the Apex in the hall, waiting to come in. "Oh fuck, please tell me you didn't go and bond them all?" Her face was aghast.

"No, no! I have only one bond, and I am happy with just that." It was the wrong thing to say apparently, because a stinging heat started up on her back. Dean sucked in a breath when she flinched. It wasn't as strong as the open wound on her back, but it was painful enough. Around her, the room stilled, the entire Apex focused on her. Carla glanced at their rigid stances before looking back at Melody, her confusion clear on her face.

She took Melody by the hands and pulled her over to her single bed, sitting down and tugging Melody down with her. "I get that you just met me, and that you still don't trust me yet, but please tell me that you've told him. He's your bonded familiar now, you can trust him with anything. Please tell me he knows what's going on and is helping you."

Well. Fuck. Talk about letting the cat out of the bag!

Now, all of the shifters were agitated, waiting for her answer. All except Dean, who gently pulled her to her feet and into his arms. "I don't know it all, but I'm starting to work out bits. I'm helping her all I can," he said quietly. His hands paused on her hips, not knowing where it was safe to wrap them around her, before he slid them down to her butt and squeezed, eliciting a squeak from her.

It was the perfect ice-breaker, making the men laugh even if it was strained, but the whole thing had turned what should have been a joyous morning into a more sober one.

Between the eight of them, they had the women packed up in no time, and with their magic, the room was spotless even faster. At least there was no furniture to move. In under an hour, all trace of them was gone from the room. It was time to move to the next stage of their lives in their new accommodation.

Melody looked at her map. If the central hub of the campus was the rings of classes, then the outer spokes were the ancillary buildings and accommodation for the students and teachers alike. In the north west quadrant were the male and female witch dorms, with a few scattered cottages behind them for bonded witches. They were all empty. In the north-east quadrant, however, were eleven cottages in arcs that would form concentric rings if they continued.

First there was an arc of three cottages, then five, but the outer ring only had three again. There was room to build more, but it seemed that there was no need for them at this time. According to the map, she and Dean would be housed at the very eastern end of the last row, while Carla and Quinn would be at the northern end of the middle row. Only the cottage at the eastern end of the middle row could have placed them further apart.

Still, it could have been worse. There were cottages

behind the main male and female witch dormitories and even a few dotted behind the shifters dormitories. On their trip to the woodhouse the other day, she had even seen one out past the glass houses, right at the edge of the academy boundaries. Yes, there were greater distances to be apart while still on campus.

The two wolves were going to help Carla and Quinn, while the two dragons would help Dean and herself. The door creaked a little when she unlocked it, and they all stood for a moment to allow the stale and musty air to escape. It was obvious that this cottage hadn't housed anyone for a very long time.

There were claw marks on the floor near the doorways from where previous shifters had rushed in or out in their beast form. Inside, it was quaint but pleasant, although a thick coat of dust covered everything.

"Well, it looks like the first thing I need to do, is put a cleaning spell through here," she said, hands on hips. "Give me a moment, gentlemen, and then Dean, you can choose which room you want."

The three men turned to look at her in surprise. "Don't you want to choose?" asked Dean.

"Nope. I know that you won't be comfortable in a room that smells of another shifter, not until you can mask it with your own scent, whereas I won't be able to smell it. You might as well pick the least smelly of the two rooms, and I'll go for the other one. Sorted."

Melody gathered her power.

"Dust and debris
Must be gone
Clean the surfaces.
Until it's done
A gleaming home
We must see.
Make it clean
So mote it be."

Nick snickered. "Is that really how you use your magic?"

"Well, no. I wasn't taught many spells, so I just made up my own."

The two dragons looked at her, aghast. "You made up your own spells? Do you realise how dangerous that is?"

"It's not dangerous, I've made up hundreds and I've never had one go wrong. Well, except for the time I turned Martha's hair purple, but that's only because I wasn't concentrating. She was being such a bitch, and I thought about how the hairstyle I was giving her made her look like a plum, and suddenly, both her hair and skin were purple." Melody giggled. "It took them a week to work out how to undo it, and I got the beating of my life, but it was funny."

The dragons looked at each other, the other shifters sensing something was awry.

"Melody," asked Justin quietly, "just how strong are you?"

Melody looked at them, the forlorn looks on their faces telling how much they wanted to challenge her. She knew if she told them the truth their beasts would push harder. It must have shown on her face, because Nick jumped in before she could answer.

"Let us worry about our beasts. Just tell us the truth, how strong are you?"

"Well, you know that my coven are beast tamers, right? That it's our specialty?"

The three shifters nodded.

"And you know that we're strong, that our witches are some of the strongest in the country?"

They nodded again.

"Well, I'm the strongest in our coven. From what we can tell, I'm the strongest we've ever had. I'm pretty sure that I could defeat the five of you at once," she said quietly.

Justin spun on his heel and left. Melody watched him go, not calling him back. What could she say or do to make things better? She'd suspected that she was stronger than a dragon before she came. All the testing her aunt had done had indicated it. But it wasn't until she got here and sensed them all that she knew just how much stronger she was.

The dragons had been stuck here for Goddess only knew how long, and here she was, their ticket out of there, and she wouldn't let them challenge her. It had to rankle. She was sure her very existence annoyed the dragon right now.

"Jus's dragon is riding him hard right now. Rather than risk destroying the cottage if he challenged you, he's gone off for a short flight."

"You can shift without a witch?" Melody asked him, surprised.

"It's different for us than most shifters. Besides, there's a spell over the school allowing us all limited freedom to shift. How do you think we're all able to challenge you? It's maintaining control over our beasts once we've shifted that we need a witch's help with, and with the spell calming them, it's easier to take control and shift back." Nick shrugged.

"For Jus and I, we can do that without the spell, but it's not worth it, the grounds here aren't large enough to allow us to get a good flight in, and being in the air makes no difference. The wards are wards, no matter how high you are."

Dean ambled off to inspect the rooms, coming back soon after. "It doesn't matter to me which room it is, the scents are so faded that neither of them bother my lion. So maybe you should have that one, it's got an en suite. The other one doesn't, and I'll just use the main bathroom."

"Are you sure? Wouldn't you want to go straight for a shower after a run?"

"Sure," he grinned, "but then I get to walk around you semi-naked. Sooner or later you're going to have to give in to my charms."

Nick punched him. "Come on, Cassanova, let's go get your shit from the dorm and bring it over. Fuck knows it's going to take the five of us."

"What do you mean?" asked Melody.

"Well, *princess* Dean has been here for just over ten years. You accumulate "stuff". And all that stuff is coming here. Just be glad you didn't bond me, I've been here for a *lot* longer."

His voice was lighthearted, but in his eyes, Melody could see a lingering sadness.

Before she knew what she was doing, she found herself hugging him. "I wish I could …" she left the rest of the sentence hanging, too afraid of the consequences of completing it.

"We'll help you get there, Mel," Dean said softly, coming up behind her and sandwiching her between the two of them.

"Hey! Is this a private party, or can anyone get their hands on her now?" asked a loud voice behind them.

Melody spun to see that the two wolves had returned. "Why don't you go unpack, Mel, and I'll take these douchebags with me to go sort out my room," suggested Dean.

There was laughter from the other shifters and some good natured teasing. Nick had Dean in a headlock when someone cleared their throat at the doorway.

"Hey, I was told to come here and tell you all that Melody and Dean have to report to the provost," a young woman said.

They all looked at each other. "Okay, thanks," said Mel. She turned to the others. "Why don't you all go get Dean's stuff, and we'll go and see what the provost wants. It's probably something she does with all newly bonded pairs. I'd say that Carla and Quinn are already over there."

Melody halted abruptly at the looks on their faces.

"Thanks, we'll be right there," Nick told the other witch,

dismissing her. Once she was gone, he turned back to her. "No, Mel," he said, adopting Dean's name for her. "The provost doesn't normally meet with newly shifted pairs. That's Mrs Hardinger, she's the counsellor for bonded witches and shifters. So, whatever is going on, we're coming with you. You might not be ours yet, but you're going to be."

21. MELODY

Melody was startled to realise that Nick's pupils were slits in golden eyes. His dragon must have been very close to the surface. Just then, Justin stalked through the door, his hair wild and his clothing slightly crooked. "So what are we waiting for then?"

Melody stared at him, how had he known to come back?

Nick must have picked up on her confusion, because he tapped his temple. "Dragon thing," he told her, motioning for her to precede him through the doorway.

Shrugging, she led the way, Dean walking beside her and the others tagging along. They made an odd procession as they walked along the outer circle towards the provost's office. Students who were between classes stopped to watch them, whispering behind their hands. Dean started growling long before they got there, and she held his hand to help keep him calm. Given his reaction, she didn't want to know what they were whispering.

The office was the same treasure trove as her last visit, but this time it wasn't the items on the shelves that held her interest. The group of teachers stationed around the edges of the room was daunting, and there in front of the provost, was Shawna.

"Provost Aer-Canticum, you asked to see us?" Looking around the room, Melody saw all of her teachers, plus a witch that she didn't know but who looked familiar. She thought it was the earthy, outspoken witch from her first day.

"I asked to see you and your bonded shifter. Unless you wish to inform me that you have bonded all of these gentlemen, they need to leave."

"With respect, Provost. She is not yet ours, but she will be. Whatever concerns her, concerns us," Nick stated calmly.

There was a rustling from the assembled staff, but nobody said anything. Many witches viewed shifters as inferior, so for Nick to have claimed that Melody was theirs, rather than that they belonged to her, was an affront to several of them.

"Very well, I will let you all remain, on the understanding that you do not interfere with what is going on. You may have a future claim on this woman, but at the moment you have no ground to stand on."

Nick nodded, accepting for them all.

"Melody, a serious accusation has been brought against

you. It has been suggested that you cheated in gaining power over Dean's lion. Shawna assures me that although she was in the wrong to attack you, you managed to defeat her and her friends with very little magic and a greater use of your limbs than anything else." The provost held up her hand when Melody opened her mouth to protest.

"Furthermore, I have reviewed your transcripts, and although your teachers assure me that you are a fast learner, active participator and cooperative, you are not at the top of any of your classes. We can all sense your power in this room. So it begs the question, Melody. How did such an average-level witch gain control over such a powerful shifter?"

From where she stood with her arms folded over her chest, Shawna smirked.

"How do we resolve this, Provost?" asked Melody.

"I am afraid that I am going to have to dissolve your bond with Dean, and you will repeat the feat here in front of witnesses. It will be slightly uncomfortable, but there will be no lasting damage to either of you, or to the bond. Because it is so new, the bond will simply renew and continue at the stage of development it was at, should you succeed in defeating him." There was doubt in the provost's voice that this would be the case.

Melody sighed and nodded, indicating that things should proceed. Provost Aer-Canticum stood behind her desk, raising her hands. "Melody, if you would…" but Melody had anticipated her. It wasn't the first time she'd had a familiar stripped from her, after all. She raised her hands in a mirror image, causing her sleeves to fall down to her elbows. Shawna shrieked in anger.

"See! I told you she cheated, those are enhancer cuffs on her wrists!"

The provost paused mid-spell, but then proceeded, breaking the bond. Melody winced as she felt the backlash of the bond slapping at her. Beside her, Dean was snarling, his beast clearly close to the surface.

"Are they enhancer cuffs, Miss Bestia?" The provost asked her.

"No, Provost, they are not."

Suddenly from her right, Melody felt a stream of power reach for her, it came from Mr Cartwright, who taught enchantments. The bangles at her wrist glowed bright blue to indicate that they were enchanted.

"They are enchanted, Miss Bestia," chided her teacher.

"Yes sir, they are. But they are not enhancers, they're dampeners." There were several gasps from around the room, and a snort from one of her teachers, although she didn't see who it was.

"She's lying, she's wanted Dean from the start. You can't let him challenge her again!" screeched Shawna.

"Silence!" shouted Provost Aer-Canticum. "Shawna, you were permitted to witness this in order to silence any grounds for further complaint. I am well aware of your history with Dean. You will not, however, interfere in these proceedings again. Is that understood?"

"Yes, Provost," said Shawna, sullenly. Her eyes glittered maliciously. No matter what was resolved here today, Melody knew that Shawna would never forgive her.

"Please remove the bangles, Miss Bestia," the provost said, coolly. It wasn't lost on Melody that the irritating Shawna, and even Dean, were referred to by their first names, but that she was referred to by her coven name.

Reluctantly she removed her bangles, Mr Cartwright stepped forward to take them from her. Instantly, the witches around the room exclaimed. Melody felt a pang of sorrow as she parted with them, but it was obvious that everyone else felt something different.

Not only were the bangles no longer masking her power, but because she had been wearing them, and the Apex had said that they wouldn't challenge her, she hadn't kept up the ward hiding her strength from others. For the first time, they were all feeling her true strength. Shawna, especially, was horrified.

"Well, I think we can see the truth of the matter now. Still, the bond must be reformed, Dean, challenge her please and then we can get to the bottom of all this."

Dean had become increasingly agitated during the few minutes that had passed, so much so, that Nick and Justin now held him back. Immediately he exploded out of his clothes and turned to her, but Melody didn't move. Because he hadn't uttered the words, technically he hadn't challenged her, so she didn't have to accept.

"Melody?" asked the provost.

"He hasn't challenged me," she said.

"I told you, she can't beat him. She's got some other enhancer stuff somewhere," sneered Shawna.

"Shawna, be silent," said the provost.

Shawna opened her mouth to respond, but nothing came out. Her eyes grew wide as she realised that she had been effectively gagged.

"Melody, do not be obstinate, this is neither the time nor the place. Dean, has challenged you, now accept and make him shift." The provost's tone brooked no argument.

Melody hesitated, and apparently the geas took it as a no, because she fell to her hands and knees when the mark hit her. This was the most brutal one yet, it felt like it sank to the bone, and she couldn't restrain the cry that escaped her lips.

The lion in front of her roared, charging her and ripping the shirt from her back, exposing her secret to all of them. Immediately, several teachers ran to her aide, trying to staunch the bleeding. But nothing seemed to work, none of their spells took effect. There were panicked cries across the room as blood rolled down her arms and onto the floor, staff debating on whether this spell or that would be more effective.

"STOP!" bellowed an authoritative voice that she recognised as Nick's. How she knew it was him after such a brief acquaintance, she didn't understand, she just *knew*.

Please don't say it, she thought.

But he did.

"There's nothing you can do. That's a geas mark!" Nick called.

This time when the second mark hit, she passed out. It was only a small mercy, because soon she was being shaken awake by a frantic Dean who had shifted back to his human form.

"Mel, please fucking wake up!"

She was in his lap, his arms wrapped around her, and he snarled at anyone who came too close, even the other Apex shifters. There were tears in his eyes, but she knew it was better this way. She had said that she would refuse him, and now she had. Now they were all safe, and the matriarchal power would die with her. Her aunt could scheme until the world ended, but without Melody and her powers, it would all come to nothing.

"Mel, please, accept my challenge," he whispered.

"You're safe," she said, and smiled weakly, her hand coming up to stroke the tears from his cheeks.

"Melody, do you remember signing the papers when you came here?" asked the provost.

"I didn't. My coven signed on my behalf," she replied.

"Well, there goes my ordering you to do it, those papers would have given me control over you while you are on my campus. Your coven signing them nulls that advantage. That wasn't supposed to be allowed, I'll have to talk to the admin staff about that," she mused.

Dean growled at her, and Melody tapped his face a little harder. "Don't you dare growl at her, she's the provost!" she whispered, unable to draw in enough breath to admonish him properly, because of the pain.

"Ok, then let me try reason," said the provost. "I gather that you are in trouble, Melody. I gather it also has to do with refusing to accept Dean's challenge, and I suspect the second mark was for revealing that you were under a geas."

Melody closed her eyes. She couldn't afford to even hint at a response, a third punishment would kill her immediately. She knew that she was dying, but she didn't want to go just like that. She wanted just a little more time in Dean's arms, surely it wasn't too selfish to want that.

"Ok, don't answer that, I suspect that I am skirting too close to the truth. But let me say this, if it is bonding him that is getting you in trouble, ignore it. *Do* it. It will at least buy us enough time to sort this mess out. Do you understand me, Melody? I think we can help you, but you have to be alive for that."

The provost, as brilliant as she was, had it wrong. She wasn't getting punished for the bond, it was for the lack of it.

"Please, Mel, accept my challenge," whispered Dean, desperately.

This was it, if she said no, now, then she was dead. But if she accepted him, then he was dead. Although, the provost seemed to think that there was a chance that she could help Melody. Could she be right? Was it worth risking the world for a chance at surviving this intact?

Nick knelt beside her, and although Dean's growls grew louder, he didn't push his friend away.

"Mel, please, give us all a chance. Let us help you. We all will, the five of us, the provost, I think even a few of the staff will try. Please, Mel, don't give up."

His earnest face and his fear; that was what finally undid her. These men had been here for a very long time, and she was their only chance at ever leaving. She knew that. They were too strong now to ever fall against a weaker witch than her, and the older they got, the stronger they would become.

"I accept," she whispered.

The healing was no gentler than the strike. Her back arched as the first gash closed up, the flesh knitting back together with a heat that was almost unbearable. Dean raised her up so that he could see her back. She knew the wound wasn't completely healed, it wouldn't be until he was bonded to her again.

There was a good chance, however, that she would now be too weakened to defeat him. The thought bolstered her.

"Nick," Dean said, hoarsely, and the dragon shifter moved forward, taking her into his arms. Dean stood, naked and proud, and a moment later, his lion regarded her solemnly. He nudged her with his head and then let out a low rumbling purr.

"Big cats can't purr," Melody said, wonderingly.

"Tell that to the dumb, furry fuck," snarked Oz, earning him a low growl from Dean.

Melody gathered her magic into her palms and then held one up toward him. "Shift," she commanded, releasing her power.

Instantly, he fell back on his naked butt, a look of surprise on his face matching the one that she knew must be on hers.

"I thought it was too late, that you were too injured, I thought…" he broke off as her back arched again. This time, the wound healed down to what felt like a scar. She knew, because she'd had many wounds heal on her before.

"What the fuck is it now?" exclaimed Ryan.

Nick inched her forward and there was a collective gasp from the room. "The wound has healed, and where it crossed the other one, it has healed across that too, so the first one is now broken into two distinct parts," explained the provost. "It seems I was mistaken, Melody. You're not in trouble for bonding Dean. You're in trouble because you refused to."

The other Apex shifters moved closer to her then, their eyes eager and pleading. She knew what they were thinking, maybe if she claimed them, then the mark would heal entirely. Melody shook her head, unable to say anything aloud.

"Right," said the provost, standing. "Under the terms of the contracts that you have all signed, I forbid anyone here to speak of any of these events outside of this room. In fact, you may only talk about it with me. This is my ruling as Provost of the college."

Melody saw a shudder pass through the staff and students alike as the spell took hold over them, although she felt nothing herself.

"Melody, you and the Apex will remain, everyone else is dismissed. Shawna, you will see me again this afternoon after classes. I think it's time we had another talk," chided the provost, and Shawna visibly shuddered. Melody felt no pity for her.

Slowly the staff shuffled out of the room, several of them looking curiously at her. That was all she needed, the staff paying her extra attention.

When the room was finally cleared of everyone else, Provost Aer-Canticum indicated that they should sit. Melody gestured at her bloody clothing and the provost sighed, flicked her fingers, and Melody found herself in repaired, clean clothing. The fabric of her shirt, though, caught at her remaining wounds, and she winced.

"Oh dear, I'm sorry, I forgot about that." With another small gesture, Melody could feel the application of some sort of dressing to her back.

Slightly more comfortable, she sat, the shifters hooking various chairs from around the room and joining her.

The provost sighed. "Mclody, it seems like we only meet when there's something dramatic happening in your life. I wish that you had come to me earlier, however, I sense that you are unable to say anything. Tell me, just what is it that you can share with me?"

Melody thought for a moment, with the wound still on her back for revealing the presence of a geas, even though it wasn't her fault, and with having had the other wound as well, she knew that she couldn't chance anything that her aunt wouldn't approve of.

"I'm from Bestia Coven. We live on a large property in

Virginia. We're one of the oldest covens in the country, and one of the strongest – if not *the* strongest. We're famous for our beast taming skills. I'm the strongest beast tamer that we've ever had, my aunt's testing has proven that. My late mother was our coven leader, but with her untimely death, my aunt took over. I, however, am the bearer of the coven's matriarchal power. My coven has high hopes of me gaining more than one familiar."

There, that was all safe and all neutral and all true. The provost regarded her warily.

"Much of that is common knowledge, Melody. Although not that you have your coven's matriarchal power. I'm sorry for your loss, I had not heard of a change of leadership in Bestia recently," she said gently.

"That is because it isn't recent. My mamma died when I was four."

Provost Aer-Canticum gasped. "You inherited the power when you were four? Even though your aunt survived? But that's ..." her voice drifted off and her gaze became speculative. "Did you understand what your mother was doing?"

"No, Provost."

"I see," she paused, seemingly unsure of herself for the first time. "Were there other witnesses to this ceremony?" she probed, carefully.

"No, Provost. It was just my mamma and me. She was bleeding, but she made me play the game where we passed power back and forth between us. She had done that with me as far back as I can remember. Only this time, she pushed back more than I had given, so much so, that at the time I thought my skin was going to split open with the power. It hurt, badly. I was four and I was terrified. She pulled me into her lap, kissed my head and hugged me until her arms fell onto the floor. She was dead."

Melody tried to recite the story clinically, it was the bare bones that she had practiced with her aunt since she was young, although this time she had said that her mother was bleeding, rather than she was sickly. She knew that the provost would see through the story, and she hadn't betrayed her coven – technically.

As it was, though, her best efforts to remain detached and neutral failed her. By the time she had finished speaking, her voice was a whisper. Dean reached out and pulled her out of her chair and into his lap again, his arms wrapped around her careful to avoid her wounds. There was something about the scent of him, the warmth of him, that made her feel safe in a way that she hadn't since that fateful day.

"You say that your coven wishes for you to gain several shifters. I gather that they wish for them to be of the stronger variety. To what end?"

"Pardon?"

"Why do they want you to gain more than one strong shifter?" the provost pushed.

There was nothing she could do or say to answer this question without risking herself. Nothing that resembled the truth, anyway. So she made no effort to hide the lie of what she said next.

"I don't know, Provost," she said wide eyed and with a shake of her head. "I guess they want the prestige of it all, our coven wants to be the best in *the land*, the best in the *world*." She stared at the woman, hoping that her hint took root.

"Were you told to aim for the Apex shifters? The dragons in particular?"

Melody shook her head, closing her eyes and blocking out everything. Her entire body trembled. This was getting too close to saying something that would kill her.

There was a long pause, and then eventually the provost sighed again. "Under the circumstances, I cannot allow you to bond another shifter until you are able to speak freely. I know that you are not bound by the contracts, so I will bind these shifters. None of you present will be permitted to challenge her until we know that it is safe to do so. I cannot impress upon you enough, the importance of obeying my edict."

The Apex shifted as the command took hold upon them.

The provost tapped her fingers against her lips. "Leave the dampeners with me, Melody, you don't need them now, your lion will protect you from any other challengers." She fixed her gaze upon him. "Dean, you are not bound by her promises, not until you swear fealty to her coven."

"I already swore fealty to her," he told her, and the provost closed her eyes.

"Well, I don't know if that was a wise move or a foolish one, and I doubt that Melody could advise us either way."

Melody shook her head.

"Very well, return to your cottage and finish settling in. You're expected to resume classes tomorrow. I suggest that you see the healers and ask for an iron supplement. Do not show them your wound, tell them that I required it of you. You are all dismissed."

They rose together, thanking her for her time, before heading toward the door.

"Melody?" the provost called, and she turned back toward the woman behind the desk. "If you were to get an offer to join another coven. Is there anything preventing you from accepting it?"

Melody's heart soared. This was something she hadn't even thought of! Her aunt certainly hadn't, there was no geas on her to stay with her coven, only to be loyal to it. Loyalty did not quite equate with staying. If she were to accept an offer to another coven, all the geasan upon her would break, instantly. Her aunt would know immediately, but providing she swore her fealty rapidly, it would be over and done with before she could retaliate. Still, Melody had to answer carefully.

"A witch is free to choose whatever coven she wishes if a coven should ask her to join. It is the first and greatest of the freedoms granted to us by the Goddess." It was also something her aunt wouldn't want to tamper with. Although Melody knew all the laws inside and out like she was required to, she had never thought of that one in this light before. It was a chance at freedom, a chance to prevent all of this without putting any of the shifters in danger! It was a chance that she would jump at, if it was offered to her.

"Very well, Melody. I admire your loyalty to your coven." The provost watched her carefully, and Melody nodded her head vigorously to indicate that yes, this was another geas on her.

The provost sighed and nodded her understanding. Melody's shoulders sagged in relief.

It seemed that they were *mostly* linked around what she said rather than what she thought. Or, to be precise, what she communicated in speech, or lack thereof. It was a fine line to walk.

"I will follow your progress with keen interest. I imagine that you will be studying very hard. The highest ranking witches have so many opportunities open to them."

The provost scrutinised her again, and Melody nodded to say that she understood. If she wanted to get an offer from another coven, then she would need to be at the top of her class.

22. DEAN

*D*ean kept his arm around her, refusing to let her go, and together the six of them left the provost's office. What he and the others had just witnessed shook him to the bone. What had he bonded to? He didn't regret a second of being bonded to Melody, but whatever was troubling her was driving him and his lion crazy, and she wouldn't even tell him about it.

His lion growled at him. Ok, not *wouldn't*. She *couldn't*.

It was obvious that more than the three geasan that they had identified had been laid upon her. One to hide them, one to force her to bond the Apex and one to ensure her loyalty to her coven. He wondered what else controlled her. Part of him wanted to test her limits to find out, the rest of him simply wanted to protect her, to ease the worry that seemed permanently etched on her face.

In the office, she had said that he was safe when she refused to bond him. Did that mean that she thought he was in danger now that the bond had been renewed? He had so many questions for her, but it seemed that her coven had bound her tongue more effectively than any gag.

Dean felt magic wash over him, it was from one of the dragons, probably Nick who liked to link them up, because now he could hear the others.

How's she doing? And how is your lion? asked Nick, solicitously.

She's ok. The worst of the bleeding seems to have stopped, although the wound isn't closed. It seems that it's clotted for now, but it wouldn't take much to open it up again I think.

Maybe we should pack it with moss? It will absorb the blood and help to keep the wound clean, suggested Oz.

Yeah, that's an idea. The provost spelled something onto her, I don't know what it is, but she's not flinching and I'm not sensing a lot of pain through the bond. Of course, it was interrupted, so I'm not sensing a lot of anything yet, not until it's finished renewing. Give me half an hour or so and I'll have a better idea of her pain levels at least, Dean told them.

I can't believe the nerve of that fucking bitch, Shawna. We should have put her in her place years ago, growled Ryan.

Yeah. I think the provost is finally going to handle her. I'm pissed that she's known all this and not done enough to stop it, Dean replied angrily, a low rumble sounding in his chest. Melody looked up at him, so he smiled at her and kissed her forehead.

To be fair, sent Justin, *there probably wasn't anything she could have done to stop that harpy. Shawna was obsessed with you from the get-go. Do you realise she's been here six years now? She keeps changing her major to prevent from graduating, hoping that she'll grow strong enough to nab you.*

Fucking hell, that's desperate, snorted Oz.

It's not just her either, sent Nick. *There's about a dozen of them. They're after all of us. He shuddered.*

Not. Fucking. Happening, sent Ryan, and they all laughed.

Melody shifted in his arms looking up at him. "What's so funny?" she asked.

Well. Fuck. This was awkward.

Nick, can you link her in? he asked the dragon.

Nope, not unless I was bonded to her, he sighed. They all sobered.

So, what are we going to do about this clusterfuck? asked Oz.

I don't know, but I think we should stop talking now while she can't hear us. We can talk when we get to the cottage, Dean sent.

The others fell silent, so he assumed they agreed. Then he felt Nick's magic withdraw.

"Sorry, we were chatting across a pack bond, we won't do it around you again," he told her. He could almost feel the shame rolling off the others at having excluded her. "We were agreeing that there was no way in hell we'd let Shawna or her lot take us. They just need to graduate and get out of here. Goddess help any shifter stupid enough to challenge them before the end of the year."

"What do you mean they need to graduate? Isn't that what they're doing this year?" she asked him, confused.

Dean steered them into the medical center, settling her into a chair in the waiting area.

"They've been changing electives and taking extra courses for a few years now, trying to delay their graduation until they're strong enough to take us on. Only, they forget that we get stronger with age too, and it's not necessarily in proportion. Our beasts have actually been actively working at getting stronger so that they never catch up. It's also meant that nobody else has been able to bond us either," he turned and looked at her, the heat in his eyes warming her from the inside. "Until you."

"Can I help you?" asked a voice behind them, and he turned to acknowledge the woman that he'd heard entering long before she spoke.

"I need to get some iron supplements. The provost sent me to get them from here," Melody told her.

"Ok, I'll be back in a moment."

The woman went back through the door that she had emerged from, and a few minutes later she emerged with a standard bottle of iron tablets with a vitamin C supplement included.

"There you go, is that everything?" she asked.

"Yes, thank you so much," said Melody, and they all filed out again.

Dean could only imagine what a strange impression they must have made in there. One woman and five hulking shifters crowding around her. Goddess knows what the healer thought of them all.

They ambled over to the cottage, meeting up with Carla and Quinn who were on their way there.

"Roomie! How did you go, are you all done? Your two wolves disappeared on me, but we managed to get our stuff all done anyway."

Dean noticed Melody flinching when Carla referred to them as *her* wolves. He hoped Oz and Ryan didn't see it.

"No, we haven't even started yet, we just came from a meeting with the provost. Shawna accused me of cheating, so I had to prove that I didn't." Melody didn't say anything else about the disastrous meeting. "The others came along to back us up."

"Ugh, she's such a bitch. I wish she would grow up and graduate already. Six years at the academy and she still doesn't have a shifter to show for it, none of them do. Now, nobody will challenge them. They've made too many enemies." Carla sneered.

Dean saw Melody do a double take. It seemed that she was surprised about her lack of knowledge of fellow students, but Dean wasn't. He could tell that she'd led a fairly sheltered life, and that the academy was her first real experience of the world without her coven around her. He also knew it was going to be a good thing for her, as long as they could keep her away from Bestia coven.

He'd read between the lines of what the provost had said too. They needed to get her an offer into another coven. It was something Dean would discuss with the others later, once she was asleep. Talking of which, it was going to be strange tonight.

He often slept in a pile with the wolves, or sat up late talking, laughing and drinking with the others. It wasn't like they hadn't graduated already, so if they were too tired in the morning, it wasn't a big deal. Tonight, however, he was going to be in an entirely different building across the other side of the campus. The thought of being so far away from his friends, his chosen pack, was sobering. The thought of finally being with a witch, though, was comforting enough to ease his pain.

Dean wondered what kind of relationship they would have. Witches without beast magic often frowned upon mating with a shifter. Fucking them in private was one thing, but forming a mate bond with them was another. Whispers of beastiality often plagued those who flouted their bondings, but at the academy there was a kind of bubble of acceptance.

He'd heard stories of witches foolish enough to mate their familiars without the permission of their coven leader and the mess that it caused. Often, coven leaders arranged matings between witches for political or magical gain, disregarding the wishes or desires of their members. A witch already mate bonded to a familiar was no longer available for breeding, losing potential advantages for their coven.

The witch involved was often left with a painful choice. Break the mate bond, or be expelled from their coven.

Breaking a mate bond could kill a shifter, which was why it wasn't taken lightly in the shifter community. Many witches, however, saw shifters as second class citizens, without any true magic of their own other than their ability to shift, so their death was seen as an inconvenience at best. But any witch who broke their mate bond, would find that no other shifter would ever challenge them for a familiar bond.

Something told him that Melody wasn't one of those who saw shifters as lesser beings. From the sounds of her coven, though, he wouldn't be surprised if *they* did. Her coven scared him a bit, but they had all year to come up with a way to get her out before he had to accompany her home.

He didn't know much about Bestia, other than the fact that they were renowned beast tamers, incredibly strong as a coven, and kept pretty much to themselves. Dean had thought it was dedication to their familiars, but now he suspected that something was darker at play. Putting a geas on another witch wasn't something done lightly, and Melody had three very strong ones on her that they knew of, and he suspected there were more than a few others that they weren't aware of.

It gave the whole situation a much more sinister feel, especially with Melody's offer of sacrificing herself so that she wouldn't have to drag him into it. He knew that was what she was doing as soon as she denied him. He'd felt the echo of her pain, even though the bond had been severed, smelled the blood, seen her physically give in as the second lash hit her. That was some fucking twisted shit, and he promised himself and his lion, that he would protect her from it. Never again would she suffer at the hands of the bitches that raised her!

His lion roared in agreement. Together, they would protect her.

23. MELODY

Unpacking in her new room was a little surreal. First of all, Melody had never slept by herself before. Back at the compound, in the cellars, there were always the other shifters to keep her company, to warn her of approaching footsteps, to ensure that her sleep was guarded.

Even in the other room with Carla – a luxury, having a room with four walls and some privacy – she still had someone with her to give her a sense of security. Here, in their cottage, Dean was in a separate room on the other side of the living room. She had no doubt that he would hear her and come running, but the fact that he would have to run to get to her, was daunting.

On the other hand, she couldn't very well invite him into her bed. For the first few weeks after a bond was formed, the beast would ride the human side hard, pushing them to mate with their bond owner. This wasn't always a fortuitous thing. It wasn't based on love or romance or even friendship. It was simply a primal response to mark someone as theirs.

Melody suspected that it was why so many witches looked down on cross-species pairings. That and the fact that shifters were seen as inferior, because they had no innate magic other than the ability to shift. It certainly wasn't how she felt at all. Familiars were a sacred gift from the Goddess. An opportunity to grow in strength and magic and develop true and deep bonds that would benefit both sides.

Sebastian had shown her how good a bond could be with a non-sexual partnering. She suspected that he was the exception to the rule when it came to a beast pushing the human side to mate. Sebastian had never demonstrated any sexual interest in her, thank goodness. Rather, he'd taken her on like a cub. Teaching her everything that he knew, and caring for her as a real father would have. In her darkest moments, long after he had been tortured to death, she could still hear his voice talking to her, giving her the courage to keep going.

She suspected that the encouraging voice would eventually grow to sound like Dean's. As their bond grew, they would form an empathic and eventually a telepathic link with each other. Melody had been jealous earlier, when she realised that they'd been sharing a pack bond. If only she could. Then maybe she could get around the geasan, she wouldn't need to say anything – they'd know. How that would work with her punishments, she had no idea. All she knew was that Dean and Nick and the others had given her a reason to fight, and to keep fighting. She had to keep them safe!

The men were still bringing in things from Dean's room when Melody finally emerged from her own. Boxes were piled along one side of the living area, the stack growing higher by the minute. Melody laughed.

"Goodness, Dean. Just how much stuff do you have?" she called out to him in his bedroom.

"About ten years worth," sounded his voice from right behind her, and she jumped a foot into the air, making him snicker.

"Ugh, you rat. You'll pay for that," she warned him.

"Shifter hearing, sweetheart, you can't sneak up on me," he said with a smirk.

"She doesn't fucking need to, mate," said Nick, adding his box to the pile. "Heads up!"

Dean looked upward, too late to do anything about the glass of water hovering above his head. "Ah, fuck," he grumbled, as it descended. But rather than raining down on top of his head, the glass moved to the back of his neck and tipped the water down inside his collar, making him shudder.

Blazing golden eyes regarded her as she giggled. "You like to play, kitten?" he asked her in a gravelly voice, and her giggles died, replaced by a feeling that she didn't recognise. Her core clenched suddenly, and she realised what it was.

Lust. It seemed that Dean did too, because he inhaled deeply before his eyelids dropped to a half-lidded look.

"Well, well, well. If you wanted me to take my shirt off, kitten, all you had to do was ask," he told her, suiting the action to words and removing his shirt.

"Oi, oi!" called Nick. "Stop giving in to your beast, you'll be rutting the fucking furniture before the day is out if you can't control him."

"Fuck off!" snapped Dean, but Nick's words had the desired effect on them both. He took a step back and put his damp shirt back on, while Melody tried not to look at how it clung to the muscles of his shoulders.

Justin dropped one more box on the pile and stood back. "That's the last of them. You're a fucking hoarder, Dean, even I don't have that much shit. Melody, you should totally make him go through that and have a big chuck."

Melody rounded on him, poking a finger in his chest. "I most certainly will not. They are Dean's possessions, and I will never take away anything that is his, unless he asks me to. He's not some puppy with his toys, he's a grown ass adult and these are his belongings. *His*, I might add, not mine."

All the time she had been speaking, she was prodding him in the chest, and he took step after step backward under her ire. By the time she was done, his back was against the wall on the other side of the room. All the others had stopped what they were doing to watch them. Melody realised what she had done, and hastily withdrew her hand, but before she could step back, Justin had grabbed her by the hips and pulled her against his own.

Melody felt the hard length of him against her, and then she felt his lips against her own, his arms snaking around her and pulling her tight until she flinched in pain from where he pressed on her wound.

"What the fuck?" Dean roared, stalking towards them and pulling her away from him by the arm. Then he had Justin by his shirt, slamming him against the wall in fury.

Justin didn't resist the angry lion, but his eyes were now molten silver, and the pupils were vertical slits. His breathing was harsh, and he trembled all over.

Instantly, Nick was by his side. "You can't shift here, you'll destroy her house. That is not what a familiar does to his witch!"

Once again, Nick had rescued her from hot-blooded shifters, and once again, Justin spun on his heel and left the room, the door slamming against the wall with his passage. She hoped that it hadn't left any damage, but more importantly, she hoped that Justin would be ok.

"Is he alright?" she asked Nick, whose eyes were glazed. She suspected that he was talking to the other dragon.

"Yeah," Nick finally said. "He needs space. He's going to be absent a few days. Seeing you here, knowing what you are, what you could be – it affects us all. Then to find out that you've been hurt and abused," Nick shrugged, "It's a shifter's worst nightmare. It's hitting us all hard, although nowhere near as hard as what was done to you. We're all struggling with this. The more we find out about you, the more desperate we are to bond to you and protect you."

Melody had to find some way to warn them. They couldn't bond her now!

"Dean will be coming home with me at the end of the school year. Ordinarily he would be required to swear to the coven, but he already swore to me. I'm sure that my aunt will work out a way around that so that we can ensure his loyalty to the coven." It was the truth, it sounded loyal, but with what they knew, it should also act as a warning.

"We'll protect you, Melody," Nick looked at his friend, "And we'll protect him too."

Silent tears of gratitude fell down her cheeks. They understood! Well, at least as much as they had discovered, they understood. Melody knew that the truth, the entire truth would horrify them.

"Come on pups, let's leave these two to settle in. I don't know about you, but after lugging all that shit and using my magic to clean his room, I'm hungry," said Nick.

"Dude," said Oz. "You're a fucking dragon. You're always hungry."

"True dat." Nick laughed, and the three shifters waved as they left to go to the dining hall.

There was an awkward silence after they left, the easy camaraderie evaporating with their departure.

"Do you want a hand unpacking? I'm done with mine," Melody asked.

Dean looked at the stack of boxes and sighed. "Justin's

right. What I need to do is go through all that and have a big chuck out, before I unpack it and give it a home." He turned to look at her. "You could help with that if you like?"

"Sure, just point me in the right direction, and I'll get started."

That was how they spent the rest of the afternoon, sorting and storing and throwing out a lot of things. For Melody, it was quite the insight into Dean's life and the way he saw the world. She loved his collection of blue glass bottles. She carefully scattered them about the shelves in the living area and kitchen. They added a sense of serenity to the place that she had never experienced before.

Carla had been surprised when Melody had no photos, no mementos, not even a handmade quilt. Her blankets were all grey and utilitarian – scratchy – although very warm. Carla's own side of the room was an explosion of colour, with posters of celebrities intermingled with pictures of places that she wanted to travel to some day, and images of predators from all walks of life. Owls, wolves, lions, and alligators, just to name a few.

Melody had no personal belongings to speak of. Her stolen travel mug, a few items of jewelry that had belonged to her mother, and her tatty grimoire where she recorded all of her simple little spells that she'd made up. Some of them weren't so simple, one made the entries look like cooking recipes. No hand, bar her own, would be able to turn the pages and find a spell inside of it.

Dean, on the other hand, had small mementos from

various sources, gifts, things that caught his eye on travels with his family, things of beauty from nature. There was a small bird's nest, complete with downy feathers, a rock that had been polished until it gleamed a brilliant blue, and a stick that had grown into the shape of a man lying on his side. There were framed photos, clay statues, and more books than the shelves in their cottage could ever accommodate. If Melody's belongings were sparse, then Dean's more than made up for it. Sadly, she wondered what would happen to them all once he was moved to the compound.

Her enthusiasm for discovering all of these facets of him suddenly waned. She remembered what had helped her to survive in the past. Never getting to know the shifters too deeply, never becoming too attached, because Aunt Georgia and her cronies would use it against her, to punish her and the shifter who had allowed their relationship to grow beyond that of witch and familiar. It had happened time and again until she had learned not to become emotionally attached at all.

It didn't mean that Melody was insensitive or uncaring when it came to shifters. She was compassionate and thoughtful, and the shifters back at the compound were devoted to her because she made their dreadful lives just a little less awful. Even if she couldn't set them free as she wanted to. It was just that she couldn't allow herself to love them as individuals, because losing them tore her heart apart more each time.

Gentle fingers tucked under her chin and raised it up.

"Hey beautiful, where did you go just now?" he asked her softly.

"Home," she whispered, and his face darkened.

He gathered her carefully into his arms, wary of the wounds on her back. "You're safe with me."

"Yes, I know. But are you safe with me?"

Wisely, he didn't respond. The two of them far too aware of the consequences of breaking the unspoken rules.

She was supposed to be keeping her distance from him emotionally, but Melody knew, for better or worse, this time, it wouldn't work. Dean was already winding himself around her heart and she no longer had the strength to resist.

24. MELODY

Walking into class with Dean at her side the following morning was an ordeal in and of itself. It was enchantments with Mr Cartwright. He gave her a wry look as she sat at the back, Dean taking a seat beside her. They had decided to come to class early, rather than trying to find seats together once the class was half full. It wasn't assigned seating, so they were free to sit where they chose.

Dean hadn't wanted anyone sitting where he couldn't immediately see them, so the back row it was. Regardless of where they sat, however, they would still get the full attention of anyone entering the class to find their own seats.

As students arrived, they endured the stares, whispers and giggles, stoically. Melody was surprised at the lack of maturity of her fellow students. These witches, who were adults and purportedly wanted a shifter familiar so much they had chosen this academy, were reduced to a set of babbling teenagers, unable to cope with the reality of what that meant. They claimed that they wanted their own, yet were quick to attack someone who had not only achieved what they sought, but had bonded one of the Apex to boot. What was wrong with them?

Melody knew part of the furor was that very few first-year students had a familiar – despite the fact everyone tried their best to get one – and almost all of those who did, had arrived at the academy with their familiar already 'accidentally' bonded. For Melody to have bonded a shifter in her first year, never mind one of the Apex shifters, was a little unorthodox to say the least. Everyone was interested, and they were all following the drama.

Dean had told her some of the rumours going around the night before so that she would be prepared to face them in the morning. Some students said that she had cheated, others said that she had seduced him first, while a third group said that he was so desperate to finally be bonded, he had convinced his lion to throw the fight. Melody knew it wouldn't be the end of the stupidity, so she did her best to ignore it.

Mr Cartwright called the class to attention and began his lecture, and that was the end of the drama ... until the end of class, of course. As they traversed the corridors between the classes throughout the day, the whispers grew. Dean's growl was so constant that it became a background noise to her, so she was startled when it became an outright snarl.

Looking up, Melody saw that Shawna and her cohorts were standing across the corridor, blocking the way. Her heart sank, but outwardly she drew herself up taller, folding her arms across her chest. She had learned from an early age that bluff could achieve what threats could not. If she projected confidence, it would undermine the other person far more effectively.

"I know what you are, whore, and I won't let you keep him. He deserves way better than you. You may have fooled the provost, but you haven't fooled me at all," her dark eyes flashed before turning to Dean. "Don't worry baby, we'll get that bond broken again, and then I'll bond you, I'll take much better care of you than she ever could. She's a frigid virgin, she wouldn't even know where to start." Shawna smirked. "She might have fucked your lion, but you know that I'm better in bed than she could ever be!"

Melody expected Dean to leap for her, instead his eyes trailed lazily up and down Shawna's body. "Shawna, you overestimate your value. At best, you were a mediocre fuck," he said, harshly. "Your constant squeaking made me feel like I was fucking a guinea pig, it was a serious turn off, but I managed to get over the line ... just. As for Melody, I'm yet to have the pleasure, but it is my deepest desire to bury my cock in her and hear her scream my name. I'm a patient man, I'll wait until the end of time for the opportunity."

Dean sneered as he looked at Shawna, while she sputtered and turned scarlet. "No shifter in their right mind would want a fucking blood-sucking harpy like you in their bed. Nobody here will challenge you, not once they've heard the truth of what you're really like. The same goes for the rest of your little horde. You lot are the joke of the school, witches who can't even graduate. Who would want to be associated with a desperate bunch of bitches like you?"

There were whistles and cat-calls from the students who had gathered to watch, and Dean smirked as he shouldered his way through the women, dragging Melody behind him and heading down the corridor to the central courtyard. In the middle of the dappled sunlight, the other Apex shifters lounged at, or on the table. Dean led her straight to them, but she pulled back against his grip.

From across the courtyard, Melody could hear them. Two wolves, howling, two dragons crooning, all of them calling her, courting her, wanting her, even as their human sides chatted and joked with one another. Melody knew the more time she spent with them, the harder it would become for them, with their need for her growing. It was best if she stayed away from them as much as possible.

"What's wrong?" asked Dean.

"Their beasts are crying for me, I can hear them from here. If I go over there and sit with them, it's only going to make things worse," she told him, and he looked at her in shock.

"You can hear their beasts?"

She nodded. "I can hear most beasts if I listen hard

enough, I just try to block them out most of the time to give them some privacy." She tugged on his hand, leading him over to the far side of the courtyard. At the table, the Apex stirred, their eyes watching her hungrily. Beside her, Melody could hear Dean's lion rumble a soft protest, but she knew he hated being apart from her more than his pack, so he acquiesced quickly enough.

"We gonna eat?" he asked her, and she heard his lion growl. Or was that his stomach?

Melody laughed. "How could I forget your appetite? Come on, let's go and satisfy your beast of a belly."

Dean slapped her on the ass, making her jump. "Be careful, kitten, or I'll show you another appetite you can quench."

Together they walked over to the dining hall, where they made impressive sandwiches from the offerings, and took them back outside to sit in the sunshine against one of the courtyard walls. There was no sign of Carla and Quinn, which was a shame, because she could have used her outgoing friend's company to distract her from the stares and pointed glares that they were getting.

"Don't let it get to you, it's just new, another drama. Trust me, I've seen this all before. It will settle down in a few days. Someone will get drunk on the weekend and throw up on a teacher's shoes, and you and I will be old news." Dean put an arm around her shoulder and tucked her into his side, still managing to juggle the remains of his overflowing foot-long sub without it exploding over his lap.

"If you say so, I can't wait to be old news," she told him, and he gave her a squeeze.

"Hang in there, kitten, it won't be for much longer."

Melody smiled up at him. "I know, thank you."

Together they ate in companionable silence, while across in the center of the courtyard, four beasts pined for her. They had to find a way to free her from her coven, it wasn't just Dean's life on the line now, it was the mental health of those four other men, and if she couldn't find a solution soon, they would challenge her!

At the doorway to her next class, however, Melody discovered that it wasn't just the Apex beasts that she had to worry about.

25. MELODY

Carla and Quinn stood a few meters away from the doorway, Carla tensing when they came into view, before striding quickly towards Melody, grabbing her arm and swinging her in the opposite direction.

"Girl, we need to get you out of here," she said, quietly, tugging her along.

"Uh, why?" Melody asked.

"Because a bunch of shifters have decided that you've had enough time to adapt to your bond with your kitty there and they're going to challenge you."

Dean growled, but Melody wasn't sure whether it was because he had been called a kitty, or that Carla doubted his ability to protect her, or simply because other shifters wanted to challenge her at all.

Melody pulled to a halt. "Not happening."

"Girl, I know. It's why we have to get you out of here," Carla said, pulling at her again. "Come on, Mel."

"Carla, it's ok. I can refuse them, and that's for the ones that get past Dean." She stroked his arm and she could feel his beast purring at her confidence. Dean merely smirked.

Carla looked at her. "I thought you were avoiding all of the shifters wanting to claim you? I'm confused. If you're not doing that, then what was the point of the cuffs?"

Damn. There was only so much that she could tell Carla, she looked at Dean for help, but as he hadn't been part of that conversation, he shrugged.

"I've been outed, Carla. People know how strong I am now. The provost took the cuffs from me and my power has been unmasked. I mean, feel it, Carla. This is close to my full power showing. It's kind of pointless to try and hide it now, everyone knows. Yes, this is what I was trying to avoid, an excessive amount of challenges, but I'm not fooling anyone anymore, I just have to put up with it."

Carla snorted. "You do realise that most witches would kill to have a familiar, never mind a second one? Quinn is amazing, but if you think I'd turn down a challenge from another shifter, think again. And you're talking about it like it's something you have to endure." She shook her head.

"It *is* something I have to endure, Carla. I'm strong enough to take down and hold every shifter in this school. Every. Single. One. And I *can't*, it's not right. So I have to reject them all. It's not just saying the words, it hurts them, physically, and it's no joy ride on my side either. I pray to the

Goddess that you never have to reject a challenge. Turning down Quinn was awful, and I *wanted* to accept him. Quinn *is* amazing, but he's not right for me, for my coven. At the end of the day, that's who I have to bring my familiar to."

Melody looked earnestly at her newfound friend, desperate for her to understand, but she could tell that Carla didn't. Instead, she could see her friend drawing back towards her familiar.

"So, you're saying that Quinn isn't good enough? Well, I would never have thought the rumours were right, but they are. You *are* a bitch, aren't you? You played me well, Melody. Shawna was right, you are a cheat and stuck-up-cow. If anyone asks, I won't hesitate to tell them what you're really like. Playing the helpless card, that's a despicable move, Melody. You really fooled me." Carla spun on her heel and walked off.

"Wait, Carla, that's not what I said at all, it's not what I meant," Melody called after her, following her back to the classroom.

"Trouble in paradise, bitch?" The voice to her left dripped malice. Melody looked to find the speaker and her heart sank.

Shawna.

"She's right. You're a cheat, a bitch and a … stuck-up-cow wasn't it?" Shawna snickered. "Yeah, that's way too preppy for me to say, but a first-year student? Well, who knows what kind of immature junk comes out of their mouths. Looks like your reputation is about to take a nose-dive. Any popularity you gained by stealing my familiar is about to rebound on you in droves. Enjoy the ride, bitch."

Shawna glared at Dean. "Too bad, kitty, you could have made a nice little pet, but if you're willing to poke your cock where the Goddess doesn't shine, don't be surprised when it gets diseased." With that final barb, she walked away, leaving Melody shell shocked and Dean growling.

Melody pulled herself together first. "Ignore her, she's never been worth our time, but Carla," she sighed. "Carla was my first female friend. I can't believe that she'd turn on me so quickly. Is that what friends do? Is that how people act?"

"No, Mel." Dean growled. "That was something else altogether. I'd almost think … ".

"What?"

"I need to talk to the dragons, then I'll let you know. Come on, we're late for class." Dean slung an arm around her shoulders and directed her to the nearby doorway, but that was as far as they got.

"Melody Bestia, I challenge you!" A voice rang out, and a wolf sat in front of her.

Silence fell across the room as Melody stared at him.

"Don't bother," Carla called from the other side of the classroom. "Melody is very picky, it's dreary for her to have to reject you all. She's too good for the shifters here. She didn't even want Dean but he tricked her into it."

"Really Miss Bestia, could you please get on with it so that we can resume class?" snapped the teacher.

"Yeah," called out another voice. "Some of us want an

education and we can keep our legs closed long enough to get it." There were titters throughout the room.

"That's enough," called the teacher. "Miss Bestia, now, please?"

Dean nudged her, and Melody came out of her shock. Could today get any worse?

"I'm sorry, I reject your challenge—" she began, but was cut off by the furor around the room.

Melody raised her voice. "I've only just bonded Dean. I need more time to accommodate my bond. I just want to be allowed to study and to work with my familiar."

The wolf in front of her whined, dropping to his belly and pawing at his ears. It was several moments before he could get up, and Melody could empathise. She didn't feel great herself. Eventually he slunk across the room and sat at the feet of another witch, the empty desk beside her indicating where he had been sitting.

"Pfft, forget it James. If you think I'm going to take being your second choice, you can think again. If I'm not the witch for you, then there's no point in even trying." She shoved him away from her side, hard, and he cowered on the floor.

"Stop it," cried Melody, rushing to his side and dropping down beside him. "Please understand," she whispered into his furred ear. "There's more at stake here than I'm allowed to say. I'm not free to choose whoever I want, otherwise I'd bond every shifter who challenged me, and I'd care for them all." She scratched his head gently, but the wolf still shook. Still, she'd skirted too near the truth and a weal appeared on her back, making her wince. Across the room, Dean growled and rushed toward her.

"Please, don't hate me," she whispered, despite the fresh pain. "I would never willingly hurt you. I hold all shifters in the highest regard."

The wolf sighed and laid his head in her lap, panting as he recovered.

"Miss Bestia, you've disrupted this class long enough, please take your melodrama elsewhere. You may see me at the end of the day for a remedial lesson."

Melody gathered the wolf's belongings into his backpack, including his neatly folded clothes. Just how long had he sat there, naked, waiting for her to enter so that he could challenge her? And she'd had to reject him, in front of everyone who had sat there and waited with him. It would be some time before the fuss died down, and there would be several witches who would never accept his challenge now that he'd been rejected. It was so unfair the way familiars were treated!

The wolf slunk along at her heels, his tail between his legs, ears flat to his head and nose to the ground. The poster child for lupine misery. Nobody said a word as they headed to the door.

Surely the day couldn't get worse.

But yes, yes it could. At the door stood a third year-witch, a male that she didn't know the name of.

"Provost wants to see you," he said, loudly, before turning and leaving.

There were murmurs behind her, and Melody knew that by the end of class, a fresh round of whispers would be going through the school.

"Here, give me his pack," Dean said, not asking, but taking it from her.

James, the wolf, however, stuck to her side like glue. He whimpered as they walked through the corridors to the provost's office.

When she knocked on the door, it wasn't the provost who opened it, but Mrs Hardinger.

"Hello Melody, oh my, have you bonded another one so quickly? That's hardly advisable." She looked down at the abject misery of the beast beside her and sighed. "Ah, no, I see that you didn't. Well, James, you'd best come with me. You're going to feel like shit for a bit."

The outspoken witch took his things from Dean and headed off with the wolf at her side. Melody watched them go until they were out of sight.

"Melody, would you care to join me?" asked a soft voice from inside.

Oh Goddess! She'd ignored the provost, again!

26. MELODY

Melody rushed into the office, quickly sitting in a chair in front of the desk, before realising that she hadn't been invited to sit and rocketing to her feet again.

The provost laughed. "Please Melody, you're welcome to sit, but I thought it might be nicer by the window." She indicated a small lounge with a high-backed armchair beside it and a coffee table with afternoon tea laid out.

Now crimson, Melody moved to join the provost who stood in front of the chair.

"Dean, do come and join us, I believe that you have a fondness for cream-filled donuts."

In a flash of movement, Dean was seated beside Melody, and she looked at him, surprised.

"What? Mel, they're *cream-filled donuts.*" He shrugged and shoved at least half of one in his mouth, moaning.

"I guess that's a yes," Melody said quietly.

"I haven't asked you anything yet," the provost said, her head tilted in confusion.

"To the donuts, they're definitely a favourite."

They both chuckled as Dean munched on the remains of the first and reached for a second.

"Well, while his mouth is otherwise occupied, you can tell me how things are going." The provost picked up a teapot and poured three cups of tea without asking them, offering milk and sugar with a gesture of her hand.

Melody declined the sugar, but added a generous amount of milk. Beside her, she could feel Dean watching, probably making note of her preference.

"I'm not sure what you want to know. We've unpacked, I'm able to participate more in class now that my strength isn't masked. I'm attending classes and handing in all my assignments on time."

Dean stiffened beside her, frowning, but Melody shrugged. She wasn't sure what either of them were getting at.

"Life is continuing, that is good to know, but what I was asking is *how are you*, Melody? You're here under unusual circumstances, you've bonded a familiar in your first year, there are difficulties, shall we say, with your classmates, and you're about to experience an absolute torrent of challenges."

"She just had a fight with Carla," Dean supplied, and Melody frowned at him.

"Indeed?"

"Well, it wasn't a fight. I misspoke, I said that I had wanted to bond Quinn but that my coven wouldn't approve, and she took it as an insult."

Dean snorted. "I'm pretty sure there was much more to it than that."

"Please explain, Dean," demanded the provost.

"I don't have magic, but I can sense things. Carla felt … off." Dean shook his head, his blonde curls flopping with the movement. "Quinn was silent the whole time, he should have rushed to her defence if he'd felt her get agitated, but he was just looking at her, confused. Like she was saying spiteful stuff, but she didn't mean it; like there was no emotion behind it."

"You think Carla has been tampered with? That's a serious accusation, Dean. Even for a shifter of your standing, there would be repercussions against you and Melody if word of this got out."

"I know, I was going to get the dragons to look into it. Shawna attacking Melody hot on the heels of that? It was just too convenient. And then as soon as we got into the classroom, James challenged her, and Carla was in there and spreading shit about Melody in front of everyone. And the teacher didn't intervene."

Melody opened her mouth to protest Dean's take on it all, but the provost held up a hand, silencing her.

"Let's take this back a moment. Shawna *attacked* Melody?" she asked, dangerously quiet.

"No, she didn't attack me," Melody said, frowning at Dean. "It was just more of her bullying tactics, but I was so surprised by Carla, that I didn't have a single comeback in me. I just stood there like an idiot and let her spew her usual rubbish."

"This has happened before?"

"Once or twice. I try to ignore her, it's not like her opinion matters to me, but I'm pretty sure she's the one behind half the rumours about me."

"And was this before or after you bonded Dean?"

"After," Dean growled. "She's been on a campaign against Melody since we bonded."

"More fool her," said Melody. "Seriously, don't bother about it, if you step in again, it just makes her think that she's bothering me and encourages her to keep going. I'm just going to ignore her and she'll get bored and move on."

"Yeah, not happening, kitten," Dean said, stroking her hair.

"And the teacher, who was it?"

Melody stilled. It was one thing for the provost to deal with Shawna, it would be a whole different shit-show if a teacher got in trouble. She put a hand on Dean's leg, warning him.

"I'd rather not say. If you were to speak to a member of staff, it could turn them all against me, even the few who don't hate me."

"They don't hate you, Melody," the provost said, taking a sip of her tea. "Some are afraid of the level of power that you have, others are simply jealous. It's not a matter of love or hate, but of fear and prejudice. Bestia is a coven that is rather secretive, there is an element of fear involved with that as well. It may be time that we shed some light on their workings."

Melody blanched. Her aunt would kill all of the shifters before allowing them to talk to anyone outside of the coven.

"No, please, don't!"

Dean stiffened beside her, growling.

"You would defend their actions?" the provost asked, incredulous.

Melody panicked. She couldn't tell them the truth, the punishment would be severe, but she couldn't let this happen either. "I'm loyal to my coven," she said, eventually, and the provost relaxed a little. "You mustn't investigate the compound." There, she hadn't said that anything untoward was happening, she was loyal, but she also hadn't said that they wouldn't find anything alarming either.

"I see, I gather that there would be repercussions for you," the provost murmured, and Melody shook her head wildly.

"Upon others?" the provost probed.

Melody froze. She couldn't answer that question honestly, and she refused to lie. "I am loyal to my coven," she finally replied.

The provost nodded as though she had shouted something. "Yes, that would be undesirable. I will think about it.

Of course anything illegal could not be permitted to continue."

Silence fell. Melody wasn't sure what else she could say. Dean was watching her carefully, she could almost feel him urging her to speak up. Or was she actually feeling him? Was that the bond at work, that fluttering pressure in her chest? Was that him urging her to say something? Finally, he spoke instead.

"Telling the truth to cleanse any reproachable actions would be the best thing you could do for your coven. A good cleansing would benefit the coven by removing the corruption."

Both Melody and the provost looked at him in surprise.

"As someone loyal to her coven, it would be her duty to cleanse it of wrongdoing," prompted the provost.

"The shifters are not treated well …" That was as far as Melody got before the geas enacted, searing across her back in a blaze of pain.

"No!" Dean yelled, pulling her into his arms. Melody could hear his lion roaring.

"Melody?" the provost asked, having dropped her tea in surprise.

"She's hurt, I don't understand. She was acting loyally to the coven. The best thing for the coven is to get rid of that bitch," Dean growled, tearing yet another shirt open to get to her back. At this rate, she was going to run out of clothing.

A large man entered bearing dressings and bandages. There was a nimbleness yet smoothness to his movements that suggested some sort of small cat shifter but certainly not a domesticated one. It wasn't until she got an image of tufted ears that Melody realised he was a lynx shifter. That was different, she'd never seen a shifter's beast in their human form before. Was this a side effect of the bond?

"Thank you, Jonas," the provost murmured, taking the supplies from him and shooing Dean off his seat. "Here, Melody, let me help."

Deftly, the provost cleaned Melody's back, removing the dressings that she had put there earlier with her magic and replacing them.

"I wanted to put some healing poultices on them this time. Bandages I can summon, herbs, not so much," she mumbled as she worked, the man, Jonas, helping her.

When she was done, Melody felt a surge of the provost's magic and her clothing repaired itself. It was a handy thing to do, she would have to ask how it was done later, especially if Dean was going to continue tearing her clothes off her.

Melody's cheeks heated at images of other circumstances where he might tear her clothes off. Now was not the time! From in front of her, however, Dean began to purr.

Jonas reached out and cuffed the back of his head. "Enough of that. The bond is new, it'll be riding you both hard and at inappropriate times. Your duty is to protect your witch, and that means keeping your beast's libido in check."

The provost looked up, and Melody wanted to sink into the ground in embarrassment.

"It's nothing to be ashamed of, Melody. Jonas and I have

been together for so long, I'd forgotten what it was like to have a new bond." She looked shrewdly at Melody then. "But you've had a familiar bond before, correct? You should have known this."

It was yet another question that she didn't dare answer. Yes, she'd had familiars before, but Melody had never held their bonds longer than a couple of hours. Even Sebastian, her first familiar ever, had only been with her for the day. He had been in his forties, and her aunt had been teaching her the fundamentals of beast taming. None of them had expected her to defeat him, but she had.

Aunt Georgia had been exultant. Sebastian had been sworn to the coven before he knew what they were truly like, so when he'd been ordered to challenge the child over and over again, he had no choice but to comply. None of the other witches had been strong enough to defeat him, but there he was, subject to the whims of his new coven mistress and a seven year old girl who had no difficulty forcing his wolf to shift back and dumping his bare ass in the dirt.

It was the beginning of a nightmare period for Melody, as every shifter in the compound who hadn't been bonded was forced to challenge her. She had defeated every single one of them, and was allowed to keep none. Every single shifter was broken before the month was out, and all of them were bonded to one of the other witches. Melody had no idea what magic they were performing, but by the end of the year, every single one of them was dead.

So, while Melody had had hundreds of familiar bonds,

she'd never truly had her own familiar. A process that would likely be repeated if they couldn't work out a way to defeat her aunt.

When Melody looked up again, it was to see all three of them watching her, the provost, her familiar Jonas, and Dean. Each of them wore grim expressions and she could only imagine what they thought of her. How on earth was she to answer the question.

"Melody," the provost began, but Dean growled over the top of her.

"No, no more questions. The wounds are too much," he snapped.

Melody held her breath, waiting for a flash of pain, but apparently Dean hadn't been specific enough in what he said to trigger anything.

"Have you had a bond before your one with Dean?" Jonas asked, before anyone could say anything.

Dean snarled, but the older shifter ignored him.

"Yes," she answered quietly.

Jonas nodded. "Have you ever held a bond longer than a day?" he asked her, again before anyone could stop him.

Melody froze. Would answering this be considered as disloyal? She didn't think so, it wasn't like they had asked her how many bonds, or why they were taken away. Then she realised that technically she had. Dean's bond, to be precise. She looked at him, hating the fear she saw in his eyes.

"Aside from Dean's," Jonas qualified.

"Mel, don't answer. For the love of the Goddess, don't answer," Dean pleaded.

She couldn't live like this and she couldn't ask Dean to live like this either. If they were going to help her find a way out of the situation that her aunt had put her in, then they needed as much information as Melody could give, and sometimes she'd have to take a risk that the information she was giving them was ok to impart.

"No, I haven't," Mel told them, and braced herself for the pain.

Nothing happened.

Dean's shoulders sagged as he came to the conclusion that she was alright. His head flopped forward, landing in her lap, and a soft mewling sound came from him. It broke her heart just a little bit more.

"Dean, sometimes I have to take risks," she told him.

"No, you don't, Mel. You don't *have* to fucking do anything." Dean's voice cracked as he spoke to her legs. Was he crying?

"I once came across a coven that was a little backwards in their thinking. They used the strongest witch they had to break familiars down. The bond was broken and they were forced to challenge again and again until they were so weak that even the weakest witch in the coven was able to defeat them. It was used as a training exercise to make the shifters stronger. It was back in the days when shifters were stolen from their covens, they were treated like possessions, like cattle to be owned and traded." There was no mistaking the growl in Jonas's voice.

Melody wondered if he knew how close to the truth he was.

"That is barbaric," the provost protested, and Jonas shrugged.

"It was the way things were back then. At least now, shifters have it better, although we've still a long way to go."

"Why would they need to make me stronger, Mel? I'm already an alpha lion, and familiars aren't poached from covens anymore."

"You're right, that's not what they're after," the provost said, and Melody froze.

If anyone voiced their thoughts right now, the geasen would kill her. Before her, Dean stiffened. Could he feel her panic?

"Enough," he growed. "No more risks until she's stronger."

The provost stared at Melody, a thousand questions in her gaze, but eventually she relented. "Yes, you're right. One step at a time." She shuddered, before redirecting her attention to them both. "Melody, as a witch with a new familiar, you'll be meeting with Mrs Hardinger once a week. The sooner you commence this, the less of a rollercoaster the whole process will be. Her methods are unorthodox, but I can guarantee that the chance of her not knowing something you need to know is slim."

Melody nodded, that was a reasonable thing to do, and probably what happened for all new familiar bonds.

"However," the provost continued, and Melody's heart began to race again as those wise grey eyes looked at her. "I think that you and I should meet on a regular basis as well. I would suggest afternoon tea once a week should be enough. Show me your class schedule please."

Dutifully, Melody got it out of her bag and passed it to the provost who examined it, frowning.

"Well, that's not going to work at all, is it? Classes finish at three and dinner is served from five to seven. Fine, on Wednesday evenings, you will dine with us here in Provost House."

Melody gaped. She was going to be interrogated every Wednesday? Never mind the fact that word would quickly get around that the provost was playing favourites.

The provost sighed. "Melody, I am not the enemy here. You are a student struggling with a very unique set of circumstances. We will meet once a week to determine how we may ameliorate the problems that you face. And," she paused, smiling gently, "I do hope that we may even go so far as to become friends."

There was a chime outside.

"Well, I think I've disrupted your classes enough for today. What do you have now?"

Melody took her schedule back and looked at it. "Herbology with Mrs Jensen," she replied.

"Ah, lovely. It was one of my favourite subjects, especially when we got to have classes outdoors in the springtime. Don't be late, Mrs Jensen has a low tolerance for tardiness."

Melody and Dean stood. "Thank you, provost," Melody said, and Dean muttered something similar.

A burning heat settled in her chest as they left, and she wondered what it was until he spoke aloud.

"There's no fucking way she's asking you questions every week. And if she doesn't realise that she's setting you up as a teacher's pet lookalike, then she's nowhere near as smart as she thinks she is," Dean growled as he stomped along beside her.

"I'm damned either way, Dean," she told him. "If I come back from these things smiling, then I'm the favourite and to be avoided. If I come back scowling, then I'm doing something wrong and they should avoid me. Either way, the provost's attention isn't going to do me any favours. The best we can do is to just get on with it."

Dean grunted.

"Besides, I have a task for you, a pet project if you like," she told him. "Something that may be of enormous benefit to me."

Dean stopped in his tracks, his expression so eager that she almost regretted manipulating him into a better mood.

"You said you were going to get the dragons to look into whether Carla was influenced, right?" she asked him.

He frowned and nodded.

"Then do it. Please, find out if my friendship with Carla really was as shallow as it seems right now, or whether there was something darker behind our fight. I hate to think that I chased away the very first friend that I've had outside of the shifters in my coven."

When they started walking to class again, there was a new purpose in Dean's stride.

27. MELODY

The next round of drama started the following morning at breakfast, and Melody kicked herself for not anticipating it sooner. Witches weren't constrained to just one familiar, not if they had the power to back it up, and now that everyone could feel her strength, the other shifters there were taking notice.

In class it had meant that she was finally able to put her full effort into the practical work, all of her teachers commenting on her improving technique, and she spent every evening studying with Dean to help with the academic side too. But in everything else, she was gaining more and more attention from the shifters.

As she was popping the last of her toast in her mouth, a man walked over to where she sat alone with Dean. Shawna's smear campaign had taken off in the last few days, and witches all over were avoiding her and giving her looks of disgust. So when he approached her, *everyone* watched. Melody knew that whatever happened, grossly exaggerated versions would be circulating through the school within minutes.

"Hi, I'm Trent," he said, looking at her.

Dean growled, but Melody opened her senses to get a feel for him. He was a fox shifter, strong for a fox, but nowhere near as strong as the larger predators. She wouldn't be required to bond him, if he challenged her.

"Hello Trent, nice to meet you and your fox," she told him, and his eyes widened in surprise.

"How did … never mind. Melody, of Coven Bestia, I challenge you!" Unlike Dean, he didn't simply erupt from his clothes. The fact that his beast wasn't yammering at him to challenge her, helped her do what she had to next.

"I thank you for the honour of your challenge, Trent and Fox, but I have a newly bonded shifter. For the immediate future, we wish to establish our bond before I even consider accepting another challenge. I'm sorry, but I decline."

Beside her, Dean tensed, obviously waiting for the backlash, but there was none, and he looked at her quizzically, but Melody was focused on Trent. She could hear his fox yip, urging him to get out of there, responding to the increasing aggression from Dean's lion, but Trent ignored his beast.

"Thank you. I look forward to challenging you again in the future, once you are more settled." Then, with more dignity than she would have thought possible, he turned and walked back to his friends, who were all glaring at her.

Well, what did they expect? That she was going to accept every challenge now just because she had bonded someone and they wanted her? These juvenile antics were beneath them, and Melody wished she had a pack master there to give them a telling off. Instead, she turned to Dean and shrugged.

"Your lion would have eaten him for breakfast," she told him quietly enough so that it was between them, even with shifter hearing surrounding them on all sides.

"How's your back?" he asked her.

"It's completely fine."

"Completely?" he repeated, disbelievingly.

"Ok, it's as fine as it was last night. How about that?" she snapped.

"Hey, easy there, I was just checking."

Melody sighed and discreetly bobbed her head in the direction of another shifter walking towards them. In the background, three more had stood from their chairs. "We need to get out of here, or it's going to turn into a circus," she told him.

Dean's lion growled, and he stood, pulling her towards the main doors that led into the outer ring. Melody, however, had another idea. She pulled him in the opposite direction, towards the side door that led into the north corridor. There she took a sharp left, heading for the tapestry. She used her knife to cut her finger and smear it on the stone before Dean could more than grunt at the smell of her blood, and the door opened.

"What the fuck is that?" he asked her.

Melody didn't answer, dragging him inside, and then hastily casting a spell that wiped his scent from the corridor. She still hadn't undone the one that was masking her own. She would have to wait and see if Carla would let Quinn help her out by checking for Dean's scent after she masked him tonight. If these shifter challenges were going to continue to happen, now that she'd been outed, then she would need to return to the corridors.

The door closed behind them, despite Dean putting his weight against it and trying to prevent it.

"Dean," she hissed, "let it go, it's fine, I can open it again from this side. Just step back here and wait for a few minutes with me."

"Where the fuck are we?"

"In a tunnel that leads from the north corridor back to the female witch dormitory, now hush, I haven't had the chance to test these for sound."

He opened his mouth to speak again, but Melody clapped her hand over it, silencing him. Outside, they both heard the distant rumble of male voices, but none of them paused, and none of them were clear enough to understand. Finally, after counting to three hundred, Melody cut her finger again and opened the door a fraction. A quick checking spell revealed that the corridor was empty, and she pushed it open wider to let them both out.

Then she turned and grabbed Dean's hand. "Hurry up, or we'll be late for shifter care," she urged, but Dean wouldn't budge.

"Melody, what the fuck is that tunnel?"

"Well, after I arrived here, I was looking for quieter routes around the school, for obvious reasons," she said, delicately skirting the truth. "I came across an old book that was written at the time of the founding of the academy. There were pieces of paper in it, a map of the school with all these tunnels on it, and a key that described how to find the doors and how to open them. So, I used them to avoid too much attention until you bonded me."

"That's how you avoided us?"

"I avoided everyone," Melody said very carefully. "I couldn't afford to be challenged by just any old shifter you know," she shook her head to show her disagreement with what she was saying. "I need to be selective about the shifters that I bring back to the coven. So, I used strategies that were tailored to help me achieve my ends."

Dean looked at her like she had three heads, and then a dawning light crossed his face. "I see," was all he said. "The dragons are going to be crushed. They've been looking for the tunnels for over a century. And you found them in your first week. That's hilarious!"

Melody smiled, glad that he could laugh at something. If she was going to be challenged by shifters all day, because she doubted that it was possible to avoid them all, then he needed to start with a positive attitude.

"You're worried about the challenges, aren't you?" he asked her, reading her face.

"Yeah, I know it's going to upset your lion. Plus, I'm bound to make some enemies today when I decline. I get it, it takes a fair amount of courage to walk up to a witch and challenge her, but to have her then turn you down, well, that must be pretty embarrassing."

Dean smirked, "Depends on the witch and the circumstances. I wasn't embarrassed when you turned me down yesterday." He frowned at her, the memory still unpleasant despite her eventual acceptance. "Besides, my lion won't be bothered now that he knows you intend to turn them all down. And if it makes you feel better, we can always get the others to come and be your bodyguards. They'd love it."

"No Dean, we can't. Their beasts are too attached to me as it is, we have to avoid them altogether." Dean recoiled from her. "They need the space to keep their heads straight, otherwise someone is going to get hurt." She had to make him understand. "We need to keep *everybody* safe." It was close as she could get to saying what she needed to.

Dean frowned, but nodded. She knew it was breaking his heart to be away from his friends, it was breaking hers as well. All she wanted to do was reach out and touch them, comfort them, *claim* them.

Melody stopped that line of thought cold. It wasn't helping her situation. What they needed to do was get through these next few months and work out a way for

Melody to protect Dean before she had to go home at the mid-year break.

Their final class of the day was defence magic, where they practiced protecting themselves against the third-year students. It was a class that she dreaded, because in the past, Shawna and her posse had made things difficult for her. She expected that today would be no different.

It wasn't Shawna, however, who came barrelling up to her the instant she set foot inside the door. Nor was it one of her cohorts.

"Keep your filthy hands off Trent! He's taken!" the woman yelled, shoving Melody backward through the doorway and into Dean. She was taller than Melody with frizzy blond hair sticking out at all angles. Melody recognised her from a few of her classes, but couldn't remember her name. "It's bad enough that you're fucking his lion, but you're not corrupting Trent's fox. He's a beautiful little animal, and he'll be mine by Christmas."

"Back off, bitch. I turned him down," snarled Melody, pushing the irate woman off her. "I don't fuck beasts, that's debased and I won't be a part of it. I earned the right to Dean's bond through my strength alone. I didn't have to ask for him, didn't have to get stronger, I didn't even have to fucking try. I am strong enough as I am, I don't have to wait until Christmas to fucking *try* and claim my shifter. So, go fuck yourself. Go on, practice your fucking ass off so that you can be good enough to claim a shifter that I could claim in my fucking sleep!"

Melody shoved the woman so hard, she fell on her ass, and then she walked into the room properly. There was a tick of claws behind her, and she turned to see Dean padding in after her in beast form. Before she could stop him, he turned his back on the woman, lifted his tail, and sprayed urine all over her. His paws swept up, as though flicking sand and grass up behind him, and then he stalked over to where she stood.

Ok then. Dean was obviously pissed with the woman. *Duly noted.*

Trying not to laugh at the now howling witch, Melody turned her back and headed for the women's locker room, only to come face to face with three shifters who blocked her way.

"I challenge you," the three of them said in unison, each giving the other dirty looks.

"I thank you for your offers, I am flattered, but I am refusing all shifters until further notice." Impatient now, she let Dean push them aside and then followed him over to the girls locker. "I'll be just a few minutes. You'll know if I'm in trouble." She smirked, and he butted her with his head. "Ok, ok, I'll be careful, but aside from Shawna and her crew talking smack, what's the worst that can happen? I'm strong enough to take them all on. I've never broken before, and I'll be damned if Shawna will be the one to succeed."

Melody turned and pushed through the door, heading for her locker near the back.

"There's the skank now. Lion cock not good enough for

you? Now you've got to try a fox one as well? What a whore. Bad enough that you corrupt their human sides, but to sink to fucking their beasts is just disgusting." Shawna might not have been able to talk about what really happened in the provost's office the day before, but it didn't stop her from making up her own version.

"Oh please, grow up." Melody sighed, sick of the drama. "What's wrong, Shawna? Did the provost finally tell you to get over yourself and graduate? Did she spell it out for you that you will never be strong enough to take on one of the Apex? Because no matter how you grow, you'll never be a match for their natural growth, so give it up already, none of you stand a chance. Or did she tell you that you have the emotional maturity of a ten year old, and that it was time you started acting your age, given that you are so much older than the rest of us?" Shawna's face turned crimson, and Melody was willing to bet that she had hit close to the mark.

"Get over it woman, he fucked you because he's a lion and he could. It wasn't a lifelong commitment. You go on about me being a whore, but you're the one who opened your legs to him willingly enough, and you're the one willing to make a fool of yourself for years trying to get him back. Get a life, Shawna, better still, graduate this year and just fucking get out. Everyone is sick of you, and none of the shifters here will ever have you."

While Melody knew that she was potentially adding fuel to the fire, Sebastian, and the other shifters who had raised Melody in the absence of any sort of care from her coven members, had taught her to stand her ground. To know when to fight back and when to bide her time. They had taught her stealth and the advantages of stalking your prey. In short, they had taught her how to defend herself as much as possible, and Shawna had no idea of the beast that she was awakening.

"So what are you going to do now, whore? Move your sights onto all of the other shifters?" asked one of Shawna's followers, snarling.

"For fuck's sake, I'm not interested in your fucking shifters. Tell them that you're a better chance, because I won't accept their challenges."

"Who the fuck do you think you are? Do you think that all the shifters want you now, that we're not good enough for them? How dare you make out that we're their second choice!" screamed a blonde woman, flying at Melody.

Yeah, she knew how to handle this.

Releasing her power, she froze every woman in the room. Rock. Solid. They couldn't gape at her, they couldn't speak. All they could do was blink and breathe. A low moan sounded from one of the women, but she couldn't move her tongue or mouth to make words.

"All of you want to know who I am. Very well. For starters, *I'm* the woman who can take on every shifter in this academy. There is not one here that I couldn't defeat if he or she challenged me." She looked around the room, the utter stillness guaranteeing them her attention. "Secondly, I'm the woman who can hold all of you still at the same time, without using a spell. This is my raw power alone. Imagine how much more I could do if I used the word with my will. I could rip your heads off and not one of you could do anything about it. Luckily for you, I have no interest in your petty little lives."

She started weaving in and around them. "They are petty little lives too, because if you didn't speak up against me, you also didn't speak up for me. You've allowed the evil in this school to spread, simply by doing nothing. So, I include you all. Petty. Little. Lives."

Melody ended her walk in front of Shawna. "I have no interest in your shit. I have gained a shifter, and I count myself fortunate that he was willing to challenge me. I expect that I will have more than one by the time I graduate. However, that is between me and the shifters that choose to challenge me. Who I accept challenges from is my own business."

She turned and faced the rest of the room. "I have no interest in stealing a shifter from another witch. There are five shifters here who I would consider of interest to me. They're known as the Apex. One of them has already challenged me and I accepted. No other shifter at this academy interests me. Do you all understand?" she asked, rhetorically. It was not like they could answer her.

"So, let me make one final thing clear. Not a single one of them is interested in any of you. If you don't have the power to help them with their beast, then they have no use for you. What the five of them need from a witch is more than what any other shifter would. I'm more than capable of supplying the magical strength that all five of them need – at the same time." She stepped even closer to Shawna, until they were almost nose to nose. "I suggest you stay the fuck out of my way, and I'll avoid you like the plague, and then we can all be happy pretending each other don't exist."

Melody released her power, and every single woman fell to the floor now that they were no longer held up by it. She quickly changed into sweats and a t-shirt and prowled out of the silent locker room. When she opened the door, Dean stood there with a huge grin on his face. Of course he had heard every last word. Stupid fucking shifter hearing.

"You're planning on bonding the others?" he said with a broad smile.

"Of course I'm planning on fucking bonding them, I'm just waiting for the right time." She waited for a lash, but none was forthcoming. The right time was apparently a vague enough reference for her to get away with it. That was worth remembering.

"This year is going to be fucking epic!"

She rolled her eyes and didn't answer. His enthusiasm both delighting and sickening her at the same time. She wanted him, she wanted all of them, she couldn't deny that, but she wouldn't take them at the cost of their safety. She had to sort that out first.

28. NICK

Watching Dean parade around with the woman that Nick suspected was his mate, was driving his dragon insane. The longer this farce went on, the more irritable he became. Oz even went so far as to comment that Nick was even crankier than Justin, and that was saying something. The other dragon was well known for his short fuse, so if he was being compared to Justin, then things were getting dire indeed.

It was all compounded by the fact that Melody wouldn't have anything to do with any of them. She wouldn't sit with them at meal times, if they came to visit Dean at the cottage, she retreated to her room, leaving her enticing scent floating behind her, ensnaring them all and switching their minds to things other than their friend.

Nick's dragon was pining for her, there was no other

word for it. The great beast was constantly sighing in his head, and every time he caught her scent, he pushed at Nick to get out. The longer they waited, the edgier he became, the harder she was to resist.

The rumours going around the school weren't helping either.

Neither Melody or Dean had said anything, but after a confrontation between the bitch, Shawna, and Melody in the locker rooms, things had gone south for the pair of them. He'd heard of pranks where chairs were pulled from beneath them as they sat, their notes being set on fire, and airborne objects darting between their legs in order to trip them up. These were minor grievances, and although they must be irritating individually, their cumulative effect would be quite demoralising.

Then there were the shifters. Dean said that the rumours going around the academy of what had happened in the locker room were utter bullshit. She didn't punch anyone, she didn't threaten to shove their tampons down their throats, and she didn't say that they had better hold on tight to their shifters, because she was after them all. He did say that she was a total badass, had held them all frozen and soundly told them off.

Now though, shifters either veered away from her in fear of being bonded against their will or challenged her outright. She was declining upwards of a dozen challenges a day, earning her the enmity of the embarrassed shifters, and the ire of the witches who actually wanted them. No witch wanted to be a shifter's second choice, or at least, not if she knew about it. With most shifters trying their luck at gaining a strong witch, it meant that there was little chance of them not discovering that their favourite had already challenged another witch.

His witch was gaining enemies left, right and center, and she wasn't reaching for him to help. It was driving Nick and his dragon mad.

And the wolves along with them. At least the four of them had each other, a sense of *pack*. Dragons moved in families, not packs, and Nick hadn't seen his one for a very long time.

Dragons tried to avoid the traps that academies had become. If a dragon wasn't accompanied by a witch, they were assumed to be dangerous and held in an academy until such time as a witch could convince the world council that they were in control. This was what had happened to his uncle and aunt, and it had been fifty years of red tape before she had finally been able to claim him back. More than enough time for hundreds of witches to try and get him to challenge them, using fair means or foul. Academies would rather say they had an unfettered dragon, than admit that they held one in error. It was a huge point of contention between the world council and the dragon council.

The world council was adamant that dragons needed a witch to control their beasts. The dragons were adamant that what they needed was a stable family. When dragons were in harmony, they didn't need outsiders coming along and controlling when and where they shifted.

Still, that was another issue for another time. Now that he had found Melody, Nick discovered that he no longer minded someone having that kind of control over his beast. Well, he didn't mind *her* having it. As far as protecting her went, though, he wasn't sure what more he could do. The petty things going on at the academy would continue until she had bonded the five of them, and she couldn't bond the five of them until she had sorted whatever issues she had with her coven.

With that thought in mind, he reached out to Justin and the wolves with his magic, linking them together.

Hey, he sent. *We need to meet with the provost. I'm thinking the only way to get her out of this mess, and us into her life is to sort this shit with her coven. From what the provost was hinting at the other day, we need to find her a new coven, but we need to talk to her first. I'm going to drop by there now and see if I can make an appointment to meet with her, you guys interested?*

Hell yeah, finally, something that we can actually do, Oz replied.

I'm in, sent Ryan.

Meet you there, Jus replied.

He took the next corridor, heading towards the provost's office. At this time of day, it was unlikely that she was in Provost House.

Dean, we're going to try and see the provost and see if we can get some more information on potential covens for her, Nick sent to the lion.

Hey, that reminds me, Dean sent. *Mel had a fight with Carla the other day, and Quinn didn't react to the shit that Carla was spewing. He wasn't growling or posturing or anything, he was just looking at her in surprise. I'm worried that Carla was being influenced, the provost is aware of my thoughts, but I haven't made an official accusation yet. I was wondering if you and Justin could do some snooping and see.*

You're right, it's odd that Quinn didn't get upset with her, but if it was a hex, then it would have worn off. Have they made up? Nick asked him.

No, Carla is now hanging around with Shawna. She already tried that scent thing on me, is there another version of that? Like a, I don't know, a BFF one or something.

Yeah, there are influencer things, but again, they would have worn off. Leave it with me, there are other possibilities. Jus and I will look into it, Nick reassured him.

Thanks man. Just be prepared that the provost may ask.

Duly noted.

Nick could almost feel the others converge upon the unsuspecting provost. He hoped that she could meet with them right now, because there was something almost offensive about the thought of making an appointment and waiting until he could see her in order to bring about a change of such magnitude in their lives. If they could free Melody of whatever trap she was ensnared in, then she would be free to bond them – and they would be *free*.

As luck would have it, the witch who sat at a desk outside the provost's office waved them through, after conferring with the provost, so the four of them sat down in the chairs that they had used the last time, the provost giving them all stern looks.

"Well," she began, "I think I can guess what, or rather who this is about. Care to enlighten me further, gentlemen?"

Nick wasn't surprised when the others turned to him to speak, he *was* the one who had suggested this after all.

"I'm sure that you agree that there's something wrong with Mel's coven, we need to get her out of there. We can't talk about it in front of her for fear of risking another mark. I've counted three so far, and they're the strongest ones I've seen in my lifetime. One for loyalty to her coven, one to prevent her from revealing that she has one, and one that prevents her from refusing a challenge from an apex shifter, whether it's the Apex here, or an alpha or dragon elsewhere."

"You think there are more?" asked the provost, curious.

"I would bet her life on it, yes. She's the strongest witch I've ever come across, even amongst those who live with my people. She should be powerful enough to break those three geasan, but she's not, which means that many more pin her down. If her mother died when she was four, then I would say that her enslavement began then."

The provost looked at him thoughtfully for a few minutes. "It is easy to forget that you are not as youthful as your appearance," she said, finally. "I had not put her situation into context like that, but then, she's not the core of my existence, is she." Her eyebrow quirked. It was obvious that the provost suspected that Melody was his mate too, as well as the witch that he was destined for. It was true that dragons often mated with their witches, but never more than one at once. He hadn't had a chance to talk to Justin, to see if his friend felt the same inexorable pull toward her.

So, at least the provost agreed with his analysis. "What do you know of her coven?" he asked.

"Very little I'm afraid, they are a very close group. I know that there are no male witches in the coven, rumour has it that the male babies are adopted out, but I've never met one." She shuddered. "I do know that they keep a large quantity of shifters at a massive compound in the westernmost part of Virginia. It's where Melody grew up, so shifters are no stranger to her, unlike many witches who walk through those doors having never encountered one." She gestured vaguely in the direction of the main gates and the arched doorway that faced them.

"What of her aunt?" he pressed.

"Georgia? She came through here, excelled academically but was only an average strength witch. It would not surprise me to learn that she had killed her older sister in order to receive the coven's matriarchal power. But I have no proof, so that is the mere supposition of an old woman. The fact that Adelaide, a brilliant and strong witch, forced her powers into her daughter at such a tender age, however, is telling of the poor relationship between them. They were always loyal to one another here, but if you watched, you could tell that there was no love lost between them."

"So you suspect that the aunt is the key to the geasan. It would make sense. As a weaker coven leader, she would need control of the matriarchal power. If it belonged to Melody, then she would need control of Melody. Would you agree with me, Provost?"

"I'm afraid that I would, Nick. I think that young woman is in a great deal of danger, not only from her aunt, but from the geasan laid upon her. I also think that the only way to free her, is to get her an offer of membership at another coven." The provost leaned back in her chair, taking off her glasses and rubbing her hands across her face.

"I've sent discreet inquiries out to a few covens. I would contact my own, but it might be seen as nepotism. If you gentlemen have any connections that might be interested in taking her on, by all means, send out feelers, but please be careful. I fear the consequences of her coven hearing of this before she swears fealty to a new one, would be disastrous."

"We will, Provost. It's as much in our interests as hers to see her freed. Believe me, we'll be careful," Nick assured her.

"Well, there's only one more thing to tell you." She eyed him shrewdly. "The better a witch's academic gradings, the more likely the stronger covens would be interested in her. At the moment, although they're improving, her marks aren't enough to make her stand out. It may make her a social pariah, but she needs to spend every spare second getting herself ahead of the others. She can go to her teachers and ask for work that will get her extra credits, and I would suggest that the five of you, with your combined knowledge, tutor her in everything. Make her the dux, and you'll have all the covens panting after her, even with only a single strong familiar."

"Study groups it is then," said Oz, contributing for the first time.

The others nodded. "We've all got our specialties, we can write study notes for her, and clue her into the things most likely to be in the exams. She'll be top of the school in no time," said Nick.

The provost smiled and stood, nodding at them and gesturing toward her door which she opened with her magic.

"I'm glad we've had this chat, gentlemen, but you must excuse me, I have many balls to juggle today."

They smiled and made their farewells, a new sense of conviction filling their hearts. Melody needed their help, and they would do everything they could to save her.

29. MELODY

After classes were done for the day, Melody and Dean took their time walking in the late sunshine, meandering between the buildings on their way back to the cottage. It was such a lovely day that she thought they might take a blanket out onto the grass and soak up the sun, but those pleasant thoughts were brought to an abrupt halt by the unpleasant sight awaiting them.

The front door stood wide open, and their possessions were strewn across the lawn. Dashing to her favourite pair of jeans, Melody saw that they had been shredded, and they were wet and stank. It took her a moment to realise that they had been urinated on.

There was destruction everywhere. Dean's bird's nest had been shredded, his blue stone crushed and scattered. All around them, precious items and objects had been destroyed.

Photos torn, their frames shattered; cushions exploded in piles of white fluff. Clothing ripped, bedding shredded, ornaments smashed.

When Melody rushed inside, she found that things were worse, and she hadn't thought that was possible.

All the furniture had been broken apart, and the cushions on the lounge and armchairs had been torn open. Melody gagged as the smell hit her, they hadn't just urinated in here. Somewhere, there were faeces as well. The enormity of what had been done was overwhelming. It was one thing to face the rumours and the sly remarks, pinches and the shoulder checks, but this was much more intimidating.

"What on earth is happening here?" asked an authoritative voice, and Melody turned around to see Mr Cartwright in the doorway, the other members of the Apex behind him.

She didn't say anything, she couldn't, and she didn't have to. Her teacher took in the destruction around him with eyes narrowed to slits. He closed his eyes, putting his fingers to his temples.

"Provost, please come to cottage eleven, I have to report that it has been vandalised," he said to the thin air.

There was no response that Melody could detect, but he nodded and said that 'he would' whatever it was that had been asked of him. He turned his stern gaze back toward her.

"I came to return your dampeners, it seems that my arrival was precipitous. Please come outside. Your familiars need to join us too."

The five shifters stood around her, grimacing at the

stench which must be much more overpowering for their enhanced senses. Together, the seven of them trudged back outside, where the provost and several teachers were approaching.

"Well, Melody, do you have any idea who would want to do this to you?" asked the provost as soon as they had cleared their lungs of the funk inside.

"No, Provost, it could be any number of people," Melody told her.

"Very well, Jonas, could you lead the other shifters through the debris and see what scents you can pick up, whether they be staff or students." The provost turned to a burly man behind her, and Melody was startled to realise that it was the provost's familiar amongst the other staff. It was strange, the teachers here were probably all bonded to shifters, but it just never occured to Melody that their shifters would also have come. They certainly blended into the populace well.

Jonas and four others stepped forward together, conferring in low voices and then splitting up. Two of them checked the outside items and the other three moved inside. Melody felt sorriest for those three, they not only had to go in there, but inhale the stench deeply as they searched it for the scents of the perpetrators.

Minutes later, the five of them gathered and conferred for a few moments before returning to report.

"I'm sorry, Provost," Jonas said formally, bowing as he did so, "but the scents have all been masked. Even the biological elements have only the base chemicals present and not individual scents. I could tell you that one of them had asparagus last night," he shuddered, "but other than that, there are no identifying scents."

The provost sighed. "Well, at least they weren't totally stupid about it. Thank you Jonas, thank you, all of you. I can't imagine that it was pleasant."

The shifters nodded in acknowledgement.

"If my staff would care to join me, we will repair this now," said the provost.

Immediately, the teachers present came forward to gather around her. Two of them laid their hands on her shoulders, others laid hands on those two, and so forth until they looked like a small peacock tail fanning out behind her in their different coloured robes. Then the provost said a spell under her breath, and slowly the pieces lifted from the ground, repairing and reforming in front of their eyes. Noises from inside of the cottage indicated that the same was happening there.

It was all done in a matter of moments, but there was a collective sigh of relief when she finally lowered her hands. It seemed that those sorts of repairs took a lot of energy. Melody hadn't used a mending spell to fix anything larger than a broken mug, so she wouldn't know. There was, however, still a lingering stench.

"Everything has been repaired, but it sits where it was dropped. There is also the matter of the biological waste. I trust that you are able to take care of those things yourself?" asked the provost.

"Yes, Provost, thank you for your help. Thank you all for your help. It would have been considerably draining to clean all of this, and I'm not sure that my grasp of repairing items would have been up to the task."

The teachers nodded to her and departed, leaving her with the provost and the shifters.

"Melody?"

She turned to the unknown and saw it was Professor Simmonds, her wards teacher. Apparently not all of the staff had left, both he and Mrs Hardinger had remained.

"I would like to see you after classes tomorrow, to go over some wards to put on your cottage. I fear that until the shifter population settles down again, you may be in for some more little pranks like this."

"I would hardly call this a *little prank*, Professor Simmonds," said Mrs Hardinger. "The place was absolutely destroyed. This isn't some high spirited witch messing around, this was the work of some seriously pissed off people!"

"Yes, yes, of course. I didn't intend to demean the psychological aspect, only that so long as there are staff here, we will be able to repair everything. The physical aspect of it, although unpleasant, is negligible," he amended.

The provost fixed him with a wry look, "Professor Simmonds, it took a considerable amount of power from over a dozen staff members to repair the items that were damaged. I would hardly call that negligible. Perhaps you should quit while you're ahead."

"I meant … yes, yes, you're right. No offense meant, Ms Bestia. I am simply glad that we are able to undo the physical elements of this mess. I will see you tomorrow afternoon. You may wish to seek additional tuition from Mr Phelps, he is more proficient at personal shields. I prefer to focus on the intricacies of protecting objects and places." He bowed to her and left.

Now, it was just Mrs Hardinger and the provost. While Melody appreciated their care, she just wanted them to go so that she could deal with the biological aspects of cleaning up – that she wasn't looking forward to.

"Melody," began Mrs Hardinger, "I know that you have a lot on your plate right now, with the extra tuition that you are about to receive, but I think we need to look at your mental health as well. Bonding Dean under these circumstances is stressful to say the least, never mind that every shifter with a cock is fantasizing about you every waking moment of the day. And my dear, I am not exaggerating. I'm counsellor for the unbonded shifters too, and I'm inundated with males who you have refused. I've heard enough sexual fantasies to last me a lifetime, let me tell you." She giggled.

Melody hadn't thought that she would like a counsellor, most descriptions had them as out of touch or trying too hard to connect to their charges, but she had a feeling that she would like the rather earthy witch. Mrs Hardinger reminded her of some of the female shifters that she had known, much more comfortable with their bodies and talking about sex than the average uptight witch. She supposed it came from having to care for so many shifters. Melody knew that her own thoughts and feelings had been shaped by the shifters that she had grown up with.

"Now, your shifters and I will get together and find slots in your timetable for you to come and see me twice a week, once with all of them, and once without. We'll manage to fit it in between your ward tutoring, your shield tutoring and the academic tutoring that they'll be giving you."

Melody opened her mouth to protest, but Mrs Hardinger cut her off.

"Young woman, they might not be bonded to you yet, but do not doubt for a moment that they are yours. You might also want to rethink rejecting Trent. He's the strongest fox shifter that the academy has ever seen, there aren't many witches who would be able to defeat him in a challenge. Ylena was trying to woo him, but she's a flighty thing and far too involved with Shawna and her motley lot. You could do worse than him."

She eyed Melody thoughtfully. "He certainly can't do better than you. Now," she turned to the shifters, "you lot will need to help her do everything, she's not going to be able to achieve all that she needs to without a lot of help. You'll need to keep her fed and rested, and if you can take on the domestic cares of the cottage then she'll have more time to study. We'll have her dux of her year in no time."

What?

Melody had no idea what they were talking about. The shifters were going to tutor her? And since when did she want to be dux of the year?

"That's an excellent idea, Mrs Hardinger. The sooner Melody tops all her classes, the better." The provost gave her a significant look, and suddenly Melody understood. The covens would pursue a witch who was top of her year. The provost had said as much, and now they were all working together to make sure that she got there.

"I'm glad that all this is settled, now, Melody, I do believe that you have a significant mess to take care of. I suggest that you use minimal magic, I think you will need it over the coming weeks for wards and shields and improving academically. The mid-year holidays are coming up. If you want to attend that advanced elemental magic course that's being offered, then you will need to improve significantly." The provost turned and left, Mrs Hardinger followed.

What advanced elemental magic course during the holidays was she talking about? Melody would have to go back to Bestia to take Dean … Oh! So even the need to return home was being taken care of.

Melody turned and looked at the shifters surrounding her, she wanted to cry with gratitude, but she held back. If they were going to be more involved with her at the insistence of the provost and Mrs Hardinger, then she had to be strictly neutral with them. It wouldn't do any of them any good if they became more attached to her before she was free to bond them.

"Well, like the provost said, we need to do this the old fashioned way, since I need to conserve my magic for classwork and study," she told them her voice husky with emotion despite her attempt at strength. "I appreciate any and all help that you might give."

Ryan, the more outgoing of the two wolves walked up to her and grabbed her, pulling him to her and kissing her soundly. "I'd be only too happy to help."

Well, so much for keeping an emotional distance!

The others watched her closely, gauging her reaction, relaxing a little when she wasn't upset. Yet another precedent had been set. Would she ever get this right?

"Now, as for the magic, I don't believe the provost said anything about us using ours. So, Justin and I will make you a deal. If you lot pick up everything out here, we'll deal with the more unsavoury elements both inside and out. Put the soiled stuff in a heap, and then we'll take care of it." Nick and Justin turned and headed inside where Melody could feel their magic swell and sweep through the dwelling.

Melody began gingerly picking up items and putting them in a pile at the bottom of the stairs. Nick's nest and stone were thankfully unspoiled, but every item of clothing had been marked with urine. This was going to take a long time.

30. MELODY

The next morning, there was a knock at the cottage door, and Melody opened it to find another student standing there with a letter in his hand.

"The provost asked me to bring this to you," was all he said, before he turned and left.

Melody looked down at the envelope in her hand, and her heart sank. Aunt Georgia's crisp handwriting was plastered across the front. This couldn't be good. With shaking hands, she opened the envelope.

Melody,

I hear that you have bonded an alpha lion. I am disappointed that this is your only success thus far. You are not trying hard enough if the shifters are not challenging you. We will expect you here for the holidays, where your shifter can swear his fealty to the coven.

In the interest of helping you focus, he will remain with us when you return to the academy. It will allow you to concentrate more on your studies and trying to encourage other strong shifters to challenge you.

We look forward to an improved attitude.

Georgia

Mistress of Bestia Coven

Of course her aunt wouldn't acknowledge their familial relationship in a letter. She would see that as beneath her. It was also all of her worst fears come true. Dean would remain behind, the subtext being that he would swear fealty to her aunt and then be put into their breeding program once he had been stripped from her and bonded to another witch.

A droplet of water hit the blurred page in front of her, and she jumped, realising that it was her own tears.

The letter was snatched from her hands and Dean scanned it before she could get it back. He looked confused and angry.

"Why would she want me to stay with them? It would interfere with our bond development to be so far apart. What aren't you telling me?"

Melody shook her head, a sob escaping her, and Dean stepped forward, gathering her in his arms. "It's alright kitten, we'll work it out, ok? Don't worry about it." Gently he soothed her until her tears stopped. "Now, let's get you cleaned up and get some breakfast in you before class."

He pulled a handkerchief from somewhere and dabbed at her face, tapping her nose, fluffing it over her eyes and her cheeks, and tickling her under the chin until she couldn't help but laugh and push him off. She was enjoying getting to know his gentler side.

Together they walked hand-in-hand to the dining hall, which was already more than half full. Heads turned and the whispers started immediately, but Melody ignored them as best she could. When Dean steered her towards the Apex, where they sat off to one side, she didn't resist. The whispers increased in ferocity and even more eyes watched their progress. Melody knew that it didn't bode well for them, but she was just over it. Frankly, she had bigger things to worry about.

Nick handed her a piece of paper. On it was her regular classes written out, but then there were sessions well into the evening where she was allotted time with three of them for individual tutoring. She had Mrs Hardinger on Wednesdays and Fridays, wards on Mondays and shields on Tuesdays and Thursdays. Then there was an hour's session with one of the men before dinner. After dinner there were two one-hour sessions with two other men, and finally an hour of revision every night.

It was a gruelling schedule, meaning that she was doing twice as much study as anyone else, but hopefully it would be enough to take her to the top of all her classes. And wouldn't the other witches love her for that too?

It was just as well, she couldn't afford to make other friends, even with shifters. As long as Melody was under her aunt's thumb, she would end up dragging everyone else down with her. It was bad enough that Dean was doomed and that the other Apex shifters were at risk of the same fate.

A plate with bacon and eggs was plonked in front of her, bringing her thoughts back to the present. Justin sat opposite, watching her closely. "Eat, then you can tell me about the battle between Morte Coven and Draskia Coven in 1592," he ordered.

Even meal times were to become revision sessions, apparently. Out of the corner of her eye, she could see the others digging into their food, although their meal was punctuated by snorts, eye-rolls and frowns. It seemed that they were discussing something, and Justin had been sent to distract her. Judging by the glower on Dean's face, she suspected it was the letter that he had seen.

She inhaled her breakfast, and then spent the next ten minutes being drilled by Justin, before they switched out seats and it was Oz who was grilling her. By the time the chime sounded for the first class, her head was spinning with information that Melody hadn't even realised she knew, and all she wanted to do was lie down.

There was no respite. Dean hooked an arm around her waist, tugging her toward her first class. They sat down together in the back row as all the students filed in. A body plopped into the seat on her other side, but she didn't look up to see who it was, Mr Phelps had just walked into the classroom, immediately launching into the lecture.

Melody's hand was a blur as it moved across the page taking notes, but in her peripheral vision, she could see the person beside her constantly turning to look at her. It was quite distracting, but she managed to persevere. However, it seemed that she wasn't the only one who was distracted. At the end of the lesson, Dean stormed past her and picked up the other person, slamming them against the wall.

"Just what the fuck is your game, fox?" he growled.

Melody spun to see that Dean had Trent pushed up against the wall, the fox wasn't resisting, his eyes fixed on her even though Dean threatened him.

"I'm a patient man, Melody. I'll wait. I'll even wait until after you've bonded your Apex. But you need to realise that I am just as much yours as they are. My fox will look at no other," he said quietly, but purposefully.

Her heart sank. She couldn't take Trent too, he was too gentle. Even as strong as he was, her coven would crush him in a month. She wouldn't corrupt him, not like the students had hinted, but in terms of taking him for her coven.

"You don't know what you're asking, you don't know …" wisely she didn't finish her sentence. She couldn't afford another lashing right now.

"Stay the fuck away from her," growled Dean, as she turned to leave.

"I can't, my fox, he's already pining. We'll wait, we won't interfere, but we *need* her."

"She's right, you don't know what you're asking," Dean replied.

"Fine, I don't know, and neither of you are going to tell me, I get that. I get it now that something is wrong, but that only makes my fox scream to protect her. Allow me that, at least. I heard what those bastards did to your cottage. I've seen what they do to her in the halls. You can't all keep protecting her without rest, let me help. At the very least, let me sit near her so that others can't." The desperation in Trent's voice halted her steps. Beneath it, she could hear his fox whimpering, crooning and groaning as she walked away.

"Let him," she told Dean, who raised a brow. "He's telling the truth, his fox is already mine, whether I allow him the challenge or not. At least let them get some relief by helping to guard me because it's too late for them to stay away." She turned back to Trent. "You know this is only going to make it harder, right? Your fox is going to push even more for you to challenge me."

Trent blinked his eyes slowly in acknowledgment, but Melody knew she had to drive the point home.

"If you challenge me again before I say you're allowed to, I'll reject you so soundly that you'll never be able to approach me again. Do you understand?"

Melody could hear his fox whining, but she waited until he nodded – at least as much as he could with the way Dean was holding him.

Dean relaxed, letting Trent's feet touch the floor again. It was an impressive feat to have held him up like that, because the lithe fox shifter was not short.

"Come on, we're going to be late for divination," she told the pair of them, and they hurried to catch up with her.

For the rest of the day, the three of them sat together,

usually with her in the corner. Dean beside her and Trent in front. When lunch time came and Dean led her into the central courtyard where the others had already gathered with enough food for a small army, he canted his head, indicating that Trent should join them.

The others looked askance at the addition of the fox shifter, but Dean just said, "He's already hers," and they nodded and left it at that. Trent, on the other hand, looked a little stunned at his inclusion into what had previously been a very selective clique.

Throughout the hour long lunch break, the men took turns at tutoring her for the remaining subjects of the day, so that when she went into them, not only was she up to date with what was being taught, but she was able to demonstrate an understanding of the material. Several of her teachers complimented her on her answers, garnering her dark looks from her fellow students.

In the hallway after her final class, the frizzy haired blonde woman accosted them again.

"What the fuck has she done to you, Trent?" she screamed at him.

"Ylena, she hasn't done anything. My fox wants her, that's the end of the story. I'm not going to deny him. I told you already that I wasn't ever going to challenge you, you're too controlling and possessive, both traits that foxes don't like. Even if Melody hadn't turned up, I still wouldn't be yours. Please, stop bothering us." Trent frowned, obviously tired of the woman.

Melody wondered if she'd been able to wash Dean's scent from her clothing, or whether she'd had to discard it. She honestly felt no compassion for her, Trent was right, no shifter wanted to be controlled. It was the biggest failing of most witches seeking a familiar. They saw them the same way that they would a domesticated animal. Shifters were wilder than humans, hell they were wilder than most of their non-magical counterparts. There was no caging them or controlling them. You formed a good partnership with them from the start, or you had already lost them.

It was one of the things she hated the most about her coven. Aside from the fact that they tortured and killed most of the shifters in their care, they actually didn't care about them as intelligent beings. Bestia saw shifters as beasts that had to be controlled. It was debasing to witness, and it was a behaviour that Melody had never adopted. It was probably why these shifters were walking all over her.

"You'll pay for this, you slutty bitch," snarled Ylena, but she was startled when both Dean and Trent growled at her, their teeth lengthening as their beasts pushed forward to answer the threat.

The two shifters closed rank in front of Ylena, leaning over her menacingly and advancing upon her for every step she took backward. Eventually, Melody took pity on her, well at least got tired of the drama.

"Boys," she called, "come on, we've got bigger fish to fry." She stepped around the frightened witch, not bothering to see if they followed her.

"I accept your challenge, Trent," screamed Ylena from behind them, and the fox shifter laughed.

"That wasn't a challenge, that was a promise. Stay away from Melody, or I'll make sure you regret it," he called back to her, not even bothering to turn around.

Yeah, Melody was back to having no compassion for her at all. The stupid bitch had it coming!

31. DEAN

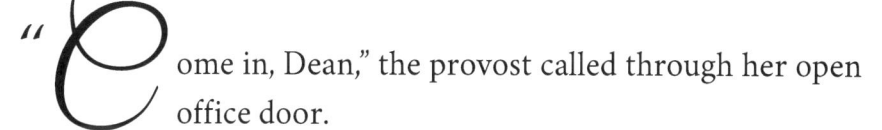

"Come in, Dean," the provost called through her open office door.

Dean nodded at the witch who sat at a desk just outside the door before entering.

"What can I do for you, Dean?"

"Melody had a letter from her aunt," he started.

"Ah yes, I gathered that that was who had sent it. I grabbed a passing student and had him take it to her. I assume that she got it promptly?"

"I don't know when you sent them, but it came this morning before breakfast," he told her, and she nodded with a smile. "It's the contents of that letter that brings me to you."

"She let you read it?" asked the provost in surprise.

"No, but I read it anyway before she could stop me. It seems that her aunt has heard that we are bonded, and looks forward to seeing me at the mid-term holidays. She made it clear that I was going to swear my fealty, and that I would be staying at the compound when Melody returned to campus after Christmas. The excuse was that I would distract her from her studies, and her efforts in procuring other shifters. Her aunt also made it clear that she was disappointed that Melody had only bonded one shifter so far."

The provost snorted so loudly, that a page blew off her desk. "That woman is far more ambitious than I had thought. It concerns me that she may have put a geas on Melody as young as four and the level of control that she seems to have over her. Several of the staff have expressed concerns too. Melody is a strong witch, and they believe that she should be strong enough to break the geasan upon her, but if it started when she was a toddler, and there are as many as I suspect there are, then Melody is in danger."

Dean's lion growled, and he felt his teeth lengthen. He struggled for a moment to reassure his beast that the threat wasn't immediate, and that they needed to use their wits to overcome it. Instead of mollifying his beast, it made his cat hyperaware, which meant that Dean's senses were heightened and there was an increased blood flow to the brain. He'd attended enough lectures on shifter psychology to understand what he was experiencing – his lion was on the hunt!

The provost waited until he was under control again, before speaking. "I've had positive reports from all of Melody's teachers, I check in with them once a week. She's shown significant progress even in just a couple of days. With a continued effort, she should be at the top of her classes by the mid-year break." She smiled at Dean encouragingly.

"Given that we need to stop you from going with her to her coven, I'm going to suggest she apply to study under Professor Ludwig over the term break. It's an advanced course in curse breaking, something that I fear Melody may have need of. The course has limited numbers, so it's a highly competitive field that she will be facing. The sooner she can top her classes, the more likely she will be accepted. I have no control over who is selected to attend. Professor Ludwig belongs to Claremont College, and as a guest lecturer, the final decision is hers. I can only send a list of recommended students, and I must be impartial. Melody's name will be on that list, providing you keep helping her to improve her grades."

The unspoken warning was clear, if Melody's marks weren't high enough, then she didn't have a chance of being accepted and Dean would be forced to go and live at the compound. From Melody's reactions, that was something to be avoided at all costs.

"What about invitations to other covens?" Dean asked her.

"Well, the only coven I can speak to at the moment, is my own, and we both know how bad that would look if she was to join us and suddenly be free to bond all of the Apex. As much as I would love the prestige for my coven, and to be able to take a much more personal interest in Melody's care, it cannot be." She sighed, leaning back in her chair.

"I have spoken to my coven mistress. She's intrigued, but she won't mention Melody to her contacts until she's doing better in her grades. Everything depends on that, Dean. You must all push her as hard as you can. She simply *must* do better."

He would see to it, Dean had a feeling that both of their lives would depend upon it – in more ways than one.

"What of the dragon's quest?" the provost asked him.

Quest? He had no idea what she was talking about.

"They were looking into a potential use of forbidden magic on one of the witches here," she prompted.

Dean realised she meant Carla and his suspicions. "Nothing yet, I've only just told them. Nick said something about influencing hexes or spells wearing off, but given that Carla has made no move to apologise, and is now hanging around Shawna, he's looking at other alternatives. Shawna tried to use a scent on me to influence my decisions. I thought she was wearing bad perfume, but Nick detected the magic."

The provost sat up stiffly. "And why was I not informed about this earlier?"

"Nick dealt with it, if she'd been more successful, he'd probably have told you. As it was, we all thought it smelled horrific," he explained, rubbing the back of his neck sheepishly.

"Dean, it's a serious offence. If she's willing to try that on you, what about another shifter who doesn't have the benefit of a friend wise enough in magic to detect it?"

His heart thumped. The possibility that Shawna or one of her cohort would try it on another shifter hadn't occurred to him and he was willing to bet it hadn't occurred to Nick either.

"So, what do we do?"

"*You*, do nothing. I will speak with Nicholas to see whether he knows which particular spell she tried to use. There are some false ones out there. If that is the case, then I can only reprimand her for her foolishness. If, however, she used a legitimate one, it's grounds for expulsion."

"I'll let Nick know that he needs to come and see you," Dean offered.

"Thank you, no. I'll send for Nicholas when I'm ready. Please keep me informed of any progress when we have dinner next week, or sooner if the matter is urgent."

Dean rose to his feet, he knew their meeting was over. "Yes, I will, and thank you again."

"Dean?" she called him, just as his hand touched the doorknob. He turned to face her. "Remember that I *am* on your side – all of you."

32. MELODY

The days flew by in a blur, with the holidays rapidly approaching. Her waking hours were spent entirely in study, with no social interaction, even with the shifters surrounding her. Meals were simply an opportunity to cram more information into her while she chewed, but all the hard work was beginning to pay off.

In history, her marks were almost always a hundred percent, and her lecturer, Professor Whitlaw, had even gone as far as to suggest that Melody do her final exam early, as she was demonstrating advanced knowledge. If Melody could complete the class early, the others had argued for her, then she would have more time to cram for the other classes. It was hardly an enticement.

"But what if I bomb out?" Melody had asked fearfully.

"Then you're still in the class and hopefully Professor

Whitlaw will let you take the test again at the end of term. We can clarify that with her before you take it if you like. A chance to complete the course early, but no harm no foul if you don't succeed," coaxed Oz. "Besides, with us drilling you, how could you possibly fail?"

That was the other part she was worried about. Just how much more could her poor brain take? Melody lived, breathed, and ate knowledge. Her only respite was when she fell into bed exhausted. She felt like a robot, spitting out facts and dates without having a true understanding of them, but that's what the syllabus required. It would be next year when this acquired knowledge would take on a more practical application. Even history.

The rules of their way of life were born from the conflicts of the past, and understanding how far they could be bent without breaking them, required not only a knowledge of what the rules were, but how and why they were created.

Still, it would all be worth it if she passed. Dean had told her about the advanced course on offer over the holidays, if she was accepted, it would give them more time to work out how to escape her aunt. Everything would be worth it if it bought them more time.

Another week passed, and the end of term date was getting closer.

Yesterday, Melody sat for her history class exam, and today she would get the results. Even as she spat out all the answers to the questions the men had given her over breakfast, Melody's gut roiled, to the point that she couldn't eat at all.

In proportion to her success, her popularity, or rather whatever had remained after bonding Dean, declined. The other witches didn't speak to her, and the shifters were politely but firmly turned away by the Apex, before they even had a chance to challenge her, yet the bullying increased. Either Nick or Justin now accompanied her to all of her classes, as well as Dean and the ever-present Trent.

The men had decided that she shouldn't waste her magic on protecting herself from the small hexes and curses that were constantly thrown at her. Melody couldn't sit down without tacks appearing on her chair, and she couldn't walk three steps without invisible objects snaking around her feet to trip her up. The attacks were so constant now, that it was a full-time job for the dragons to protect her.

At the same time, there had been more attempts at damaging their cottage. The two wolves now patrolled around it whenever she wasn't there, with either Nick or Justin sleeping inside. The dragons guarded her day and night. Her tormentors, having discovered that their taunts didn't work during the day, now timed just as many attacks after she retired for the night. So Nick and Justin took on twelve hour shifts.

Two nights ago, someone had attempted to burn down the cottage while they were all in bed. Nick had tried to go outside to see who it was, but all the windows and doors had been sealed shut with spells. He had been easily able to defeat the flames licking at the outside walls, but this was a much more serious attack, and he had met with the provost the next day.

It seemed that there was nothing they could do. Without knowledge of who the attacker was, there was nobody to expel. It only meant that Professor Simmonds and Mr Phelps worked her even harder in their tutoring sessions. The provost was determined to protect her, but was helpless to do so without an eye-witness account.

Not all of the teachers were sympathetic either. Most of them ignored the pranks pulled on the group, saying that it was too petty to pay attention to, and that they had enough on their hands trying to instil the knowledge that they had to impart. In truth, it was. Individually, the events were negligible, but when you considered the effort that the group of them had to put in to counter them, the overall effect was something a little more sinister.

There was nobody stepping forward to claim credit either. Shawna had backed off, her cronies leaving Melody alone to the point of deliberately turning their backs. Even Ylena subsided, although she gave them dark looks. The attempted fire while blocking them in the cottage, however, was a little more serious, and the provost had called a staff meeting to make sure the teachers understood that the pranks were getting out of hand.

Melody wasn't sure that it was going to fix things. If the students suddenly got in trouble for pranking her, then it would be seen as favouritism. It would need to be a blanket policy of no pranking, and half of the events occurred in the corridors where there wasn't a staff presence anyway. Still, Melody knew that after the fire, it couldn't be ignored anymore, she just didn't know what the right answer was.

Halfway to her history class, Melody heard her name called out. She turned to see Carla walking over to her, with Quinn at her side.

"Look, I don't know who did it, but I just wanted to make it clear that I had nothing to do with the fire. You might be a stuck-up bitch, but Mrs H said they sealed the windows. That's some fucked up shit and I don't want to get the blame, ok?"

Melody blinked. It was as close to an apology that she would get, and she took it with both hands.

"Carla, I just wanted to say again, what I said, it wasn't meant as an insult to Quinn. I've been ordered to only bond alphas and dragons, that's it. If I'd bonded Quinn, they would have taken him from me and given him to another witch," Melody paused, waiting for the lash that never came, while Dean trembled beside her. Some risks were just worth taking, and the chance of getting Carla back was more than worth it in her book.

Carla glared at her. "So he's good enough for you, just not for your coven? I don't see how that's any better. Fuck, you really are the living end." Carla spun on her heel and walked away, while Dean rounded on her. After giving her a searching look, Quinn followed his witch.

"What the fuck, Mel?" Dean growled, grabbing her arms and shaking her. Around them, people stopped to watch.

"I had to, and it was fine. It's done now," she said, pulling away from him.

Nick stepped up beside them. "Not here," was all he said, nodding to their audience.

Dean growled and Melody sighed. She didn't need more drama right now, all she had been doing was trying to reduce it. It seemed that she was damned no matter what she did. She turned to go, but a shifter stood in her way.

"Provost wants to see you, asap," he grunted, before turning and walking away, his gait stiff.

Even the shifters hated her.

"I guess we're going to the provost then," she murmured, biting her lip. Nick shrugged, but Dean took off, not waiting to see if she followed.

When they arrived, the woman at the desk waved them in, so they knocked and entered when they heard the provost give permission.

"Of course, I should have expected you all to come," she said with mild humour. "Well, this affects you all, so I'll get straight to it. I wish to offer my congratulations on two accounts, Melody. Not only did you pass your final History of Witchcraft exam with flying colours, meaning that you no longer have to attend lectures, but in doing so, you gained acceptance by Professor Ludwig into her Advanced Curse Breaking course being held over the term break. There are only ten students accepted each year, so this is a significant offer. I am afraid that the course runs over the entirety of the holidays, so you won't be able to go home for Christmas, or New Year, if your coven celebrates them."

The provost said all of this with such a straight face, that Melody wondered if she really knew how momentous this was for her. This course gained her another few months to work out how to evade her aunt's clutches.

Then suddenly, the provost smiled and winked at her, before schooling her face to its usual seriousness.

"Why do I get the impression that this isn't the only news that you have for us? And that the other news isn't so great?" asked Melody.

"Well, that would be because you are a perceptive witch, Melody," said the provost wryly. "While technically this isn't bad news, I fear that it will impact upon you, so I wanted to give you as much warning as I possibly could. There will be a student transferring here from Mayfield Academy in the south. As you are aware, Mayfield is our sister academy for shifters, but that isn't why this news is important." She paused, but Melody already knew what was coming.

"He's an alpha shifter," she said in a neutral tone.

"Yes, Asher is an alpha wolf. That isn't the only point of concern, though. Asher has already graduated from Mayfair, he's been there for six years now, no witch has been able to defeat his wolf, although he seems to have made his mark in sexual conquests. My concern is; that in his application for transfer, Asher cited you. It may have been indirect, but I fear that his intention is to come here for the sole purpose of challenging you."

There were low growls from around the room, and Melody's stomach twisted.

"What did he say?" she asked.

"He said that he had exhausted all of the potential of Mayfair Academy and had heard that Adolphus had better offerings." She looked sternly at Melody. "He's obviously heard that a witch has bonded one of the Apex and he's coming to throw his hat in the ring, so to speak."

Melody nodded, it sounded like an alpha shifter alright. They would do exactly that, without even thinking through the consequences for the witch.

"When does he get here?" she asked.

"Sometime in the last week before the holidays. I won't know until the week before." The provost looked down at her desk to a diary, flipping the pages. "Which is the week after next. My goodness, the end of term comes so fast. Now, as for the advanced course, there is a fee to remain at the school over the holidays, and another for the course itself. I imagine that your aunt would simply refuse to pay, despite the honour that it would bring to your coven, so I'm simply going to pay the fees myself. I hope that that is acceptable to you."

Her tone of voice left no doubt that whether it was acceptable or not, it was what was going to happen.

"I am very grateful, Provost, that is generous indeed, but I don't understand why you would do such a thing." Melody looked at the older woman in curiosity.

The provost smiled at her. "Melody, I don't know what you see when you look at me, but I can imagine. I'm an older woman, happy with Jonas, but we were never able to have children. Instead, we tend to think of the students here as ours. I'm quite attached to your shifters, having known them for many years now, and you too are someone that I am becoming quite fond of." She smiled at Melody's surprise.

"Your strength in the face of your adversity is admirable. When faced with a challenge, you step up without hesitation, and when you come across an opportunity to help someone, you do so without question. You are a remarkable young woman, Melody, and I look forward to seeing who you will grow into."

Melody was taken aback. Of all the answers the provost had given her, that was not one she had even considered. She almost sounded like … well … a mother. Her eyes filled, her breath hitched, and suddenly she was sobbing. All these years Melody only had the shifters who were as much prisoners as she was. Now, here she was, away from the cancer that her coven had become for the first time, and the people here, who barely knew her, cared for her more than the blood family that she had left behind!

Dean pulled her into his arms, and she allowed herself to find comfort in his embrace again. He hadn't pushed her for a physical relationship, although his beast must have been begging him to commence one. He'd simply been there for her. They all had been, and not one of them had asked her for anything in return.

"Trent," the provost said quietly. "I suggest that you return to classes. I'm giving Melody the rest of the day off, but unlike the rest of the Apex, you have yet to graduate. You must apply yourself, as Melody is, for she's going to need familiars who are as strong mentally as they are physically."

"Yes, Provost," he said, ever obedient, however, he let his fingers trail across the back of Melody's neck as he passed her on his way out. Melody shivered from his seemingly casual touch. She knew it was more than that, however, and so did the provost. When Melody raised her eyes to the older woman, she had a wry smile on her face. Yes, she knew that he was hers just as much as the others were.

"Gentlemen, I suggest that you let Melody relax today. Too much study can be just as detrimental as not enough. I have spoken again with her lecturers this week, and she is now at the top of all her classes. I can now begin on the other plans that we discussed recently."

Her gaze returned to Melody. "You have made remarkable progress, but you must not rest on your laurels now. I would suggest that you focus on completing as many of your subjects as early as possible. Next semester, you will commence the intermediate history class. As such, you have a whole half term of work to catch up on. Let that be your first priority. Then, once you are up to date, I would suggest that you pick another subject and seek to complete it. It would be my advice, Melody, to graduate from here as soon as you are able."

"Yes, Provost," she said, and they all rose, recognising the dismissal for what it was. It seemed that while she had gained a reprieve from her first-year history class, it would be replaced with her second-year one, and she had the three weeks remaining of term, plus the three week end of term break to catch up on six months worth of work. Easy peasy.

33. MELODY

The next two weeks passed in the same blur as the last few had. Study and sleep became her entire life, and meals were inhaled with as little concentration as possible. The bullying had not let up, but there were no further attacks on the cottage. The new wards that Professor Simmonds had taught them meant that the dragons were now able to sleep during the night, and instead they focused on protecting her during the day.

Oddly enough, Melody had difficulty with the personal shields that Mr Phelps had been trying so hard to teach her after class. They were advanced level, way beyond what she could have expected to be learning at this stage, but she didn't think that was why she was struggling.

Several elements of personal shielding seemed to just elude her. The desire to repel a spell directed at her, the ability to detect magic approaching her and the ability to actually force her will into the spell. After weeks of trying, Melody threw her hands in the air with a grunt as she fell, when Mr Phelps' hex hit her squarely in the chest.

"I can't do it!" she growled. "I don't know why, but my body and my magic refuses to do this. What is wrong with me?"

Mr Phelps looked at her consideringly for a few moments. Then he looked away. "Sometimes, magic fails, because there is a block," he said carefully, looking back at her.

"Like a mental block?" she asked.

"Mmm, it can be, yes."

Melody turned the thought over in her head. What on earth could possibly be blocking her magic from working to defend her? Why couldn't she defend herself? What could block her magic? And then it hit with the force of a bomb. Of course. A geas. Either the cumulative effect of all the geasan her aunt had put on her, or a specific one. It didn't matter which, the result would be the same. Melody would be vulnerable to a direct attack from her aunt!

Mr Phelps nodded at the look of dawning comprehension on her face. He knew enough not to say anything aloud, and for that, she thanked him silently a thousand times over.

"Whatever the cause of your block is, Melody, it is important to keep practicing, to keep trying to cast defensive spells. You are of no use to your coven if you cannot even defend yourself." He winked at her to take the sting out of his words, but Dean growled anyway.

"Easy there, kitty," she told him. "He makes a valid point. I'm no use to my coven," she pointed at Dean and then to the other shifters who stood to one side, watching, "if I cannot even defend myself."

Dean blinked, and the others stood taller. It was the first time she had publicly acknowledged that they were hers. She knew Dean had passed on her comments from the other week, but it wasn't the same as hearing it from her own lips.

There was a knock at the door and everyone turned to see who it was. "Ms Bestia, the provost asked me to give you this." It was Mrs Hardinger. She passed over the slip of paper and stood watching while Melody read it.

Ms Bestia,

The parcel should arrive some time on Tuesday of next week. I trust that you will take the necessary steps to ensure that you are aware of when it arrives.

Provost Aer-Canticum.

Melody read the letter a second time. Parcel? She wasn't expecting a parcel, just this new student Asher. And then it clicked, leaving her feeling stupid. Well, at this rate she was going to run into the fucker in the first five minutes! She turned to the other shifters.

"Tuesday next week," she said obscurely, but they all immediately understood what she meant, if their low growls were anything to go by. She felt stupid, they had grasped it without pause, while she had to think hard about it before the penny dropped.

"Don't be hard on yourself dear, the provost had to *explain* it to me, even though I knew about this in advance. You've been working so hard my dear, it's no wonder that it didn't occur to you straight away," Mrs Hardinger explained.

Mr Phelps looked unimpressed by the disturbance to his private lesson.

"I'm sorry John," Mrs Hardinger pre-empted him. "I need to have a talk with Melody, and no, it won't wait until tomorrow. In fact I may need to usurp your time on Thursday as well."

"I see," was all he said, but he made no effort to stop them from leaving, and he looked annoyed. "Whatever it is, if it's this important, I wish you the Goddess' blessing on it."

Melody looked gratefully at him. He was one of the few teachers who seemed to have taken her side. "Thank you, Sir."

"Come along then, you lot are welcome for once," she called out to the shifters, and they all followed Melody and Mrs Hardinger back to the counsellor's office.

"Now that we can speak a little more freely, Asher arrives on Tuesday next week, and the provost has sent me to make sure that you've taken all of the necessary precautions. In other circumstances, I might pull him aside and have a talk with him, but we don't know who he's loyal to, and until we're sure that's you, I have to keep mum." She sniffed, obviously displeased. Melody was willing to bet that the provost had forced that concession from her, because the forthright woman would have done exactly that; sat Asher down and told him everything that she thought he needed to know.

"So, what precautions have you taken?" she asked Melody.

"Well, I got Carla to mask all of their scents. Quinn checked them all and he confirms that he can no longer smell any of us," Melody said.

"You got Carla to do it?"

Melody sighed. "Well, yes, before we argued. I'd been trying to conserve my energy for class, and for practice with Mr Phelps and Professor Simmonds. So, anything non-essential to my studies, like say, defending myself from hexes, the dragons do instead. Or, as in this case, Carla. Although I can't rely on her anymore."

The older woman's lips thinned, but she said nothing, for which Melody was grateful. She wondered if the provost had told her of their suspicions, but it was better if she hadn't. Either way, she wasn't going to mention it. She had to remember to ask Dean later if there was any progress on that front. She was pretty sure that they would have told her immediately if they had found something, but even ruling things out meant that they were one step closer to the answer.

"What else?" Mrs Hardinger asked, and it was a moment before the question clicked in her head. What other precautions had she taken.

Melody didn't know if Mrs Hardinger knew about the

tunnels, but she was willing to bet she did. However, the provost had distinctly asked her not to tell anyone else, and so far, she had only shown them to Dean, before swearing him to silence on the matter.

"That will stop him from scenting you out, but surely you have done other things?" asked Mrs Hardinger, concerned.

"Well, yes, we've devised a way for me to get around most of the campus, unseen," explained Melody.

"Oh Goddess, you found the tunnels, didn't you?" cried Mrs Hardinger, and Melody flinched at the volume. "For goodness' sake woman, this room is warded for sound, I could murder you all with a bomb blast and nobody would hear anything. Although they'd probably notice the smoke. Hmmm, I might have to work on that."

She said it so matter-of-factly, that Melody half believed her.

"Ok, so he can't see or smell you, good. Now, what about your cottage? How are you defending that?"

Melody blushed, screwing up her face at the same time. How on earth was she going to explain that the men had taken great care to urinate all over the place, the smell so strong to other shifters, that they wouldn't be able to approach.

"Ah, scent marking, good, good. I gather all of you took part in that?" She grinned when they all nodded, even sweet Trent had done several laps around the perimeter of the territory they were marking out. "The more scents, the more put off he'll be. How close is the nearest tunnel entrance to your cottage, Melody?"

"The closest one is probably the north-east corridor, but they don't all connect directly, and that one doesn't take me anywhere useful, except on the days when I've got herbology."

Mrs Hardinger eyed her hungrily. "I cannot tell you how excited I was to learn that the tunnels were real, and that you had found them. Apparently Augusta knew about them, part of being provost and all that. Another time, I shall ask you all about them, but for now let us focus on what else you can do to protect yourself from this asswipe."

Melody giggled. "Well, the men are already guarding me, they've had the last few weeks to come up with their own system of who does what, and when."

Mrs Hardinger snickered, "I'd be willing to bet that it's not all about who guards you when, either." She winked at Melody, who blushed again.

Their sessions had been refreshingly open thus far, with the older woman advising her on many things regarding handling a bonded shifter. Mrs Hardinger had been sympathetic upon learning that her first familiar, Sebastian, had died when she was young. It was something that all witches dreaded, outliving their familiar, but apparently not as much as shifters dreaded outliving their witch. Most shifters went insane and had to be put down, and that was if they survived the shock, the backlash of the shredded bond wreaked havoc on their open minds.

Melody opened her mouth to deny the claim, until she saw the sheepish expressions on the men's faces. Well! That was something to think about another time, maybe when she wasn't hiding from her aunt, a randy wolf, and whoever it was that tried to kill them all.

"Over the next few days I'll be teaching the men all of the tunnel entrances and methods for opening them. Some require magic, so the dragons or I will need to be there for that, but others should be accessible to them if the need should arise. They know not to use them unless they're sure that they're unobserved. On top of that, Justin and Nick are going to take turns in using their magic to create a pack bond between them all whenever we are separated."

"They can do that?" exclaimed Mrs Hardinger, obviously impressed.

Justin smirked at her. "We're more than just pretty faces, counsellor."

Mrs Hardinger laughed. "Aye, and I bet you think you've a mighty fine cock there and you're just dying to show it to Melody. Well, you keep your junk in your pants, this woman has got other things that need 'seeing to' first."

Justin blanched, then blushed furiously, his wry expression saying all that needed to be said.

Mrs Hardinger snorted. "Typical male. Hundreds of years old, and you're still thinking with the wrong head!"

The two women laughed, but the shifters didn't join in much, although Trent chuckled, even more so when the others frowned at him. "What? You know she's fucking right.

We're more primal than humans, we're ruled by our cocks. I'm not going to deny it. Mine is constantly rock hard, and my fox is pushing me to just shove her against the wall and slam it home. If you're honest, your beasts and your cocks are doing the same. We're shifters, it's part of who we are."

"Back off little fox, if anyone is getting near Melody, it's me. I'm her *bonded* shifter. My lion won't let any of you near her." He turned to face Melody. "You know, lions can mate over a hundred times a day." Dean's voice was a veritable purr.

"Yes, I know, and they average about twenty seconds a time. Are you trying to tell me something?" Melody snapped. It was the wrong time for this kind of argument to break out between the men.

As if there would ever be a good time.

"Dude! Twenty seconds? That's hardly enough time to get your pants down." Justin laughed.

Dean scowled at the dragon, and they all laughed at him.

"You're not going to let this go, are you?" He growled at them.

Nick smirked. "Fuck no. This is a golden opportunity to rip shit off you for centuries. Of course we're not going to let it go!"

"Best laugh I've had in months," agreed Ryan.

Melody rolled her eyes and Mrs Hardinger huffed.

"Maybe it was a mistake allowing them to come here," Mrs Hardinger muttered under her breath, well aware that all of them could hear her.

She turned her attention back to Melody. "Well, it looks like you've done all that you can to protect yourself, now we just wait to see how it all pans out."

"It's not going to work, is it?" asked Melody, suddenly forlorn.

"No, love. Not long term. But in the short term, yes, it should give you a couple of weeks. Hopefully by then the provost and I can talk to him."

Melody nodded.

"Now," said the counsellor briskly, "as this isn't our normal time, and as you have your harem here with you, how about we call it a day. Go and get some rest, love. You look peakish."

On that note, she gave Melody her customary hug, and left.

Seven days, that was all she had left until Asher arrived, and then she went back into full hiding again. Seven, fucking, days.

34. MELODY

The day in question had dawned brightly, with no sign of any sort of chaos. Melody wondered what time of day Asher would arrive. Would it be before lunch? Or maybe in time for dinner? She trudged between Dean and Justin, who were having a lively discussion on what the likely breakfast offerings would be, and what they would partake of. Melody felt nauseous just listening to the vast quantities of food they planned on devouring, but they managed to do it every meal and still be fit.

There was a rustle of grass behind her, and before Melody could turn to see what it was, a weight hit her between the shoulder blades, quickly knocking her to the ground and rolling her over. Seconds later, there were teeth on either side of her neck, and hot breath was bathing her skin.

Apparently Asher was already here.

Dean and Justin snarled, but didn't dare reach for the wolf. While challenging, the shifter would have less control over his beast, he was just as likely to tear out her throat as he was to let her go.

Melody knew that she couldn't refuse him. Although she had been conserving her magic, the wound on her back from showing the staff and her shifters that she was under a geas, weakened her more than she let on. It was a constant dull ache, and if she moved too fast, it tore open again. From experience with an actual whip, Melody knew that it would take weeks to seal properly, and the fact that it was a punishment from a geas meant that it would take even longer.

She couldn't afford to say no to his challenge, she would be too weakened to finish her classwork and even worse, she wouldn't be well enough to participate in the special holiday program with Professor Ludwig. But to accept him now, would be to doom him as well as Dean, she couldn't do that to him, even if he was an asshole. She would have to compromise.

"I will accept your challenge at the beginning of next term. Right now, I need to focus on my studies and the special course I just gained entry to. I don't have time to work with a second new bond." The lash wasn't as bad as the one where she had refused Dean, but it seemed that saying 'not today' wasn't an acceptable response either. She grunted in pain, her back arching as the weal seared across her skin.

Asher took it to mean something else. The weight on her

shifted, as he sat on her, his firm cock rubbing against her lower belly as he ground his hips against her and groaned.

"I can't smell you, why can't I fucking smell you?" he whispered huskily, still dry humping her slowly. "But I can smell pain. Why can I smell pain?"

"Get off her you fucking cunt!" roared Dean, bodily lifting him away from her and holding him still so that Justin could start laying into him. Blow after blow slammed into the shifter, but he did nothing to defend himself, his entire attention was fixed on her.

"What's wrong with her? Why is she in pain?" he roared.

That alone made Dean and Justin pause in their beating, Dean stepped up to her and gingerly gathered her in his arms. "How bad is it, Mel?" he whispered to her.

"It didn't break the skin, but it hurts like a bitch," she told him, and he sighed, stroking her hair gently while the other two looked on. "It's ok, this one will heal faster."

Dean stirred. "I can't even fucking pick you up, can I?" he growled.

"Nope, even a fireman's carry is going to make the other one split open."

"Fuck!" he roared into the sky.

Melody became aware of the crowd they were gathering, students whispering and pointing, witches especially checking out Asher's naked form appreciatively.

"Four weeks, wolf, stay away from her until it's time for the challenge, or the rest of us will rip you to fucking shreds. You got that?" growled Dean.

"I got that you're jealous and possessive, cat, but I don't take orders from you." Despite the pounding he had just taken, he stood tall and proud, Melody had to respect that, even if he was a douche.

Justin stepped up to him until they stood chest to chest. "Well, puppy, I think you'll fucking listen to me. Stay away from her until we say you can come near her."

Asher paled, but he didn't back down. Melody could sense his wolf with its tail between its legs, so this bravado was all him.

"She's accepted my challenge, I have every right to spend time with her," he countered.

Even as they argued, the fire in her back settled to a dull ache.

"Help me up please, Dean," she asked him quietly, but the other two shifters turned and watched her.

"Why is she in pain?" Asher asked again.

"I can't tell you," she said, and left it that, turning to go back to the cottage.

"Kitten, you need to eat breakfast. You've got a full day of classes," Dean tried to coax her to the dining hall.

"I just need to sleep it off," she told him, ignoring his tug on her arm and going back inside. Her body ached, her head ached, and she felt useless and hopeless. She hadn't even lasted twenty minutes before Asher had found her. So much for evading him for a few weeks! This was impossible. Not only did the marks on her back hurt, but they seemed to drain her of energy. It wouldn't surprise her if her aunt had worked out a way to do it. It would totally fit with her desire to break Melody down into something more manageable.

She slung her bag onto the floor and then collapsed face down onto her bed. She wriggled and fidgeted, trying to find a comfortable position, but it was pointless, it *hurt*. Resigned to just lying there, she fell asleep within moments.

The next thing Melody knew, there was a cool hand on her forehead, and voices that seemed far too loud. The light seemed too bright as well.

"It seems to have been broken now, that was a close call, gentlemen" said a stern voice.

"I'm telling you, it wasn't external. It must have come with the you-know-what. I didn't detect any magic coming towards her, or I would have blocked it," protested Dean, loudly, and Melody groaned.

"Melody, can you hear me?" asked the voice.

"Too loud," she mumbled.

"Ah yes, audio and photo sensitivity can be expected for the next few hours. You should rest for the remainder of the day. Gentlemen, I hope that I can trust you to watch her to see that she doesn't relapse?"

"Yes, Provost," came a chorus of voices that reverberated through her skull with the force of a sledgehammer. "Give her this when she can swallow, it will help with the pain."

There was the thundering of feet as they left the room, and then it lapsed into blessed silence, but the light was too bright and her head pounded. Melody couldn't sleep for the pain, but she couldn't get up because of it, either.

Stomping of feet announced the arrival of someone, and then a gentle voice whispered to her. "Mel, you need to drink this. I can feel your pain, love. This will help it to go away." Dean's voice was husky, like he had been shouting, but it was soft.

Obediently she opened her mouth and a straw was placed in it. Then she sucked down whatever it was, the taste irrelevant in the face of her sudden all-encompassing thirst. There was a screech, which she realised was the straw sucking air, but still her body cried out for more.

"I can't give you more, Mel. You don't muck around with healing potions. That's the entire dose," Dean told her.

"Water," she whispered, but his shifter hearing heard her. He didn't move, but a second later, more thundering footsteps announced someone else. The straw was placed back in her mouth and she drank until she could hear it sloshing in her belly. Some of the pain in her body seemed to ease, and she sighed in relief.

"Wha' happened?" she slurred.

"The provost thinks you were hit with a curse at the same time as the you-know-what, but Justin didn't feel anything coming. *We* think it might have been part of the you-know-what, but we're not sure. Either way, it was so strong it almost killed you. You've been unconscious for three days, but your fever finally broke an hour ago."

"Tired," she muttered.

"Yeah, love. Just sleep it off," Dean whispered quietly.

"Bright."

"Jus, can you do something to dim the room? She's photo-sensitive right now." Dean whispered a little louder.

Melody felt a gentle whisper caress her skin, and then the light was gone. Beside her, Dean huffed.

"Yeah, didn't think of that, that'll work too."

"Wha'?"

"It's ok, love, he's just dimmed the area around your head, the rest of the room is normal, but no matter where your head is, it'll be dark. One of us will be here with you at all times, ok?" Gentle lips kissed her temple, and it was as if he had flipped a switch. The last of her resistance left her, and she drifted off to sleep.

35. MELODY

The next time she woke, Melody felt considerably better. There was a presence next to her, on the bed but not in it. She could tell because the sheets were pulled taut across that side. She rolled over, but it was so dark she couldn't see anyone. Was it the dead of night? Whatever time of day it was, she desperately needed to go to the toilet.

When Melody rolled back and pulled back the covers, a sleepy voice spoke behind her. "Mel, you ok?" he whispered.

"Ssh, go back to sleep, I just need to use the bathroom," she told him. It wasn't Dean, but her brain was still too fuzzy to tell who it was.

"Oh, hang on, let me get Jus, he'll lift the spell and then you can see where you're going," said the voice.

"Who is this?"

"Ah, it's Oz, hang on."

It wasn't like she could navigate blind, she hadn't spent any time walking around after dark, she'd usually been at the table studying until her brain cried for mercy, and then she would simply collapse into bed. Often she woke with her bedside lamp still on. Melody had never had to think about where the furniture was, or the door. She didn't fancy trying to do it now with her bladder this full, so she sat on the edge of the bed, waiting.

"Mel, I'm going to raise it a little at a time, I don't want to suddenly blast you with light." This voice must be Justin.

"Ok, just enough for me to see, to get to the toilet before I burst my kidneys," Melody said, and he laughed. It was still a little loud, but she wasn't as sensitive as she had been the last time she woke.

Gradually everything became grey, and then she could just make out shapes. Melody could see the bathroom door, the chest of drawers on one side of it, and a chair on the other. That was enough detail! She shot to her feet, wobbled for a moment, but before anyone could grab her, she was pushing open the door and running to the toilet. She ripped down her underwear, flipped up the lid, spun and sat – just in the nick of time. She groaned in relief as what seemed like a torrent, poured out of her.

There were snickers from her bedroom, making her realise that she hadn't closed the door in her haste. She didn't care, the aching pressure in her lower abdomen began to ease, and finally she was done. Melody finished her business and washed her hands.

"I thought you were going to flood the bathroom," said Justin.

"You moaned so loud I thought you were having an orgasm," joked Oz.

"You can both leave if you're going to be like this. I still feel like shit, but at least I'm not going to rupture anything now."

"Come, sit down Mel, I'm going to raise the light levels for you, let's see how much you can tolerate, it's a bright day outside," said Justin.

"How long since I last woke?" she asked them.

"That was late yesterday afternoon. It's mid-morning now," Oz told her.

"Where's Dean?"

"We drugged him, he's barely slept, so he's currently out for the count in his room. Nick is with him, we won't leave him unguarded while he's so out of it."

Melody sat on the bed and Justin came and knelt before her. She couldn't make out his face, just that he was there. Gradually the room became brighter until she called a halt. "Stop there please, that's starting to hurt," she told him.

"Well, that's not too bad, you're almost free of the spell," Justin told her with a broad smile. "Now, the provost came this morning and left another dose of the healing elixir. She said you're to drink it all no matter how bad it tastes."

That made Melody pause. Just how bad did it taste? She

hadn't noticed the draught last night, she'd been far too thirsty. Hesitantly, she put the small bottle to her lips after Justin removed the stopper. It had no odour, so that was a bonus. The first drop hit her tongue – but there was nothing. It slid to the back of her throat and there it was, a sickly sweet strawberry taste. Still, she'd had a lot worse. Quickly, she threw back her head and downed the lot with a brief shudder.

"Too sweet," she told the men, when they looked at her questioningly.

"Try these," said a new voice, and she turned to see that Ryan had entered the room with a pair of wraparound sunglasses. Melody put them on, instantly halving the light of the room.

"Thanks Ryan."

"No problem, Jus said you were still a bit light sensitive." Ryan's concern was palpable

"Ok, Melody, I'm going to lift the rest of the spell," Justin warned, "those glasses should give more than enough protection until you're ready to deal with full daylight again."

The effect on her was minimal, she really was close to tolerating full sunlight. Melody lifted the sunglasses experimentally and shoved them back down just as fast. No, she wasn't quite there yet. The men chuckled at her reaction.

"Don't worry, Mel, you can borrow those for as long as you need to. I've got another pair," Ryan told her.

She nodded, she would be keeping these babies alright, maybe even after she healed. Melody had never had a pair of sunglasses before, it hadn't really been necessary since she spent most of her time in the cellars with the shifters, but even if she had been outside, her aunt wouldn't have seen the point in supplying her with a pair. Melody just wasn't worth that kind of attention in her coven mistress' eyes.

"Are you hungry?" asked Oz, and she nodded. He sprung up from the bed and disappeared.

"How about a shower? Do you want help with that?" asked Ryan, with a smirk.

"Thanks Ryan," she said, drolly, "but I think I'm good with that."

"Let me get you some clean clothes out," Justin offered.

"I'll get the underwear!" Ryan almost shouted, as Justin went to her small closet and started rifling through her shirts.

Melody rolled her eyes, then realised that none of them would see it behind her mirrored lenses. Then she rolled her eyes at herself. She got up and went to the drawer with jeans in it, hesitating for a moment when a thought occurred to her.

"Is it Friday today?" she asked them.

"Yeah," said Ryan beside her, holding up a black lacy thong and practically salivating.

She snatched it from him and stuffed it back in the drawer, grabbing a beige pair of boyshorts and a matching bra. At least her aunt had seen fit to make sure that she had respectable underwear, although she'd been told to use the lace sets if that's what it took to get the shifters to challenge her. Like she was some sort of prostitute. She supposed in a way, she was. She gave them her magic in return for her life. It wasn't really a fair deal, but Bestia was hardly a reasonable coven.

"The provost said you could take the rest of the week off, and besides, it's almost lunch time, you'd only have one more class left anyway." Ryan's expression showed that he was obviously disappointed with her choice of underwear.

Melody racked her brain to try and remember what she had on Friday afternoons.

"Defence magic," Justin told her, before she could set off her headache again.

"Yeah, so not up to that today," she told them, and they hummed their agreement.

Armed with underwear, a pair of jeans and a black T-shirt that Justin had chosen for her, she went into the bathroom and locked the door behind her.

"You know that wouldn't keep any of us out, Justin wouldn't even need to destroy the door, he could just magic that unlocked," called Ryan.

"It's not meant to keep shifters out, it's to remind them not to come in," Melody spat back, and the men laughed. She supposed that she couldn't blame them, their beasts were riding them hard, she could practically see the wolves pacing around the house, and every now and then Melody thought she caught the shimmer of scales on Justin's skin.

She had to find a way to get out of her aunt's clutches before these men all went insane. Their beasts would only wait for so long before taking matters into their own hands so to speak. Or paws, or claws, or whatever the fuck it was that dragons had.

Melody turned on the shower, peeling off the pyjamas that she knew she hadn't changed into. She didn't want to think about who had done that, and all the scars that they would have seen when they did. Her skin was criss-crossed with silvery lines from various beatings over the years. When she was younger, they would heal without a mark, but it seemed that even at twenty-five, her skin was no longer supple enough to survive unscathed. Every whipping resulted in new scars. In some places, the marks were so numerous and so close together they formed patches of silver skin, rather than stripes.

The heat was welcome on her stiff body, loosening muscles that she hadn't even realised were tense. It also felt good to simply be clean. Having lived in the squalor of the cellars, where sometimes the ability to bathe at all was withheld as a punishment, Melody always appreciated the chance to get clean. She wondered how the shifters put up with the stink of her unwashed body for three days! Although, knowing shifters, the increased levels of her scent probably drove them crazy to bond her, rather than to hurl her into the nearest body of water with a bar of soap.

When she had washed, shaved, rinsed and scrubbed herself into a blissful sort of submission, she finally turned off the water, letting it travel silkily down her body before it swirled around the drain hole.

Back at Bestia, showers weren't only a means of cleansing herself, they were cherished moments of privacy, a luxury, where a door was shut and nobody could see her. Otherwise, she slept in a cage that was just a little larger than the ones the shifters were kept in, even if her door was left unlocked, it still wasn't pleasant, and it wasn't remotely private for any of them. Often all she had to bathe with was a bucket of cold water and whatever rag she could find.

Reluctantly, Melody stepped out of the cubicle and grabbed her towel, rubbing it vigorously through her hair before using it to dry herself. She applied some basic vitamin E cream to her body, and then deodorant before she stepped into her clothes. Next she took a comb to her tangled brown locks.

They were brushing her shoulders now, and she would have to cut them soon before they became too unmanageable. Finally, feeling clean and whole, she unlocked the door and stepped out, only to see that the men had left her in peace. Her bedroom door was even closed. She was really tempted to revel in the privacy a bit more, but the smell of food cooking in the next room drove her to ignore the luxury and head on out.

36. MELODY

The dining table had been cleared of all her study materials, and set with five places. Melody paused to think it through. Oz, Ryan, Justin, herself ... was Nick coming? She presumed that Dean wasn't awake yet, she couldn't feel much of him through their bond.

The front door opened, and Melody whirled to see Trent coming in. He had an envelope in his hand which he gave to her, and the handwriting on the front made her shudder. It was her aunt's.

Melody,

I hear that you have been accepted into a prestigious course over the term break. We are very disappointed that we will not be meeting you and your new familiar. We expect that this course will raise Bestia's prestige significantly, or we would protest that you were perhaps working yourself too hard.

It seems that you have still to adjust your attitude in terms of what is best for the coven. We were expecting you to have bonded another shifter since our last letter. Word has reached us of another alpha wolf arriving at your school. It would be hoped that you would hasten to make his acquaintance.

I hear that you have been unwell these last few days. I trust that you are now recovered and committed to doing your best for your coven. We have high hopes of you, Melody. Do not *disappoint us.*

Georgia

Mistress of Bestia Coven

Well, if there had been any doubt that her aunt had caused her illness, it was now dispelled. Melody sighed and handed the letter over to Justin and Ryan, while Oz began dishing up. Trent walked over to them and read over their shoulders. It seemed that while he was welcome, he still wasn't an integral part of their group yet.

"She wants you to bond all of us and him?" asked Justin incredulously. "Just what does she want you to do with so many shifters?" His stare was pointed.

Melody turned away, she couldn't answer him, but she couldn't not answer him. This was tearing her in two.

"Leave her alone, dragon. Can't you see it's hurting her?" Trent's warm body wrapped itself around her as he pulled her into his embrace. He buried his face in her damp hair and inhaled deeply. She could feel his fox purring in contentment.

In contrast, Ryan's growl ripped through the room. "Be

careful little fox, there is only so much leeway our beasts will give you," he warned.

"Unlike you," chided Trent, "my fox would do nothing that would cause Melody distress. If you were to attack me, I would let you, because fighting back would only hurt her more."

Ryan's rippling growls ended abruptly, and he scowled. It seemed that there were many more bridges and bonds yet to be built between the fox and the Apex.

In silence, they sat down to eat the meal that Oz served up for them. Melody took a generous helping of fried mushrooms, bacon and eggs, the men waiting until she had filled her plate before digging in and taking everything else. There wasn't even a crumb left! She had to stifle a giggle at their appetites.

"Where did all this food come from?" she asked, before digging in.

"Shifter kitchens," Oz told her. "The academy supplies us meals in the hall along with the witches, but each dormitory has a well stocked larder because we eat more than three times a day. It just works out easier, rather than all the shifters going at different times to ask the kitchen staff to make them something. We're responsible for cooking and cleaning up whatever we make, and we have to note down what we've used so that staff can keep the larder stocked."

Well, that made sense! It was a practical solution to an awkward situation. At Bestia, the shifters were fed three small meals a day to keep them compliant. Sometimes, it seemed that whatever activities they were taken out for, were too much for the little food they ate.

They always returned ravenous, and the other shifters would give up their portions to the affected one. No matter how many times she asked, they would never tell her what happened. She didn't know if they were forbidden or not, but Melody got the feeling that they just didn't want to expose her to it, not when she had been responsible for defeating so many of them in the first place, especially as it happened against her will.

"What about all my exams that I missed this week?" she asked them, trying to turn her thoughts away from darker subjects that she could do nothing about for now.

"Told you she'd ask," said Oz.

"Your teachers graded you on your classwork instead. You topped every class except defence magic," Justin Grimaced. "It's the one we're going to have to help you with the most. We need to get past your block."

Melody nodded, she needed to get past it too. Especially now that her punishments were turning more sinister. Somehow, she knew that if she defied the geasan again, the punishment would be even worse. There wouldn't just be the welt and the illness, there would be something else as well. Aunt Georgia was like that, and she would know every time the geasan were activated.

"And the asshole?" she asked, and the men snickered.

"He's been sniffing around here every day, but we won't let him in. Shawna seems to have gotten her claws into him though, I've seen them together quite a bit" said Trent.

"Ugh, they're perfect for each other, she's welcome to him," grunted Melody, and the men nodded in agreement. There was a distinct snore from behind Dean's bedroom door, and she giggled. "Was that Dean or Nick?"

"That was the fucking lion," growled Ryan. "You try sharing a room with him, fucking impossible."

Melody laughed even harder. "The poor man, he's drugged, he can't help it!"

"Yeah? And what about the rest of the time? I usually get one of the dragons to put a mute spell around him so that Oz and I can get some sleep." Ryan sounded fierce, but she could see the twinkle in his eye, and she appreciated his levity. They all laughed with her, except for Ryan and Oz who pretended to scowl.

"Well, he's here now, so I don't know what you're complaining about," said Trent, grinning at Ryan. "I'd be more worried about where he's sleeping than how much noise he used to make in your room!"

That little comment sobered up all the shifters, and they turned and looked at her with hungry gazes.

"Don't even go there," she warned them. "He's sleeping in his own room, thank you very much."

The men nodded and returned to their meals, but the tension was still there. They all wanted to be sleeping in this cottage with her, no matter what that meant. Couch, floor, bathtub, she knew they wouldn't hesitate if it meant sharing a house with her. Next would come the flirting, then the touching, and then the pressure would really be on them all.

"So, if I don't have class for two days, what are we going to do?"

"You're going to study," Oz told her. "Well as much as you can tolerate, anyway. You still have second year history to catch up on, and you have this course to prepare for. The provost said something about an expected reading list. I'll get it from her when we've finished eating, and then we'll split the textbooks up into our specialties. Just because we can't do magic – well, aside from the dragons – doesn't mean we haven't sat through all of the classes a time or ten."

Melody groaned. She'd hoped for another day of respite, but they were right, she'd missed enough work already this week.

She shoveled the last of her food in and stood up, taking her plate to the sink and filling it with hot water and suds.

"What do you think you are doing?" Oz asked her.

"The guys and I will wash up while you go and get that list. You cooked it, so the least we can do is clean up," Melody responded.

"Nope," said Justin. "Ryan and Trent are going to wash up, and I'm going to tutor you in history."

"Shouldn't I be learning that too? If I can catch up to Melody, it's one more body to protect her in class," asked Trent.

The others looked at him for a moment before Justin

nodded. "Yeah, that would make sense. From now on, her study load is yours. Keep up."

They all helped clear the table, and then Oz set off to get the reading requirements while Justin got out her history books. For the next hour he drilled her in the witch wars of the 1800's – the ones not mentioned anywhere in the human textbooks.

They had started as a rivalry between the US and Canada, but the conflagration had ended up spreading around the globe. It lasted for twenty years before the fighting finally simmered down, and witch populations everywhere had been decimated. Oddly, shifter numbers had increased during that same period, with witches bonding large numbers of them where they could.

It gave Melody pause for thought. These days, with the two populations more in balance, witches either bonded one familiar at a time, or none at all. It was a rare exception for a witch to have two. Bestia coven had a history of bonding three or four, but as the strongest beast coven, that was hardly surprising. Still, she wondered just how many shifters she would be allowed to bond if she joined another coven? A light sting hit her shoulder, reminding her that she shouldn't even be wondering about other covens. Damn Aunt Georgia to hell and back!

The list of textbooks that Oz had returned with wasn't as long as she had feared. The men had already covered several with her, so they were able to focus on the four that she hadn't come across yet. Those were advanced texts on curse making and casting.

A hex or a curse not only had to be made, it had to be cast. The will had to be woven around the word in a perfect manner, before it could be hurled at the desired target. It took a skilled witch to cast a curse, slightly less talented for a hex. Even the most basic of witches could cast a simple hex, for example, an invisible object to trip someone over. The curse that her aunt had managed to bind into the geasan upon her, showed a very high level of skill in the technique.

Melody handled the study well, or so she thought. It seemed like the men were going a little lighter on her than usual, but Trent was struggling a little to keep up. He never complained, he just worked determinedly beside her. He might get more wrong answers than her, but he never made the same mistake twice, something that Melody couldn't say for herself.

For the rest of the weekend, they worked and ate in the cottage. Dean and Nick joined them for dinner on Saturday night, the lion grumpy that they had forced him to sleep, but happy that she was better.

He and Nick joined in the tutoring, with Trent gradually getting better and better until he was working at the same level that she was. She could see that his fox enjoyed the challenge enormously.

The men had agreed that while she was on her special course – which Trent would not need, as he couldn't perform magic – one of them would remain in the house and continue to tutor him so that he could take his final exam after the holiday.

37. MELODY

On Monday morning, they set off across the grass towards the dining hall. It crunched beneath Melody's boots, and she was startled to realise that it was frozen. There was no snow yet, but the weather had turned decidedly chilly.

Crunching off to one side alerted them to the approach of Asher, who said nothing, but dogged her all the way to the dining hall. The men surrounded her, so that he wouldn't have any access to her at the table. Asher growled, but didn't push the issue.

Melody couldn't care less, she was so excited to start this new class. From the reading that they had done over the weekend, it seemed that it would be very advanced indeed. With her defence magic so poor, Melody wondered if it would interfere with the practical side of the class, but she could only wait and hope that it didn't.

Finally, with ten minutes to go before the chime was due to sound, Melody got up and cleared away her crockery. She was too keen to get started to be late.

Looking around the dining hall, she realised that there weren't many others there, and that most of them were shifters. Several gave them dark looks as they passed, angry that she had turned them down when they challenged her. Others looked at her wistfully, the hope in their eyes painful to observe. She turned her eyes down and made her way toward the central courtyard. The class was being held in one of the indoor sports areas, where they normally attended defence magic classes.

There was nobody there when she arrived, and Melody panicked, thinking that she had the wrong room.

"Relax, Mel, this is the place, you're just early," Nick told her, massaging her shoulders.

"Aah, keen to start. This is good, yes?" asked a woman's voice with a thick German accent.

Professor Ludwig wasn't anything like Melody had expected. The witch was tiny for starters. It looked like she would blow away in a strong wind, but it was her eyes that captivated Melody. She felt measured and assessed by the green-eyed gaze that seemed to be so full of knowledge and power. This was a witch not to be crossed!

"Your name, please?" asked the little witch.

"Melody Bestia," she said.

"Ah yes, the girl that Augusta was raving about. Very good. We shall see if you live up to your reputation. Hmm?"

Melody had the feeling that the class wasn't the only thing that Provost Aer-Canticum had discussed with her new professor. She had the distinct impression that she was interviewing for another coven. There was now even more pressure on her to work hard and do well in this course.

The doors opened and the other students walked in. There were ten of them altogether. This really *was* a select course!

"Gut, gut, we begin, yes?" the professor asked, and immediately launched into her lecture without waiting for a response.

The dragons had gained permission to attend, but not to participate, and they stood against the back wall as Melody and her fellow classmates began weaving their will around the words that the professor gave them. By the time they paused for lunch, she was panting with exhaustion, but beaming from ear to ear. It seemed that her issue with protecting herself did not extend to attacking others. Indeed, she seemed to also have an affinity for creating wards and shields to keep others safe – just not herself.

After lunch, they returned and sat on the floor of the large gymnasium while the professor lectured them about what they would be attempting tomorrow. She warned them not to practice unless supervised by herself, she even gave examples of what happened to witches who had ignored her.

One poor girl had cursed her own nose off, and had to spend months in isolation, regrowing it.

At the end of the lecture, they were assigned more reading, and dismissed for the rest of the evening. Except for Melody.

"Bestia, you will stay. I will talk with you."

The other students gave her a curious glance, but couldn't stay to eavesdrop as they had been so clearly dismissed. When the door closed behind them, the professor turned to Melody.

"Augusta says you have a block. Come, we shall see."

The professor guided her towards a chair and had her sit. "Cursed in height, but not in power, eh?" she asked Melody with a wicked grin.

She placed her fingers lightly on Melody's temples. "Do not move, even if in pain. Yes?"

"Yes," said Melody, fearful, but not even nodding her head.

"It will be fine. I will be gentle, no?" she didn't wait for an answer, closing her eyes and sending her magic over Melody's skin like a blanket.

"Good natural defences. Now, for the thought ones."

Little sparks of electricity travelled across her skin. It took her a while to realise that they were pausing on her scars, traversing their length and in some cases width. Finally, after some time, the professor looked at her consideringly.

"There are always two sides. A good witch will listen to

both. I know your aunt well, we studied at school together. A hungry witch, yes? She leads your coven now?"

"Yes, and yes," replied Melody.

"Your loss was great. My sympathy," was all the professor said. "I will observe. You will prove yourself, do your coven proud. Then I will speak to my own coven."

Melody's heart thudded. She had been right. Professor Ludwig was testing her to see if she was worthy of her coven. If Melody could prove herself in these classes, then she might end up with an offer!

When Melody finally emerged from the building, it was to the sight of Asher standing toe to toe with Oz.

"I don't give a fuck. She said next term, that's still three weeks away, douchebag. Come near her again, and I'll end you myself. At least you can be sure that I'll be fast. Dean is going to take days to kill you," growled Oz.

"You can't tell me what to do, I'm not in your pack, you've all made that very clear." He turned to Melody then, his face crimson with anger. "Just what is it that's so special about you that you've got them wrapped around your little finger, huh princess? Is your cunt that fucking good?"

The shifters never even got a chance to respond, Melody had him pinned against the opposite wall in an instant. She sent little electrical charges across his skin, much like the professor had done to her to check her defences, but these were stronger, and she made sure that they bit into him on a regular basis. He grunted every time one hit his diaphragm, but other than that, he made no sound.

"We haven't had the pleasure," Nick drawled, "but as you can see, even without it, she's well worth the wait. Keep this up, and you'll never get the chance to challenge her, I promise it won't be Oz or Dean that you have to worry about. I can practically kill you and heal you again and again, and again, and I'll enjoy every fucking second of it!"

Asher blinked, but wisely, he didn't respond.

"Stay. Away. From. Me!" Melody enunciated slowly and clearly. Then she turned and walked away, leaving him hanging there until they had turned the corner. Only then did she let him go without warning, enjoying the thud and his grunt of pain when he landed.

"My dragon wants me to fucking jump you right here and now. Do you have any idea how hot it is for us to see a dominant female?" Justin asked her in a heated voice. When she looked at him, his pupils were vertical slits in large golden eyes. He trembled, and Melody knew that he was on the brink of shifting and challenging her. All the blood rushed away from her face.

"Would it really be so terrible?" he asked desolately, noticing her reaction.

"You don't understand," she whispered.

"Then make me, explain it, tell me why?" growled Justin.

"Dude, back off. You've seen what happens. You really want her in a coma for another three days?" snarled Dean, grabbing her and pushing her behind him.

"She's mine!" roared Justin.

"Yes, brother, she is," Nick said soothingly. "We just have

to be patient. We're doing all we can to speed this up, ok?" He grabbed Justin by the back of his neck and pulled them together until their foreheads were touching. "Come on brother, breathe with me, breathe deeply. Get your dragon to listen. He's not stupid, he knows that the best prize is gained by those who wait for the perfect opportunity."

He continued to murmur and soothe Justin, at the same time, flapping his free hand behind his back, indicating that they should go, before he brought it forward and rested it on Justin's shoulder, urging him to breathe together with him.

Dean tugged her arm, and together they all walked silently back to the cottage where Trent and Ryan waited.

38. MELODY

The next three weeks flew by. Melody excelled at the class, enjoying it immensely. In the evenings she did her required reading and then practiced whatever had been set for them to learn for an hour. Then, before she was too exhausted, the men would take over and drill her in history and in herbology. It was the next subject that they had decided to tackle for advancement.

Melody's brain often felt like it was going to explode under the tough regime, but by the end of the three week period, she had caught up in history and was well on her way to finishing herbology.

In a nod to Christmas, the men had chopped down a large pine tree and set it up in the corner of the room. The dragons had used magic to decorate it with garlands of popcorn and small cherries. Justin said that given their appetites, the decorations had to be edible. Melody countered by saying that if the trunk was made of chocolate, and the needles made of mint lollies, she would agree. The men laughed and threatened to make it real, but had subsided when Ryan pointed out that the heat in the cottage would melt it all in a puddle anyway.

They constantly had a fire burning, the men taking turns to either collect the allotted wood from the stores or gather it themselves in the forest. With Trent staying home so often while she was in class, she was guaranteed a warm welcome after trudging through the first drifts of snow.

Ryan hung up a garland of mistletoe from the ceiling, each of them trying to grab her underneath it, the dragons resorting to moving it to wherever she was, by magic. They didn't celebrate with gifts or a feast or anything like that. Melody had explained that in her coven, Christmas was a day off, where her entire coven went out and feasted at other households. She was never invited, and neither were the shifters, so for her, it was a welcome break. She had no need for gifts or grand gestures. It wasn't like they believed in the event anyway.

New Year, however, was a different matter. The men set up a bonfire outside their cottage, a respectful distance away from the other buildings, and they sat around it toasting marshmallows and making 'smores until Justin announced that it was midnight. Then each and every one of them lined up to hug her, Ryan and Justin sneaking in a kiss as well, making them all laugh at their shenanigans.

At the end of her course, Melody was awarded a distinction grade, and the professor had promised that she would be in touch. They had celebrated that night with a feast, and no studying, the men telling stories of their childhoods and their families. Trent had suggested that she wrote to her aunt with her grade, but Melody had assured him that she either already knew, or she wouldn't care to. She would care for the prestige, but didn't need to be notified of everything that Melody was doing.

Melody could see that her upbringing bothered the shifters, but if they knew the truth of what she had done, their anger would probably outweigh any of their affection for her. She was the cause of countless shifters being caught and worked until an early death. It was the one part of her potential escape that she dreaded. Dean was already bonded to her, and Asher soon would be, but the others, if she could get away from her coven, then they would have the chance to escape her.

It was this thought that enabled her to keep her distance from them all, even when they so obviously sought affection from her. The concept of them spurning her, even the two that she would be bonded to, so terrified her, that she walled her heart against it, and against them.

That weekend, the other students returned to the academy, full of a vitality that had never been a part of her relationships with her own coven. With them, came Shawna and her crew, refreshed and eager to take up where they had left off when it came to torturing her.

Melody wondered what would give first? Her shifters? – For she was ready to acknowledge that they were *all hers* in spirit, if not reality even though she should never dare to claim them – Her health? Or her sanity? Something had to give, because Melody couldn't keep all of this up indefinitely.

Somehow, they had to find a way to set her free, only then would she be able to claim the men that she had been born to bond. That is, if they still wanted her.

THE END

A NOTE FROM JADE:

This is my first foray into the "academy" genre, but it's a little different in that in my universe, the students are older. There are four women whose stories will be told in this universe (so far), but the first three books belong to Melody and her men alone. (Ok, yes, Aunt Georgia and her cohort as well).

I'd like to say that things get easier for Melody in the next book, but really, they just become a different kind of complicated. There are things that you can probably guess that will happen, and some that will come out of left field. But, that's half the fun, right? Reading about the unexpected.

I would like to say a huge thank you for reading my book and I do hope that you liked it enough to leave a review. I look forward to sharing more of my stories with you.

A NOTE FROM JADE:

Jade
 xoxo

OTHER BOOKS BY JADE THORN:

The Siren Saga

Catriona is a siren. They're supposed to be extinct, but they've been hiding for a very long time. Now, a chance encounter in a bar has led to her being claimed by a pack of wolf shifters, and it's the flashpoint of a war between those who want a chance to live, and those who want everything. Catriona and her fated mates must find a way to stop the horrors that will arise, while finding their own way forward in their strange new relationship.

Book 1: Siren

Book 2: Sovereign

Book 3: Saviour – coming late 2020

CLUB FRENZY

Erotic Novella Series

Club Frenzy is a vampire run club that is a registered feeding place. Humans flock there for the thrill of it, and vampires linger for a meal. Explore three short stories of love and lust and plunge headfirst into the Frenzy.

Double Frenzy

Lust Frenzy

Lycan Frenzy

Or get the entire set here:
Club Frenzy Boxed Set

OF MAGIC AND CONTEMPT

A slave of her coven, Melody is being sent to Adolphus Academy, AKA Shifter Academy with a mission: she must defeat and bond The Apex. Five incredibly powered shifters, they will make the perfect breeding stock for the army her aunt is building. If she fails, she dies - if she succeeds, they will.

Book 1 - Beneath Contempt - coming soon

Book 2 - Held in Contempt - coming February 2021

Book 3 - Civil Contempt - coming April 2021

THE BROTHERHOOD

Grace isn't your ordinary witch and neither are the members of the Elite Squad in the Brotherhood. Can they discover why seven US cities have been attacked by hordes of demons?

Book 1 – Kurt's Honour
Book 2 - Grace's Guys (A Christmas Novella)
Book 3 – Levi's Fury
Book 4 – Nick's Envy – mid 2020
Book 5 – Gage's Languor – late 2020
Book 6 – Trent's Desire – coming 2021
Book 7 – Jack's Need – coming 2021
Book 8 – Sam's Lust – coming 2021
Book 9 – Saving Grace – December 2021
Book 10 – Grace's Gift – December 2021 (A Christmas Novella)

THE PORTAL SERIES

Being revealed as a Portal is like finding out you have the plague. Nobody wants to be anywhere near you, especially if you're as strong as Jacinta is proving to be. As if she didn't have enough things on her plate already - like her new lecherous boss, now she has to contend with her Events increasing in frequency and strength.

Then there's the Pure Human movement who see all Portals as mutants who should be destroyed. At least her protective detail is on her side. They're not friends, but they like her, right? Right??

Book 1 - Stellar - coming May 2021
Book 2 - Supernova
Book 3 - Black Sun

EXCERPT FROM "SIREN": CHAPTER 1

Catriona

Shayla and I are on the prowl. The club is heaving, the music is amazing, and there are more men than a girl could need in a night, but finding the right man is proving more difficult than you would think.

The song beats into the next one, and we both smile and walk up to the bar, landing against it with loud huffs and giggles. Her red wrap-around dress looks amazing against her coffee coloured skin and her tight dark curls bounce wildly. Although I'm not overly tall, she's tiny compared to me. It's not the only difference between us either. Her hair is almost black and springy while mine is long, mostly straight with a slight wave, and the colour is more a walnut brown. It really makes my eyes pop, and I think that they are my best feature.

I am not difficult to look at, but I wouldn't call myself beautiful. Besides it's not our faces that men usually look at. When you fuck to eat, well, you don't tend to get fat, now matter how good a streak you are on. I'm not saying that I don't have curves, I've certainly got enough to hold on to, and if I were more of a feminist, I'd be constantly telling guys where my eyes are, but I don't want them to remember my face, so I'm happy to show a rather daring amount of cleavage. The little black dress I've got on tonight highlights my alabaster skin, and I know that I'm getting plenty of attention. Well, at least my body is, and that's all that counts, right?

"How about that one?" she asks me, nodding towards a guy at the back.

"No, too short."

"Well, that one then, he's not short at all." She's not wrong, he's got to be nearly seven foot. Probably not human then, but I can't say that aloud. "I bet his cock is proportional too!" She grins at me.

"Ha. Probably not, but he's got that unibrow thing happening, and he's got hair, like, everywhere." I shudder. "He can be someone else's shagpile, thanks."

Shayla tips her head back in laughter. The guy next to her lifts his beer and takes a sip, sneaking a glance at us as he does so. He's playing it cool, but he's definitely listening.

"OMG! Kat, that's just wrong, so wrong." She scans the crowd again. "What about him, in the pink shirt?"

I look at the guy she's indicating. His shirt is impossibly

tight against a well-defined chest, his short blonde hair curls a little in a cute little boy way. He'd be totally my type if he wasn't gay.

"Gay."

"What? No way." Just then a guy walks up to him and they lock lips passionately, grinding against one another as they dance. "Well, damn. I did not see that one coming."

I laugh at her. "Yeah, I saw them together earlier."

"Over there, electric blue. He's been checking you out, too."

"Yeah. No. He's either a kisser, or a crier. I'm not in the mood for either."

"Kat. There's a room full of men here, seriously, just find one and fuck him. All you need is his cock's undivided attention for half an hour, and then we can really get this party started." She laughs, poking me in the ribs. My actual target is right beside her and she knows it, and she's getting bored with the charade. "I know, what about the twins in the corner over there. They're quite hot!"

"Yeah, but they're already with someone. I don't need the drama. Fuck why is it so hard to find a good strong cock in a place like this?" I moan. If my target doesn't take the bait now, I'm moving on, we've already wasted enough time on him. The night is still young, and Shay and I want to *party*! Then there's my hunger. I've left it too long between feeds – again – and I'm in bad shape although I don't show it. My skin feels too tight, I'm freezing inside and I'm only functioning on the most basic of levels. If I don't feed soon, my body will switch to survival mode and things will get seriously ugly.

"Are you two for real?" he finally asks, and we turn to look at him.

"About as real as it gets, sugar." Shay tells him. I can see he's unimpressed with her sass.

"What, do you think only men have needs? We're modern women, we have needs too. The difference between us and most men, is we have standards as well. I'm not just going to fuck anyone, if he's lucky enough to get between my legs, then he's got to be able to get me off too."

His eyes flash golden at me, fuck, he's a shifter! "You're pretty full of yourself, aren't you?" And that there, ladies and gentlemen, is where he loses. You don't throw down a gauntlet like that to a Siren because we cannot resist and we will win every time, one way or another. Of course, he doesn't know that I'm a Siren, just that I'm bruising his male pride.

Shayla likes to find a man, *croon* to him until he's rigid and salivating, and then just fuck him dry or until he passes out. It's too easy. But me? I love me a challenge. This shifter, a wolf I'm thinking and alpha to boot, well, he's just begging me to come and make him submit. And I will, but not before I've hooked him, and I refuse to croon to do that. I normally steer well clear of anything paranormal, but I'm starving and in the mood for something different, and his body is just my type. Broad shoulders, lean hips, dark brown hair long enough to run my fingers through, and just enough of a hint of asshole to him that I know I'm going to love taking him down a peg.

"Sweetheart, I know exactly what I have to offer, and if I fuck a man... well let's just say I've never had a complaint, and I always leave them begging." I smirk at him. I'm betting that that's a line that *he* would normally use. His nostrils flare and I know I've hit my target. A challenge to his ego. "But if a guy wants some of what I have to offer, then he has to work a little for it. Manscaping at the very least. He needs to look after his body if he wants mine to worship it, and he needs to understand that I'm not after a relationship, I don't even want to spend the night. Just an hour of bliss together and I'm gone."

His pupils have dilated, and his breathing has picked up. I think I've started leaking some pheromones, not much, but he's a shifter, so he'll smell them more easily. I'm so hungry that my body is taking over. The club is loud and dark, but I can tell. It's wired into me. His attention is so focussed on me that he hasn't even noticed that Shayla is gone, she's out on the dance floor bumping and grinding with the twins she pointed out earlier. There are two women back in the corner glaring daggers at her, but she wouldn't have gone after them if there was a bond there. That's another thing that sirens can do, we can sense the bonds between people. No point in luring a man if his woman is pointing a gun at your temple, right? Shay and I tend to steer clear of the taken ones, too much drama. If I hadn't already had my sights on the wolf, I might have walked past them to check their bonds out myself.

"So, you just want a good hard fuck, huh?" He growls into my ear, sending pleasant shudders through me. Yep, alpha, and not afraid to let a little alpha rumble accompany his words. Mmmm, this is going to be fun. I know it's taking a risk, shifters can get addicted to us, but I don't plan on hanging around long enough for that to happen. A quick feed or two, and I'm gone, he's empty, and we're both very happy.

I lean my body into him and we fit together like a hand and a glove. "Why? Do you think you're up to it?" I purr into his ear. I lean back pressing our pelvises together, he's hard as a rock and I haven't even put any real effort into him yet. I look him in the eye, issuing a challenge with my raised eyebrow. He grabs me by the hips, pulling me even harder against him before his mouth crashes into mine. He doesn't even realise how far he's under my spell, and I haven't had to do anything beyond what my natural allure and a hint of my scent does for him. Of course, being a wolf shifter, he can also smell my arousal and that probably has something to do with it as well.

"Hey, I know you!" A hand clamps down on my shoulder. Seriously? Now is not a good time. Whoever he is, he's more than a little drunk. "You're that girl, the hot girl!"

I break the kiss with Mr Tall Dark and Wolfy to look at the drunk human. There's no way he remembers me, I make sure to erase the memories of those I take to my bed, or my bench, or my wall. They can remember everything but my face. I don't want a relationship, I just want to feed! "Sorry buddy, I think you've got me confused with someone else." I turn back to my wolf, but the guy has grabbed me again and spun me around.

"Yeah, it's you! My friend Pete fucked you like a month or two ago, and he's been looking for you ever since! It's like you're a drug and he's addicted. He can't stop talking about you, just wait until I tell him you're here." He pulls his phone out and sends a text before I can stop him.

Now, here's where being a Siren sucks. I can't wipe this guy's memory of me tonight unless I fuck him, and if I fuck him, I won't come because he just doesn't do it for me, but it's what I need to do. This guy just doesn't appeal to me at all. Worse than that, I'll miss out on Mr Wolf here, who's still interested enough in me to growl at what he perceives is the competition. Well, that could work for me in the short term, as long as this thing with the drunk dude doesn't escalate.

I consider my options. I can ignore the guy and grab my wolf and try to go, but from now on, Shay and I will have to avoid the club, at least for a couple of months until the post-coital thing wears off on the guy and he loses interest. I can repulse him, send him away dazed and confused, except that will tip off the wolf that I'm not human and it will probably make him too cautious to proceed with me. If the wolf wasn't an alpha, I could invite the jerk to join us for a threesome, but there's no way this bad boy is going to share me with a puny drunk human. Or, I can just walk away from them both and start hunting again, but Shay is already impatient with me to just fuck and be done with it so that I have enough energy to party with her tonight.

I don't like giving up a hunting ground as fertile as this one, but right now, staying away for a few months is the option that sucks the least. Shay is going to be pissed, it's not like me to leave loose ends like this, but I've been stringing out my feeds too much and getting careless it seems.

"I'm sorry I can't stay to see him. My friend and I were just leaving, tell him I said hi." I grab the wolf and we start heading for the doors, but the drunk dude is following us. Here's hoping that his friend isn't close by, because this could get awkward if he finds me, the charm wiping his memory would be undone, and the only way to redo it would be to fuck him again. Which would also mean I'd need a stronger charm because, hey, I'd fucked him on two occasions – that's the beginning of a bond. Yeah, not happening.

Of course, the universe is against me. Before I can get through the doors, an excited looking guy who seems vaguely familiar is pushing his way in. Now, to be clear here, seeing me won't trigger the release of the charm. I'd have to be actively pointed out to him. So, I do the only thing I can, I put my head down and barrel past him, dragging my wolf behind me. And that's when I hear him, the helpful buddy at the bar.

"Dude, that's her, you just walked right past her." Fuck. He hasn't seen my face, not yet, there's still a chance.

"Run." I growl to the wolf. I let him go, kick off my heels

and grab them up before I bolt for my car. He's a powerful wolf shifter, so of course he heard me over the ruckus, and of course he kept up with me.

"Just why are we running?" he growls.

"Ex. Stage five clinger. I cannot do this tonight. Let's just go somewhere and fuck." I huff at him. Of course, it's the wrong thing to say to a protective alpha, even if I don't know him. I can hear said stage five clinger calling out desperately to us, running behind us as I flick the fob on my car keys and unlock it. When I open my door, I realise that I'm alone. The wolf has gone all alpha on me, he's stopped in the middle of the street and he's about to face off with the poor guy who can't let a good ride go.

Well, that blows that. I put my car into gear, do a screaming u-turn, and get out of dodge, leaving both men staring at my tail-lights in shock. Yep, wolf should have listened to me, and now we've both missed out. Worse still, I'll never be able to go back to the bar. The clinger will eventually forget again, because he didn't see my face, but the wolf? Yeah, I'm so on his shit list now and I know if he finds me again there'll be questions. Damn I'm so hungry!

FUCK! I bang my hands furiously on the steering wheel while at a red light. Halfway up the next block is a supermarket, so I pull into the carpark and text Shay.

Got outed, lost the mark. Starving, off to hunt elsewhere. Club is OoB for me for a couple of months, more if the wolf hangs out there. FUCK. Off to croon, see you soon. It's her favourite catch-cry.

You going home after? She responds.

Yep. Sick of this fucking shit.

I pull out onto the main drag and lose myself in the motion of traffic until I find what I'm looking for, a small bar advertising a big screen television. It's not a game night for anything that I'm aware of, but there will be some sort of sports on there. Probably not a high IQ level, but that's ok, like I said before, I want a meal, not a relationship.

Of course, my outfit for the club is a little too skimpy for a place like this. The guys here will hit hard and heavy if I flash too much flesh, and that's how you get into trouble. Because of course the fuckers couldn't just take responsibility for their actions. Oh no. It must be the girl's fault for showing too much flesh. I reach over to the back seat and snag a pair of leggings, wriggling into them before I get out of the car. I switch out my heels for a pair of flats from the passenger side floor, and I'm good to go. Glittery sexy black dress is now a glittery slightly long top. Hey, I'm a Siren, I want *a* guy, not *all* of them!

Inside the lighting isn't much brighter than the club, which suits me fine. It makes everything more alluring when you're trying to pick up. I do a quick scan of the place, sure enough, there's a hockey game playing on the big-screen tv, and a bunch of muscled-up guys are hooting and hollering along with it. Better still, a path to the bathrooms leads right under the screen. So, all I have to do is have a drink and then make eye contact with the guy of choice as I head towards the bathrooms. It will be quick and dirty, more a snack than a meal, but it will tide me over until I can find something better. I'm so desperate right now, I'm seeing stars.

I watch the jocks while I sip at my coke, I don't want alcohol to cloud my judgement, this is a place where things could go wrong fast. While I can look after myself, and if worse came to worst, I could take down every male here with one move, I'm part of the supernatural world, and it's like fight club. You don't talk about it unless it's to someone who's part of it. To save myself, I'd have to out myself, and it's a last defence thing. With careful planning, that's not an issue.

There are five in total, all broad-shouldered and smouldering. See, I told Shay that a place like this was a better hunting ground, but she wanted to dance. Frankly, any one of them would be handsome enough to turn me on. In this case, beggars *can* be choosers. If I were feeling stronger, I'd suggest all five of them follow me and I could feed enough to last me a few weeks, but I'm too weak to keep them all in line.

In the end, I do 'eeny meeny miny mo', because they're all just as appealing. 'Mo' turns out to remind me a little of my lost wolf. Slightly shaggy dark brown hair, and just a bit taller than the others, his eyes are blue, totally opposite to the hot brown ones from the club. I flick him a glance and a wink as I head to the bathrooms, his buddies notice and slap him on the back as he gets up to follow me, but thankfully someone scores a goal on the big screen above me, and all five of them look up. Good, the friends shouldn't remember me if I take a path away from the toilets that doesn't take me into their line of sight.

The place is pretty much empty aside from the jocks and a couple of older guys at the bar, so I head straight into the ladies' room and lock the door when he follows me in. I might be able to have more than a snack after all.

"Well, hello sugar." He drawls at me. "What's your name? I'm Toby, just so you know what to scream out when I make you come."

Oh yes, he's going to be just perfect! "Just call me 'Baby'. Tonight is a one-off event. You won't need anything more than to groan out that, when you come again, and again, and again." I grin wickedly at him. He smirks back and undoes his belt which is fine by me, saves me having to do it. He shucks his jeans and I'm pleased to note he's commando underneath. I turn my back to him, flip up my dress and lower my leggings and underpants before I wiggle my ass at him. "Wrap it up and you're good to go Toby." I know he can see the evidence of my arousal already, and he stares at my glistening pink bits.

I brace my hands on the countertop of the sinks and watch him in the mirror. He's moving so fast now that he's a little clumsy, it's cute. He rips the first condom in half he's so desperate to get it open. Discarding it on the floor, he pulls out another and opens it more carefully before sliding it over a glorious cock. He puts his hands on either side of my hips, his tip lining up with my opening.

"You ready for this Baby?" he asks me softly. In answer, I

thrust back sending him plunging deeply. One great thing about being a Siren, I'm always ready to go. I don't need foreplay, although it certainly doesn't hurt. He feels amazing inside of me and I gasp, while he groans. "Fuuuuuuuuck." Just then, his eyes shimmer gold, and my brain wakes up from its lust filled haze. Another shifter? Really? Then I smell him. Another wolf. Well, what are the chances of that? Astronomical as they are, I no longer care as he sets a brutal pace, pounding into me, filling me and easing the hunger that had made my skin start to sting.

His cock stretches me wide as it rubs back and forth across my g-spot, a slow burn starting to build inside of me, flashes of fire travelling up and down my legs, my arms and my spine. I arch my back, allowing him to drive deeper, and he leans forward, wrapping himself around me, his hands settling on my breasts as he palms them and squeezes. It sends a jolt of pleasure down to my core and I groan loudly.

"Cum for me Baby," he growls, and I'm there with him, right at the edge.

"You first Toby, I need to hear it, I want you to roar so loudly all your buddies will know that you just came inside me." I clamp down on him tightly, when you orgasm a lot, you get lots of muscle. It's like doing kegels.

His hips slam into me and the roar that he releases makes all the mirrors rattle. There, the energy that he releases with that roar, that's what I feed on. I scream my own release triggered by his fulfillment.

"Oh yeah. Now that's what I'm talking about." I grin at

let my power flow to the surface again. "You will submit and let me go." I tell him, my croon rumbling with authority through my voice. I really do hate compulsion, but I'll do whatever it takes to keep safe, and something tells me that this bunch of wolves is anything but safe. I could let go with my siren call, but the humans outside would hear that and be affected too. I'm not explaining how I managed to make a stack of people deaf with my voice, so it's not an option just now.

They all drop to their knees, the others even going down flat to the floor. One, I think his name was Joe, even rolls to his back and presents his belly. Curly brown hair flops back from his face and his brown eyes watch me closely. It's a calculated look until he smiles and flashes a set of dimples at me. Seriously. Dimples! I said jump and he did it as hard as he could. That boy has 'trap' all over him, if he got his hands on me, I think he'd claim me before I could blink twice. Definitely dangerous. The alpha though, he stays on his knees, but he doesn't let me go.

"Stay." He commands using his full alpha strength against me, only it doesn't work like that. Not when I'm embracing my power. It does tickle though, insanely, and I cannot hold back the giggle to save his dignity, no matter how much I try.

"Sorry baby," I tell him, "it just doesn't work that way, and it really tickles. Please don't make me command you any harder, because I can, and I don't want to hurt the others." My eyes find Joe on his back, his expression is now a little dazed. He's not a weak wolf by what I have sensed from the others, but he's certainly the weakest wolf in this room.

"Phone." The alpha mutters, pulling his out of his pocket and opening it up to add a new contact before handing it to me.

"Fine." I growl back, giving him my details. First name only and my mobile number. "But if you bug me, I'll block you and change it." I warn him. He nods, but he's still holding me. I frown at him when I see that he's dialling the number. Huh, I hadn't thought of giving him a fake, but my phone is on silent. He glares at me until I pull it out of my pocket showing that it's ringing, and his number is on the screen.

I reject the call and quickly add him to my contacts. He growls when he sees his listing as Alpha Hole. I laugh. "Well, it's not like you gave me your name now, is it? You're lucky to be getting my number at all." He lets go of my wrist, and it's odd, but I miss his grip. Who knew I had a fetish for being dominated? Because that's all it is, right?

As I turn to go, he growls at me again. "Marcus."

"What?"

"My name is Marcus."

I nod and spin on my heel, heading out towards the manager to deal with the situation there. There's a bounce in my step that hasn't been there for a while, and I can feel the flush in my cheeks, I even swagger. Rather than a day or two, I think it will more likely be four, maybe even a week, before I need to do this again.

Using my extra energy as compulsion, I smooth things

over with the manager, and I'm out of there in minutes. I wonder how Shay's doing with her twins and I laugh. I think I did better than she did tonight. It's time for me to head home before the wolves emerge from the back, no point in undoing what I managed to achieve. I press the fob on my keys as soon as I'm clear of the door. My car beeps a little forlornly, a bit like my heart does leaving these men. All the more reason to leave them, I can't afford to get attached. Within minutes I'm in my car zooming home and for once I'm glad I let Shay drag me out to a nightclub.

EXCERPT FROM "SIREN": CHAPTER 2

Marcus

I can tell as soon as she leaves, there's an attraction, like a magnet, pulling me towards her. It started as a hum in the bar earlier, and it's getting stronger the more time I spend around her. It shouldn't, but the fact that she could withstand an alpha call from me turns me on, and her compulsion? I've never felt anything like it. It took everything my wolf and I could pull together to resist even an inch of it, and she said she could have used a stronger one but didn't want to hurt the others.

My wolf shivers inside me, a tingle running from his snout to his tail and then down into his balls. He wants her, he wants to do what Toby nearly did, he wants to sink his teeth into her, leave his mark, and make sure she understands that she belongs to him. It's totally fucked up, because we both know she's not our mate, she couldn't be, she's not a wolf. I shudder again, if this is what I'm feeling, then Toby is in for hell. The bastard had a taste of her, three by his account at least. We're going to have to chain him up, and this woman and I, we're going to have words. Lots of words.

And then I'm going to fuck her.

Joe

She's a goddess, and I want her with a longing I've never felt. When her alpha call rolled through me, my cock went rock hard and my wolf rolled us onto our backs. She wanted us to submit? We would do anything for her, endure the ultimate humiliation, humble ourselves so much she couldn't help but be pleased with our response. Maybe she would bend over and tickle our belly, our cock. Maybe she would ride us.

But no, that fucker Marcus had to keep taking her attention. I know she saw us, saw us doing this to please her, and boy, would we like to please her. Anything to get inside of her, and then, when she was relaxed and limp against us, then we'd claim her. Fuck the others, this female was ours.

"Fuck Joe, get up off there, it's a fucking bathroom man, it's like a sewer in here." Growls Matt. I roll on my side and get up awkwardly and the others laugh. "Can't you even do a crunch to get up?" he laughs.

"Fuck off," I growl, "My cock is so hard if I did that I'd snap the fucking thing in half." I lift the bottom of my shirt showing the head and a good part of the shaft above the waistband of my jeans. I undo the button and heave a sigh of relief. The imprint of the back of it and the fabric around it is clear. I slide a hand in to protect myself while I edge my fly down. The individual teeth have left their own imprints. Damn, that feels so much better, even with my brothers looking on though, it's still not going down.

"Put that shit away damnit," says Felix, "if Toby sees you with that out while he still thinks she's here, he's going to rip your fucking throat out."

"I can't dude, I've never been so hard, there's no room in my pants, it's killing me."

"Then go into the men's and deal with it. We don't need him freaking out."

"Knock him out." Orders Marcus, and we all look at him in surprise. "You're all sporting boners, even I am, I don't know about you, but my wolf is slobbering stupid for her." He winces, his wolf obviously having something to say about that. "We're all releasing pheromones, fuck, we're all responding to hers. This is just a clusterfuck waiting to happen. Sock him, and we'll pass him off as drunk. Joe, sort that fucking shit out, and maybe buy some bigger pants if they're too small for what you're packing. Do I have to wipe your fucking ass too?"

"Hey, it's never been an issue before, I've just never been so fucking hard. I'll be back in a minute, this isn't going to take long at all, and don't try and tell me that the rest of you are any different."

I push the door open to the men's room. At least I can breathe clearly in here. The smell of sex in the other bathroom was overwhelming, even with the door busted off its hinges. I grab some hand towels and remember what I saw as I came into the room. Toby was balls deep in her, I could see the muscles in his ass clenched tight as he tried to get even deeper, she was sitting on the counter between sinks, her breasts heaving with her breath, her skin flushed, her green eyes blissful... and I come. Just like that, without even touching myself. I barely get the towel there in time before I mess my pants, and I just come, and come, and come. I imagine myself in Toby's place, balls deep, and before I catch my breath my balls draw up and I come again, so hard my vision blacks out for a bit. I feel my canines lengthening and I let out a roar.

"MINE!" My wolf growls through me, and I come again. Marcus appears in the doorway, a shocked expression on his face. The fucker thinks he can take her from me. I drop the soaked piece of paper and lunge for him, my teeth going for his throat.

"Back off." Growls Marcus with a full alpha tone, and it hits me like a brick wall, but I'm able to push through it. I have to protect my mate. He barely manages to get his hands up in time, he'd expected me to drop and submit. I'm not a weak wolf, but of all the wolves here tonight, I'm the least strong, and yet here I am, snapping at the fucker's neck. Damn straight he's not taking her from me. I'm so confident, I don't see it coming, I just feel the impact of his fist, and once again my vision goes dark.

Click here to buy "Siren".

Printed in Great Britain
by Amazon